D0359524

# TO FETCH A THIEF

Also by Spencer Quinn

*Dog on It*
*Thereby Hangs a Tail*

# TO FETCH A THIEF

A CHET AND BERNIE MYSTERY

SPENCER QUINN

**ATRIA** BOOKS

New York London Toronto Sydney

**ATRIA** BOOKS

A Division of Simon & Schuster, Inc.
1230 Avenue of the Americas
New York, NY 10020

First Atria Books hardcover edition September 2010

**ATRIA** BOOKS and colophon are trademarks of Simon & Schuster, Inc.

For information about special discounts for bulk purchases, please contact Simon & Schuster Special Sales at 1-866-506-1949 or business@simonandschuster.com.

The Simon & Schuster Speakers Bureau can bring authors to your live event. For more information or to book an event contact the Simon & Schuster Speakers Bureau at 1-866-248-3049 or visit our website at www.simonspeakers.com.

Manufactured in the United States of America

10  9  8  7  6  5  4  3  2  1

Library of Congress Cataloging-in-Publication Data

Quinn, Spencer.
    To fetch a thief : a Chet and Bernie mystery / Spencer Quinn.—1st Atria Books hardcover ed.
        p. cm.
    1. Dogs—Fiction. 2. Private investigators—Fiction. I. Title.
    PS3617.U584T6 2010
    813'.6—dc22
                                                    2010021384

ISBN 978-1-4391-5707-7
ISBN 978-1-4391-6306-1 (ebook)

*This book is dedicated to Diana*

# To Fetch a Thief

# ONE

I smell trouble," Bernie said.

Better stop right there. Not that I doubt Bernie. The truth is, I believe everything he says. And he has a nice big nose for a human. But what's that saying? Not much.

It's a fact that trouble has a smell—human trouble especially, sour and penetrating—but Bernie had never smelled trouble before, or if so he hadn't mentioned it, and Bernie mentioned all kinds of things to me. We're partners in the Little Detective Agency, me and Bernie, Bernie's last name being Little. I'm Chet, pure and simple.

I took a quick sniff, smelled no trouble whatsoever, just as I'd expected, but did smell lots of other stuff, including burgers cooking on a grill. I looked around: no grill in sight, and this wasn't the time to go searching, although all at once I was a bit hungry, maybe even more than a bit. We were on the job, trailing some woman whose name I'd forgotten. She'd led us out of the Valley to a motel in a flea-bitten desert town. That was what Bernie called it—flea-bitten—but I felt no fleas at all, hadn't been bothered by them in ages, not since I started on the drops. But the funny thing was, even though I didn't have fleas, just the thought of them suddenly made me itchy. I started scratching, first behind my ear, soon along my side, then both at once, really digging in with my claws, faster and—

"Chet, for God's sake."

I went still, one of my back paws frozen in midair. Bernie gave me a close look. "Don't tell me I forgot the drops?" I gave him a close look right back. Bernie has these faint lines on his forehead. When he worries, they get deeper, like now. I don't like it when Bernie worries. I pushed all thoughts about scratching clear out of my mind and sat straight up in the shotgun seat—my very favorite spot—alert and flealess.

We were in the Porsche. There are fancy Porsches out there— we see them on the freeways; we've got freeways out the yingyang in the Valley—but ours isn't one of them. It's very old, brown with yellow doors, and there's a bullet hole in the back license plate. How that happened is a story for another time.

There was one palm tree on the street in front of the motel, a small one with dusty leaves, and we were parked behind it. That was part of our stakeout technique, hiding behind trees. Maybe it was our whole technique: I couldn't think of any other parts at the moment. Beyond the palm tree stood the motel, horseshoe-shaped—just one of the many strange things about horses, that they wore shoes—with parking in between. Two cars in the lot, parked far from each other. One, a red convertible, belonged to the woman we were tailing. The other, a dark sedan, had been there when we arrived.

We gazed at the motel door closest to the red convertible. The woman—short, blond, curvy—had jumped out of the car and gone straight inside. Since then—nothing. That was one of the problems with divorce work: no action. We hated divorce work, me and Bernie—our specialty was missing persons—but with the state of our finances we couldn't turn down anything. How our finances got this way is a long story, hard to keep straight in my head. Early on, there'd been the Hawaiian pants. Bernie loves Hawaiian shirts—right now he was wearing the one with the trumpet pattern—and he got the idea that people would snap up Hawaiian pants. In the end, they got snapped up by us. We've got a closet full of them, plus lots more at our self-storage in Pedroia. Later on came the tin futures. The tin futures looked good after some find in Bolivia, but then an earthquake buried everything, so here we were, back on the divorce beat.

Our client was a sad-eyed little guy named Marvin Winkleman who owned a ticket agency downtown. Don't ask me what a ticket agency is. What's important is that he thought his wife was cheating, and coughed up the $500 retainer. Don't ask me about the cheating part, either. It's a human thing; we operate differently in my world. "Just find out, one way or another," Winkleman said. "I've got to know."

Later, driving away, Bernie said, "Why do they always have to know? What's wrong with ignorance is bliss?" I had no idea.

We sat. Nothing happened. The dusty palm leaves hung motionless. Bernie got fidgety. He opened the glove box, checked behind the visor, patted his pockets. Poor Bernie. He never bought cigarettes anymore, was trying to quit. After a while he gave up, sat back, folded his arms. Bernie has nice strong arms. I kept my eyes on them. Time passed. Then I heard a faint metallic sound and looked out. The motel door opened and out came the blond woman, patting her hair. I glanced at Bernie. Hey! His eyes were closed. I barked, not a loud bark but the soft kind I swallow in my throat. Bernie's eyelids flew open. He put his hand on me, sat up straight, reached for the camera, and took her picture.

The blond woman got in the convertible and checked herself in the mirror. Bernie took another picture. She put on lipstick, gave her mouth a nice stretch. I gave my mouth a nice stretch, too, for no reason. "Looks pretty happy, doesn't she?" Bernie said. She backed out of her space, drove out of the lot and down the street, away from us. Bernie took pictures of the motel, the blinking sign outside, the palm tree, and me. Then we went back to watching the motel room door. "Maybe there's no one in there," Bernie said. "Like she just enjoys a solitary little nap out in the desert now and then, making this a wild goose chase."

Wild goose chase? I'd heard that one before, wanted to go on a wild goose chase very badly, but there were no geese in sight. Once—was this back when the Hawaiian pants returns started coming in?—I'd heard Bernie say, "Our goose is cooked." But no cooked goose ever appeared. Meanwhile, I was hungry. The smell of burgers on the grill, while not as strong as—

The motel door opened. A man stepped out, a tall man in a white shirt and dark pants, knotting his tie. "Bingo," said Bernie, I'm not sure why. I knew bingo—a game they played at the Police Athletic League fund-raiser, an event I'd been to only once and probably wouldn't be back to, what with how exciting it turned out to be, and that unfortunate incident with my tail and all those little plastic chips on the chief's card—but was this a time for games? Bernie aimed the camera at the man, gazed into it, and said, "Oh my God." He slowly lowered the camera.

The man glanced around in a quick way that reminded me of lots of perps we'd taken down and walked to the dark sedan at the other end of the motel parking lot.

"Recognize him, Chet?" said Bernie in a low voice.

I wasn't sure. Nothing wrong with my eyes—although Bernie says I can't be trusted when it comes to color, so don't put any money on the convertible being red—but they're really more of a backup to my nose and my ears, and the man was too far away for me to get a whiff, plus he wasn't saying anything. Still, he moved in a way that was kind of familiar, stiff and long-legged, like one of those birds that can't fly, their name escaping me at the moment. The man unlocked the sedan. "Those software geeks," Bernie said. "I should have known from the flip-flops. It's Malcolm."

Malcolm? This divorce case dude was someone we knew already? I checked those feet: long skinny feet with long skinny toes. I remembered the smell of those feet, somewhat like a big round piece of cheese Bernie had once left outside for a day or two. Yes, Malcolm for sure. I didn't like Malcolm, even though I like just about every human I've ever met, even some of the perps and gangbangers. Malcolm didn't like me, either; he was one of those humans who got nervous around my kind.

Malcolm climbed into his car and drove away. "What the hell are we going to do?" Bernie said. Huh? Weren't we going to do what we always did when a divorce case worked out like this, which was deliver the evidence, collect the final check, grab a bite somewhere? "Specifically, what are we going to do about Leda?"

Leda? What did . . . ? But then I began to see, sort of. Bernie was divorced himself. He has a kid, Charlie, who we only get to see some weekends and holidays. Charlie mainly lives in a big house in High Chaparral Estates, one of the nicest developments in the whole Valley, with Bernie's ex-wife, Leda, and her boyfriend. The boyfriend was Malcolm. What else do you need to know? Maybe just that Bernie misses Charlie a lot—and so do I—but he never misses Leda—and neither do I. And then there's Suzie Sanchez, a reporter for the *Valley Tribune* and sort of Bernie's girlfriend. Suzie smells great—kind of like soap and lemons—and has a full box of treats in her car at all times. She's a gem.

Bernie felt under the seat, found a mangled cigarette, lit up. He took a deep breath, blew out a big smoke cloud. I love the smell, would smoke if I could. His whole body relaxed; I could feel it. I could also feel him thinking, a nice feeling, like breezes brushing by. I waited, my own mind empty and peaceful.

"We could tell her," he said after a while. "Or not tell her."

He smoked some more.

"If we tell her, what happens? Something, for sure. If we don't tell her, maybe nothing happens. Nothing is often the best policy." Bernie's hand reached out in that absentminded way it does sometimes and gave me a pat. Bernie's a great patter, the very best. "Still, it's a time bomb, ticking away. But do all time bombs go off?" Bombs? Bombs were somehow in the picture? Wasn't this divorce work? I knew bombs, of course, could sniff them out, something I'd learned in K-9 school. I'd done pretty well in K-9 school, up until the very last day. The only thing left had been the leaping test. And leaping is just about my very best thing. Then came some confusion. Was a cat involved? And blood? I ended up flunking out, but that was how Bernie and I got together, so it worked out great. But forget all that. The point is I can smell bombs, and there was no bomb smell in the air outside the motel. Detective work could be confusing. You had to be patient. "Got to be patient, big guy." Bernie said that a lot. It meant just sitting, not always so easy.

Bernie took one last drag, then got out of the car and ground the butt into the dirt. He had a thing about forest fires, although there were no forests around out here in the desert, just this palm tree, a few shrubs, rocks, dirt. Bernie turned to me. "Is ignorance bliss? Hits a little closer to home now, doesn't it, Chet?"

Didn't quite get that. Were we going home? Fine with me, but shouldn't we swing by the client first, pick up the check? Otherwise why bother with divorce work?

Bernie got back in the car, started to turn the key, then went still. "And what's best for Charlie?" he said.

We left the desert, rode up and over the mountain pass where the air is always so fresh—I had my head stuck way out—and back into the Valley. The Valley is huge, goes on forever in all directions. The air got less fresh and started shimmering, the sky turning from blue to hazy orange. Bernie's hands tightened on the wheel. "Imagine what this looked like when Kit Carson rode through," he said. Kit Carson comes up from time to time. I couldn't remember what he'd done, but if it was bad we'd bring him down eventually. Message to Kit Carson: an orange jumpsuit is in your future.

The downtown towers appeared, just the tops of them, the rest lost in the haze. Soon we were down in the haze ourselves. We parked in front of one of the towers and went into a coffee shop on the ground floor. No one there except Marvin Winkleman, sitting at a front table and gazing into his coffee cup, head down. Hey! He was one of those comb-over dudes. Love comb-overs! Humans can be very entertaining, no offense.

Winkleman looked up. "You've got news?" Human sweat is a big subject, but for now, let's just say the nervous kind has a special tang that travels a long way, very easy to sniff out, and I was sniffing it out now.

Bernie nodded and took a seat at the table. I sat on the floor beside him.

"Good news or bad?" said Winkleman.

Bernie put the laptop on the table, turned it so Winkleman

could see, and plugged in the camera. "These are in sequence," he said, "time stamped at the bottom left."

Winkleman looked at the pictures, his face gray in the laptop's light. His sad eyes got sadder. "Who is he?" he said.

Bernie was silent for a moment. Then he said, "Does it really matter?"

Winkleman thought. His thoughts weren't like soft breezes, were more like dark shadows that I didn't want near me. "Guess not," he said. "What's the point?" He put his head in his hands. This happens sometimes, maybe like the human head can get to be too much to support.

"Um," said Bernie. When he feels uncomfortable he bites his lip; he was doing it now. "Do, uh, you have any kids?"

"We were waiting for the right time." Or something like that: kind of hard to hear, with Winkleman's hands covering his face.

"Well," said Bernie. "Then, uh . . ."

Winkleman uncovered his face. A tear rolled out of one eye. Waterworks: I was always on the lookout for that. Human tears taste salty. I know from this one time Charlie cried after he fell off his bike, and I licked his face. I had no desire to lick Winkleman's face. "You're telling me things could be worse?" he said.

"Maybe a cliché," Bernie said. "Not very helpful, in retrospect."

Winkleman wiped away the tear. "Sorry," he said. "Crazy to take it out on the messenger." He opened his checkbook. "How much do I owe you?"

Bernie checked his watch. "Today doesn't count as a full day." *Oh, Bernie.* "Let's call it eight hundred."

Winkleman handed over the check. "Got any kids yourself?" he said.

"One."

Winkleman reached into his pocket, produced a big wad of tickets, gave Bernie two. "Here," he said. New tears welled up in his eyes, trembled at the edge of the lower lids. "Kids like the circus."

Bernie rose. At that moment I noticed a little something on the floor. I couldn't think of the name of that little something for the longest time, not until after I'd snapped it up and swallowed it down. Croissant: that was it. Not the sausage-and-egg kind, which I'd had once behind a Dumpster at the North Valley Mall, but still: delish, and I'd been hungry since the stakeout. Could have downed another croissant, in fact, and maybe even another after that.

"Chet? You coming?"

We headed for the door. Just as we went out, I glanced back and saw Winkleman standing by a trash receptacle. He took the gold ring off his finger and dropped it inside. Bernie had a gold ring that looked just the same. He kept it in a drawer in the office. I came very close to having a big thought, but it didn't quite come.

The phone buzzed just as Bernie started up the car. Bernie had the phone rigged so the voice came through the speakers. "Bernie? Amy here." I knew Amy. She was the vet. A nice woman, big and round, with soft hands, but I never liked going to the vet. "I've got the lab report on that lump." Bernie leaned forward.

# TWO

Lump? There was Lumpy Clumpinello, of course, a truck hijacker from South Pedroia, now breaking rocks in the hot sun—I could still remember how he'd squealed when I grabbed him by the pant leg, which is usually how we closed our cases at the Little Detective Agency—but other than that, no lumps came to mind. Meanwhile, out on the street, I saw one of my guys, on a leash—I'd hardly ever been on a leash, the last time being in court, when I'd been Exhibit A and Exhibit B was a .44 Magnum I'd dug up out of some perp's flower bed—lifting his leg against a fire hydrant. I wanted to do that, too, lay my mark on top of his, and right now. Was there any way I could somehow jump—

"And?" Bernie said, at the same time putting his hand on me, in fact around my collar.

Amy's voice came through the speakers. "And—the results were negative."

The blood drained from Bernie's face. All at once he went from looking great to looking terrible, like this sick old guy who sometimes goes past our house in a wheelchair. "Oh, God," he said. "Negative?"

"That's good news, Bernie," Amy said. "The best. Negative is good."

"Negative is good?"

"It means no malignancy," Amy said. "It's just a benign growth, may shrink and vanish on its own, and easily removable if not."

The blood came rushing back to Bernie's face. It turned bright red—I had no doubt about that, no matter what anyone says about me and color—and he smiled a smile so big his eyes practically disappeared. What the hell was going on? "Thank you," Bernie said. "Thank you, thank you, thank you."

Amy laughed and said good-bye. Bernie patted my head, kind of hard, actually. "Good boy," he said. "Way to go."

Nice, but what had I done? Was this about taking down Lumpy Clumpinello, or something else? The Lumpy Clumpinello case seemed like a long time ago, but maybe it wasn't—time plays tricks on you, Bernie says. I didn't know, didn't really care, but Bernie was excited about something, so I started getting excited, too. At that moment we came to a stop sign. Looking back, I could still see the fire hydrant, partway down the block. Have I mentioned that the Porsche is a convertible, in fact it has no top at all? The next thing I knew I was lifting my leg against that hydrant, marking it from top to bottom and then back up again, doing a proper job. The air filled with soft splashing sounds, kind of like a fountain. I love fountains. One of my favorites is in the lobby of the Ritz, this fancy hotel in Beaumont Hills, the nicest part of the Valley, where Bernie and I once worked a case, although that particular fountain had actually led to problems with the management, too complicated to go into now. A woman in a passing car gave me a look, maybe not friendly. I gave her a look back, not friendly or unfriendly, just this polite look I have for when my mind is elsewhere.

\*   \*   \*

Home is our place on Mesquite Road. Our part of the Valley isn't fancy like Beaumont Hills, but who would want to live anywhere else? For one thing, we've got the canyon out back, open country that goes on and on, plus more lizards, javelinas, and coyotes than you could shake a stick at. That's something humans say, but I've gotten lots of sticks in my mouth and could have shaken them at all kinds of creatures if I'd wanted. Once I actually did shake a squirrel. Was that bad? I was so surprised I'd caught the little bugger, first and only time!

Another good thing about our place is that my bowls are in the kitchen. And then there's Iggy. Iggy's my pal. He lives next door with this old couple, Mr. and Mrs. Parsons. Not too long ago they got an electric fence and Iggy had some problems with it. Now he doesn't come outside, just watches from the window, which was what he was doing when Bernie and I drove up. He barked and wagged his tail. I did the same. Iggy barked back and wagged some more. I did the same again. We could keep this up for ages, me and Iggy, and I was looking forward to that, when he suddenly disappeared from the front window. A few moments later he popped up in the side window. Maybe he could see me better from there or maybe—what was this? Now Iggy had something in his mouth, possibly a bedroom slipper. Yes, a bedroom slipper for sure. I wanted badly to take it away from him, but how could I? So when I heard Bernie saying, "For the last time, Chet, get in here," I went bounding into the house.

"This calls for a celebration," Bernie said. I knew celebrations—and wasn't at all surprised when Bernie opened the cupboard over the sink and took out a bottle of bourbon—but why were we having one now? He also took out a box of chew strips from Rover and Company—a great company where I'd once spent some time in the testing kitchen—and tossed me one. Beef-flavored—I could tell while it was still spinning in midair. I caught it and darted under the kitchen table, like . . . like it was the bedroom slipper or something. I worked on the chew strip, a bit confused. An ice cube in Bernie's glass made a tiny hiss and then a tiny crack. I loved when that happened. I forgot whatever I'd been worrying about and polished off that chew strip.

And was wondering if I could have another one, and if so, how to make that happen, when someone knocked at the door. Uh-oh. I hadn't even heard whoever it was coming up the walk, and that was part of my job. I ran to the door, barking this sharp-sounding bark I have, a bark I've noticed scares some people, kind of strange since I mostly do it when I'm a little mad at myself. But then, at the door, I smelled who it was and went quiet.

Bernie opened the door and blinked, the way humans do sometimes when they're taken by surprise. "Uh, Leda?" he said.

"What the hell is wrong with your phone?" she said. Leda has pale eyes, like the sky in winter. She was one of those humans who never seemed to look at me, like I wasn't there. "Both phones, home and cell. I've been calling and calling."

"You have?" said Bernie. He took his cell phone from the pocket of his Hawaiian shirt. Leda's pale gaze took in the shirt; for a moment I thought she was going to say something about it—she'd said plenty about Bernie's Hawaiian shirts, and his clothes in general, when they'd been married, but she didn't. Leda herself wore dark pants and a short jacket with interesting buttons, the color of bone. What would one of those buttons feel like between your teeth? You couldn't help wondering. Meanwhile, Bernie was giving his cell phone a smack, the kind of smack he gives the toaster when the toast starts smoking and won't come up, but not so hard. "Something seems to be . . ."

"Did you forget to pay the bill?" Leda said. "They probably cut off your service."

"No, I'm sure, almost sure I—"

"It doesn't matter," Leda said. "I'm here now."

"Right," said Bernie. His expression changed, like he'd had a thought, maybe a big one. I'd seen that before, and got ready for anything. "Did you want to, uh, come in?"

"Come in?"

"Like, inside the house."

"Why would I want to do that?"

Bernie raised both hands, palms up; something he hardly ever did. "I don't know," Bernie said. He cleared his throat, but that didn't mean he had a bone stuck in it, which is the only reason I have for clearing my throat. I was pretty sure it meant something. "How are things?" he said.

Leda squinted at him. Squinting never makes people look better. "How are things? What kind of question is that?"

"Just routine."

"Routine?"

"You know. Polite back-and-forth."

Leda stopped squinting, tilted her head back. "Making fun of me, Bernie? That never gets old?"

"I wasn't. Sorry if . . . and I never—"

"Skip it." She made a little backhand gesture. "I had a proposal I thought you'd like, but if this is your attitude, I don't—"

"Something about Charlie?" Bernie said.

"Yes," she said, her face smoothing out, looking not so irritated anymore, "something about Charlie. I know it's not scheduled, but can you take him for the weekend?"

Bernie's eyebrows—he has nice thick ones; you can tell a lot by watching them—went up and he smiled at the same time. I always like seeing that one! "Yeah, sure," he said, "of course." Bernie gave her a quick look, not the kind of look I'd ever seen before from him to her, more the kind of look he had when we were on the job. "Something come up?"

"A weekend getaway," she said. "We're leaving tonight."

"You and Malcolm?"

"Who else? Of course me and Malcolm."

"Going anywhere interesting?"

"Isn't that the norm for weekend getaways?"

Back in the house, Bernie tried the kitchen and office phones, pressed buttons, smacked the phones around a bit. Then he started digging through a big pile of papers on the desk. That got me going a bit—especially when the pile tipped and all the papers went sailing—so I had to take a little break out back on the patio. We have a nice patio, surrounded by a high fence and a high gate at the back. And beyond the gate: the canyon. I went to the gate right away. Locked. A very high gate, but what no one knows is that I've jumped it more than once. There was an episode with she-barking, for example. I stood still, ears up, listened for she-barking now, heard none. We have a small lemon tree in one corner of the patio. I lay down in its shade, took in the lemony smell. My eyelids suddenly got very heavy very fast. Don't you find it hard to keep them open when that happens? And also, why bother?

I had a dream about that she-barker, a very exciting dream, but for some reason at the most exciting moment of this exciting dream, my eyes opened. The dream broke into little pieces and the pieces faded fast. I was on the patio, under the lemon tree, and Bernie was sitting at the table, the checkbook open in front of him. I knew the checkbook. It's a small thing with a cover that looks like leather, but I happen to know is not; a small thing that always seems to cause big problems.

"Can't believe I did that," he said. I rose, gave myself a real good stretch, getting my front paws way out and arching my back—did that feel good or what? Bernie glanced up at me. "My goddamn handwriting. I took a three for an eight and bounced the phone bill check." Three? Eight? Those are numbers, but what they mean isn't exactly clear to me. I don't go past two. Two is enough. I went over and stood by Bernie. He scratched between my ears. I hadn't realized how much I needed scratching right there. Ah. He was an expert. "How can I be so dumb?" Bernie said. Bernie? Dumb? No one dumb could scratch like that. He gazed off into the distance. "We need a case, big guy." I went closer, sat on his foot, waited for a case.

Soon after that, the doorbell rang. We went to the front door, opened up—and there was Charlie, wearing his backpack. "Hi, Dad," he said.

"Hey," said Bernie. He looked past Charlie to the street, so I did, too. Leda was watching from the passenger side of a car; the dark sedan, actually, that we'd seen earlier at the motel. And I could make out Malcolm beside her, at the wheel. A strange feeling, a kind of pressure, sometimes happens in my head, especially when things are getting complicated. I was feeling it now. Leda gave a little wave. Bernie waved back, a funny look in his eyes. But no time to figure that out, because the very next thing, Charlie had thrown his arms around me, and right after that I was giving him a ride on my back, charging all over the yard.

"Chet the Jet!" he yelled. "Chet the Jet!"

Was anything better that this?

We went inside and had a snack. Charlie loves snacks and so do I. "Guess what I've got?" Bernie said.

"What, Dad?"

"The circus is in town," said Bernie. "Out at the fairgrounds." He laid the tickets on the counter.

"Yes!" said Charlie. He examined the tickets. "Do they have elephants? We're studying elephants in school."

"Got to have elephants," Bernie said. "What's a circus without elephants? But we can check." He flipped open the laptop, tapped away. "Here we go. How about we watch this on the big screen?"

We went into the living room. Bernie tapped away some more, played with the remote, said "What the hell?" a few times, hit more buttons, and then a man appeared on our wall TV. He had a big head, wore a big top hat, held a cigar in one hand and a whip in the other.

"Ladies and gentlemen," he called out, "and children of all ages, I'm Colonel Drummond and it's my pleasure to welcome you to the Drummond Family Traveling Circus, the biggest and greatest and oldest and most award-winning, family-owned three-ring circus in not just the good ol' U. S. of A. but indeed in the whole world and the solar system to which it—"

"Let's fast-forward," Bernie said. Images flew by on the screen: a dude on a one-wheeled bike—the name of those bikes escaping me—juggling lots of bowling pins; tigers jumping back and forth through a ring of fire; a crowd inside the huge tent clapping their hands; a woman standing on the head of a man who was standing on the head of another man who was standing on the—; a woman in what looked like a bathing suit riding two horses at once, a foot on each one—and was she really keeping all those plates spinning at the same time? I wasn't sure. Everything went by too fast, a woman breathing fire, and was that possible? a man getting shot out of a cannon and flying through the—? and a bear on a motorcycle—whoa!—and then Bernie said, "This should be it," and the speed slowed down to normal.

"And now, ladies and gentlemen and children of all ages," said Colonel Drummond, "if you will direct your attention to the east ring, the Drummond Family Traveling Circus is proud to present the world's greatest elephant tamer and the world's greatest elephant, brought together under the Drummond Family Traveling Circus big top at great expense for your viewing pleasure. Please welcome Mr. Uri DeLeath and Peanut!"

A light shone down in the darkness behind Colonel Drummond, music played ta-da!, and there stood an elephant and a man in a tight sparkly costume. I knew elephants from Animal Planet. Would I ever forget that show they did on when good elephants go bad? And that whole house falling down? The man in the sparkly costume—Uri DeLeath, unless I'd missed something—had a big smile on his face, a dark face with big dark eyes and one of those pencil mustaches, always interesting. He looked tiny next to Peanut. Peanut's face was hard to read. I couldn't get past that trunk, so amazing. Peanut raised one of her huge front feet. Uri DeLeath lay down under it. Peanut lowered her foot onto him, just touching and no more. After a moment or two, she raised it, stepped back, and in one quick but gentle motion of her trunk scooped him up and set him behind her head. Then Peanut started walking around the ring, Uri DeLeath smiling and waving his sparkly hat, and what was this? Peanut reaching her trunk into the stands and grabbing somebody's popcorn right out of the bag and offering it up to Uri DeLeath? He ate a handful and then Peanut's trunk curled to her mouth and she scarfed down the rest, and . . . and now she was, yes, kind of prancing, like she'd pulled a fast one. Hey! I knew that prance, meaning Peanut and I had something in common. The crowd laughed and cheered. Peanut returned to the center of the ring and bowed and Uri DeLeath slid off, bowing, too.

"Wow," said Charlie. "I can't wait."

I knew that one.

# THREE

"Peanut is an African elephant," Charlie said. "That's the biggest kind."

"Yeah?" said Bernie. We were in the Porsche, and everything was great except Charlie was in my seat, the shotgun seat, and I was on the shelf in back. But I loved Charlie, so I was being pretty good about it, hardly nipping the back of Bernie's headrest at all.

"She has big tusks, Dad. The Asian females don't. And her ears are big, too. The Asian ones have smaller ears."

Bernie shot Charlie a quick glance. "Had a pretty good look at that video, huh?" Bernie said.

"Ms. Creelman says their ears help cool them down. We have to protect the elephants, Dad."

Protect the elephants? I didn't get that. Even if they don't go bad, just think of the size of them. Why couldn't they protect themselves?

We drove across the Valley, the sun shining bright, warm breeze blowing across my coat. I was feeling tip-top, lost in all the freeway smells going by: burning oil, grease, gasoline, hot rubber, hot pavement. Love freeway smells! Before I knew it, we were on an exit ramp, headed toward the fairgrounds—I could tell from the giant Ferris wheel in the distance. We'd worked a case at the fairgrounds once, not sure what it was about, maybe cotton candy. That was what I remembered most, the trouble I'd had with cotton candy, the way it got stuck all over my nose and even up inside: I'd had to breathe through my mouth, and the smell of cotton candy stayed with me for days.

"There's the big top," Charlie said as we drove through the gate. I could see it, too—a tent beyond the Ferris wheel, not far from the hills that rose at the back of the fairgrounds. We have a tent for when we go camping—my job is to carry the mallet for hammering in the pegs—but there's a stuffy smell I don't like inside the tent, so I always sleep outside. Bernie often leaves the tent in the middle of the night. He loves to sleep under the stars. He tells me lots about them, not easy to follow, but no problem: his voice is so nice to hear that often I don't even bother trying to understand.

We came to the big top and parked near the ticket booth. "The big top kind of looked bigger in the video," Charlie said.

"I was thinking the same thing," said Bernie.

"And whiter," Charlie said.

People were milling around the ticket booth in the way groups of humans do when something's not quite right. Charlie pointed to a sheet of paper stuck on the window of the booth. "Hey," he said, "does that sign say 'No Show Today'?"

"Yeah," said Bernie, stepping up to the booth; it was empty inside. "'Please come back and see us tomorrow.'"

"How come, Dad?" Charlie said. "What's going on?"

Bernie looked around. "No idea." He took Charlie's hand and walked away. I trailed behind, smelling lots of smells, some of them completely new to me. They all seemed to be coming from inside the big top. Soon I was right alongside the big top, sniffing along the bottom where the canvas met the ground. Animal smells for sure, but what animals, with smells so ripe, so rich, so strong? I squeezed my nose down under the—

"Chet?"

I looked up.

"Is Chet trying to get into the tent, Dad?"

"I'm sure he wouldn't do anything like that," Bernie said.

I trotted over to them, tail stiff and up high. We were partners, me and Bernie, had confidence in each other. My behavior was beyond reproach, whatever that was.

"Let's take a recon behind the tent before we go," Bernie said.

"How come?" said Charlie.

"Just curious," Bernie said.

Fine with me. Recon was one of my specialties. We circled the tent. On the back side sat a whole bunch of trailers, parked right up to a low chain-link fence at the base of the hills. Some of these trailers were huge, the biggest I'd seen, and what was this? Metro PD black-and-whites, and some uniformed cops laying down crime-scene tape? I knew not to go anywhere near crime-scene tape, one thing I'd learned for sure in K-9 school.

One of the cops looked up. I recognized him: Sergeant Rick Torres, our buddy at Missing Persons. "Hey, Bernie," he said. "You working this already?"

"Working what?" said Bernie.

Rick Torres crouched under a strip of tape, came toward us, shook hands with Bernie. "Hey, Chet," he said, and gave me a pat. "Lookin' good. Is he still growing, Bernie?"

"Hardly seems possible," Bernie said. "This is my son, Charlie. Shake hands with Sergeant Torres, Charlie."

Rick held out his hand. Charlie gazed down at the ground.

"I won't bite," Rick said. Of course he wouldn't! Hardly any humans did, their little teeth not being much of a weapon. I did remember a perp named Clancy Green chomping on some other perp's arm, but that was on a Halloween night, the only holiday I don't like—Halloween brings out the worst in people, Bernie says. Thanksgiving is my favorite, except for that one time with the drumstick incident, maybe a story for another day.

Charlie raised his hand, a little hand that disappeared in Rick's big one. Rick shook it gently.

"There's a gun on your belt," Charlie said.

"Yeah, but I've never fired it," Rick said, although I didn't know why, since I could smell it had been fired, and not too long ago.

A trailer door opened and a cop looked out. "Ready for that witness, Sarge?"

"You're really not working this, Bernie?" Rick said.

"Don't even know what this is," Bernie said. "We came to see the circus."

"Bad timing," Rick said. "The elephant tamer's missing. And the elephant's gone, too."

"Peanut?"

Rick took a notebook from his chest pocket, leafed through. "Yeah, Peanut."

"How can an elephant be missing?" Bernie said.

Rick shrugged. "Care to sit in?"

Bernie shook his head. "Seeing as how there's no circus, maybe we'll—"

"Dad?" Charlie's eyes were big. "Did something happen to Peanut?"

Bernie glanced down. "No reason to think that, Charlie."

"But then where is she?"

"That's what Rick's going to find out," Bernie said.

"I'll bet Corporal Valdez would be happy to entertain Charlie for a few minutes," Rick said.

Bernie thought for a moment. I can always feel when he's thinking, although what he's thinking about is anybody's guess. "Just a few," he said.

Rick waved one of the cops over. Corporal Valdez told Charlie to call her Mindy and that she had a kid named Charlie, too, now in Iraq. That was where Bernie got his wound—he limped sometimes when he was tired—but he never talked about it, so that was all I knew about Iraq. "Want to work the blue lights?" Corporal Valdez said. She led Charlie toward one of the cruisers. Bernie and I followed Rick up the stairs and into the trailer.

That was when I got a bad shock. We were in a kind of office—desk, chairs, computer, none of that shocking—and standing by the desk was the cop who'd spoken to Rick, also not shocking. The shocking part was the clown sitting in one of the chairs. I'd seen clowns on TV. They scare me every time, and this was much worse. The clown had a horrible white face with a red mouth and green eyes and nasty orange hair sprouting out of his head here and there. And it wasn't just the sight of him: how about the smell? Partly he smelled like Livia Moon, who operated a house of ill repute, whatever that may be, in Pottsdale, and partly he smelled like a human male. I hardly ever go backward, but I was going backward now, and barking my head off.

"Easy, Chet," said Bernie.

"Dogs hate me," said the clown.

He had a soft voice, actually sort of nice, although not as nice of Bernie's, of course. I stopped barking, not all at once, more this gradual dial-down thing I do.

"Popo," said the cop, "this here's Sergeant Torres from Missing Persons."

"And my associate Bernie Little," Rick said.

I barked the last of the dial-downed barks, low and rumbly.

"And Chet," Rick added.

"Nice to meet you," said Popo.

"And your real name?" Rick said.

"Real?" said the clown. "John Poppechevski." Or something complicated like that. "But everyone calls me Popo."

"Even in normal life?" said Rick.

"The distinction between normal life and circus life eludes me," Popo said. He had this big red smile on his face, but he didn't sound happy. His eyes were small and dark; everything else about him was big and brightly colored. My barking almost started up again.

"Okay, Popo," Rick said, "let's hear your story." The uniformed cop went to the doorway and stood there, looking out. Rick sat down, reaching for his notebook. Bernie leaned against the desk, arms folded across his chest. I sat on the floor beside him, picking a spot that turned out to be sticky. I shifted over a bit; that was better.

"Well," said Popo, "my great-great-grandparents, in search of a better life, came to Ellis Island early in the twentieth—"

"How about we fast-forward to the events of last night?" Rick said.

A quick smile crossed Bernie's face, not sure why. But I got the feeling he was having fun, which put me in a very good mood, and I'd been in a good mood already.

Popo nodded, the big red ball at the tip of his nose bobbing up and down. Balls are a big interest of mine; I couldn't take my eyes off it.

"You want me to skip Trumpy?" Popo said.

"Who's Trumpy?" said Rick.

"My mentor. He taught me everything I know about the profession."

"Was he here last night?"

"Oh, no," said Popo. "Trumpy passed away years ago."

"So he couldn't have had anything to do with these disappearances," Rick said.

"Not even if he'd still been alive," Popo said.

"I'm sorry?" said Rick.

"Trumpy was a man of the highest moral character," Popo replied.

Bernie spoke for the first time. "And did he pass that on to you as well?"

Popo turned to Bernie. "I try," he said. Yes, Popo had a nice voice, and there was also something nice about those dark eyes.

"Good to hear," Rick said. "So getting back to last night."

Popo licked his lips. The sight of his tongue—a normal tongue, at least for a human—touching those red smiley lips was very strange. I stuck my own tongue out, gave the end of my nose a lick, not sure why. "After the show," Popo said, "the late show, I'm talking about, which went pretty well—pretty well considering the times, the house maybe not quite half full—I relaxed for a while with the Filipoffs and—"

Rick held up his hand. "The Filipoffs?"

"You don't know the Filipoffs?" Popo said. "The Fearless Filipoffs, First Family of the Flying Trapeze?"

Rick shook his head.

"That says more about the state of the circus than about you," Popo said. "A hundred years ago their names were on everyone's lips."

What was this? More lips? I was confused. Were we even on the job? I started panting a little bit.

"The Filipoffs' trailer is next to mine, near the cages. The setup is the same in every town. After a drink or two, I went to bed. Sometime in the night I woke up, thinking I'd heard trumpeting. I listened but heard nothing more and thought it must have been a dream, and so—"

"Trumpeting?" said Rick. I knew trumpets. We listen to a lot of music when we're on the road, and the trumpet is my favorite instrument, although the slide guitar is pretty good, too. The trumpet does things to my ears that are hard to describe, especially when Roy Eldridge is playing on "If You Were Mine," which Bernie went through a stage of playing over and over.

"I'm talking about elephant trumpeting," Popo said.

Whoa. Elephants could play the trumpet? I knew right then that this case was headed off the cliff.

"You're telling us it wasn't a dream?" Rick said.

"In retrospect," said Popo, losing me completely. "But at the time I just went back to sleep. In the morning I got suited up first thing and started working the fairgrounds."

"Working them how?" said Rick.

"Drumming up business," Popo said. "Part of my job."

Trumpeting and now drumming? I didn't like this case, not one little bit. Were we even on it? If we were, who was paying? I felt a sudden urge to yawn, too strong to fight, so I gave in and yawned, a nice big mouth-stretching one, and felt better for it.

"About half an hour later Filomena came running over and broke the news," Popo said.

"Filomena?" said Rick.

"Filomena Filipoff, granddaughter and current star of the act."

"And the news was?"

"That Uri was nowhere to be found."

"The elephant tamer?"

"He doesn't think of himself as a tamer."

Bernie spoke again. "How does he think of himself?"

Tears rose in Popo's dark eyes. "As a friend. But he has no objection to the word *trainer*. Uri DeLeath is the best and most humane animal trainer in the business."

"And the elephant was missing, too?" Rick said.

Popo nodded. "Vanished without a trace."

"A little premature," Bernie said.

"I don't understand," Popo said.

"Bernie means it's too soon to give up on finding traces," Rick said. "This elephant, uh—" He checked his notebook. "Peanut, how does he normally travel?"

"She," said Popo. "She has her own trailer—like a horse trailer but much bigger."

"It's gone, too, I assume?" Rick said.

Popo shook his head. I always watch for that: it means no.

"What about other trailers, trucks, any kind of vehicle?" Rick said.

"All present and accounted for as far as I know," said Popo.

"So what are you saying?" Rick said. "They just up and walked away? We've got an elephant roaming around the Valley and not one single citizen's bothered to call it in?"

"I have no answers," Popo said.

One of Bernie's eyebrows rose a tiny bit. His eyebrows sometimes do the talking—have I pointed that out already? "Where did the trainer sleep?" Bernie said.

"When we're on the road, you mean?"

There was a slight pause. Then Bernie said, "That's right."

"His trailer's on the other side of the cages."

Bernie turned to Rick, maybe waiting for Rick to say something.

"How about we check it out?" Rick said.

"Sounds good to me," said Bernie.

We went outside. Charlie was sitting behind the wheel of Corporal Valdez's cruiser—his head barely visible through the windshield because he was so small—with Corporal Valdez beside him and the blue lights flashing. Charlie's voice came over the cruiser's PA: "Hands where I can see them. You're under arrest for murder in the first degree."

# FOUR

We left the trailer—Bernie, Rick Torres, Popo, and me. There was a moment of crowding around the door, a bit of getting tangled up, and I burst out first. That happens a lot when we're leaving places, not sure why. Popo lost his balance and almost fell; glancing back—something I can do with hardly turning my head at all—I could see the reason: his feet were huge, those floppy polka-dot shoes going on forever.

We crossed a strip of ground—rich with powerful animal scents, all unknown to me—and walked up the stairs at the back of the next trailer. The door was open and I caught a familiar powdery smell—they'd been dusting for prints, and not long ago.

"Hold it," Bernie said, raising his hand in the stop sign as we were about to step inside, "have you dusted for prints yet?" We'd worked together a lot, me and Bernie, so I shouldn't have been surprised. He had a nose, even kind of big for a human, but what did it do?

"Yup," said Rick. "Bupkis."

Bupkis? I remembered no perps of that name.

"Where'd you learn a word like that?" Bernie said.

"Counterman at the Brooklyn Deli," said Rick.

Bernie laughed. Whatever the joke was, I'd missed it, but I knew the Brooklyn Deli, a downtown joint I didn't get to nearly enough.

We entered the trailer. I was trying hard not to think about pastrami. We were in a small space with a bed and a rocking chair on one side—I stayed away from rockers, on account of this one incident involving my tail—and a desk and a hot plate on the other; I stayed away from hot plates, too.

"No signs of forced entry or violence," Rick said. "For a crime scene it's about as tidy as they come."

Bernie went to the bed. "Looks like he didn't actually get under the covers."

"Uri has trouble sleeping," Popo said. "He often reads long into the night."

Bernie picked up a book that lay on the rocker. *"Twilight of the Mammoths,"* he said. He opened it, turned a few pages. Bernie gets this still and quiet look on his face when he's interested in something: he had it now.

"What's up?" Rick said.

"Nothing," said Bernie, closing the book. But he didn't put it down.

Two pictures hung on the wall. In one, Peanut stood in a field, the man with the pencil mustache, now wearing jeans and a T-shirt, standing beside her—actually sort of leaning against her—and smoking a cigarette.

"Uri with Peanut," Popo said.

Rick bent his head toward the picture. "He seems pretty relaxed around such a . . ." He went silent the way humans sometimes do when they're waiting for a word. Never happened to me.

"Trust," said Popo. "Uri's method is all about establishing trust."

In the second picture, Uri, again smiling and looking relaxed, stood next to another man, arms over each other's shoulders.

"Who's the other guy?" Rick said.

"Me," said Popo.

The other guy was Popo? He didn't look at all like Popo. He looked like a normal guy, with dark hair and glasses, wearing normal guy clothes. And—way different from Popo—he had happy eyes: happy eyes are one of those things we pick up right away in this business. I didn't like this case, not one bit. Was it our case? I didn't know. I had no memory of anyone cutting us a check—something I don't forget—so maybe not.

Bernie went over to the bed, turned back the covers, gazed at the sheets.

"Already did all that," Rick said.

"Just getting the feel," Bernie said. He bent down, checked under the bed. I went over and sniffed around. Checking under beds was basic: we'd found stuff under beds before, me and Bernie, but not this time. Did Bernie get the feel? His face was blank.

We went outside.

"This way to the cages," Rick said.

We followed him back behind the trailers. The cages stood in a row. They were like big boxes, with roofs and walls, the only barred part being the fronts. The smells hit me first, so strong, some a bit catlike, but to the nth degree, whatever that means. And then the sights: oh, boy. Creatures I'd seen on Animal Planet: tigers and lions and—

Actually, in the first cage, just two tigers, and in the next cage, only one lion, and in the last cage, nothing. The tigers and the lion had big rubber balls to play with, but they weren't playing. They just lay on the floor and watched us with huge yellow eyes. The fur on my neck stood right up; their fur, now that I noticed it, looked kind of dull and ratty. Bernie opened his mouth like he was going to say something, but he didn't speak; he got a hard look on his face. I wasn't sure why, but I hated cages myself: bad guys had gotten me into them a couple times in the past. Maybe Bernie's mind was on that.

"Thought there'd be more animals in a three-ring circus," Rick was saying.

"We're a one-ring circus now," Popo said. "Haven't had three rings in years."

"How come?" said Rick.

Popo shrugged.

We stopped outside the third cage. What a smell! It drove all the cat scent clean out of my nose.

"Peanut's cage," said Popo.

The smell of Peanut filled my head, unforgettable.

"The way it works," said Rick, walking around to the other side, "you unlock that padlock and this whole wall slides back. But apparently it was closed when the first witness arrived."

"And who was that?" Bernie said.

Rick gave some kind of answer, but I missed it, on account of how I'd picked up Peanut's trail—what could be easier?—and was starting to follow it. The trail began by the side wall of the cage, right where Rick was standing, and led toward—

"Chet? C'mon back, big guy."

But—I went back, stood beside Bernie.

"Here she comes now," Rick said. A small woman in sweats appeared, walking fast. Human movement is a big subject—amazing they don't fall down more often—but for now let's just mention that some humans move better than others, and she was one of those. "Bernie," said Rick, "this is Filomena Filipoff. Ms. Filipoff—Bernie Little, private investigator."

She reached up, shook hands with Bernie. She had a ponytail, tied back in that real tight way you see sometimes, kind of stretching the skin around the eyes; doesn't that hurt?

"Everyone calls me Fil," said Filomena. They did? We already knew a Phil: Phil "Shoulders" Schraft, now breaking rocks in the hot sun. This Fil was very different.

"Uh," said Bernie. "Er." Some women did that to him. "I'm Bernie," he said.

"Caught that," said Fil.

"And, um, this is Chet."

Fil turned to me. "What a handsome fellow," she said.

I knew one thing right away. If this was a case and something bad had happened, this woman was not the perp. She held out her hand, a small hand but beautifully shaped. I gave it a quick lick, caught a faint taste of oranges; very nice.

"You were first on the scene?" Bernie said.

Fil nodded. "I went jogging—it was just getting light—and when I came by, Peanut was gone. I ran right to Uri's trailer and he was gone, too. I called the colonel and I guess he called you guys."

"Who's the colonel?" Rick said.

"Colonel Drummond," Fil said. "He owns the circus."

"Is he around?" Rick said.

"He's on his way," Fil said.

"From?" said Bernie.

"The colonel's got a place in the north Valley," Fil said.

"He lives here?" said Bernie.

"None of us really lives anywhere," Fil said. "We're on the

road forty-eight weeks a year." She turned to the empty cage. "It's a cliché, I know, but we're like a family."

Popo moved closer, put his arm around her. He wore white gloves, made of some material that looked soft; I couldn't help wonder how gloves like that might feel, in my mouth, for example. While I was in the middle of wondering, Rick said something I missed, and then Popo and Fil were walking away, his arm still around her.

"Like a family—there are upsides and downsides to that," Bernie said.

"Thinking the same thing," said Rick.

Bernie reached out, tried the padlock. "Who has keys for this?"

"Still checking on that."

Bernie gazed down at the ground. There were tire tracks all over the place, crisscrossing and mashed up, a big mess.

"Not going to get much out of that," Rick said. He glanced over at me. "Wonder if Chet might pick up something."

"I don't know," Bernie said. "He's never worked with elephants, and if we're operating on the theory that Peanut didn't get out of here on foot, then—"

And more of that kind of talk, but I wasn't listening. There's a time for action—pretty much any time, in my opinion. I took a quick sniff at the base of the wall, picked up Peanut's scent again no problem, and started following it. A piece of cake, as humans say. I'm not a big cake eater myself, although if cake just happens to be sitting there . . .

I pushed all thoughts of cake clear out of my mind—even Charlie's last birthday party, lucky thing about that second cake arriving so fast—and trotted along the scent trail, a nice slow trot I can keep up all day.

"Hey, Chet, ease up, for God's sake."

The trail led back toward the trailers, then made a sharp turn onto a paved road that ran inside the fence at the edge of the fairgrounds. There were lots of other smells on the paved road—including cotton candy—and lots of other smells can sometimes confuse you, but not this time: Peanut's smell overpowered them all. I followed that smell right up to where the road came to a closed gate and stopped there. A man standing in a gatehouse peered out.

Bernie and Rick hurried up behind me, huffing and puffing; always fun when you can get humans huffing and puffing. Suppose you have something in your mouth, a magazine, say, and when some human makes a grab for it, you twist away, letting them come closer and closer every time: humans start huffing and puffing pretty quick in a game like that. But this was no time for games. We were on the job, and besides there were no magazines in sight.

The guard stepped out of the gatehouse. Hey! He had a toothpick sticking out of his mouth. Hadn't seen that in way too long. Humans: you just had to like them.

Rick flashed his badge. "Torres, Missing Persons," he said.

"Heard what happened," the guard said, the toothpick bobbing up and down. "Don't know nothin'."

"In my experience," Rick said, "nobody ever knows nothing."

"Huh?" said the guard.

Bernie's lips curled up a bit, like he was about to smile. I didn't know why, just knew he and Rick were pals.

"This gatehouse manned at night?" Rick said.

"Twenty-four seven," said the guard.

"Who was on last night?"

"Yours truly. Weekends we go midnight to noon."

"You work for the circus?"

"Uh-huh."

"Got some ID?" The guard handed over his ID. Rick gazed at it, then looked at the guard. "Darren P. Quigley?"

"Yup."

"Mind losing the shades, Darren?"

Shades? Hadn't even noticed them, what with that toothpick. Darren took off his shades, maybe in a way that was a little too slow; I felt Bernie stiffen beside me. Darren had small bloodshot eyes with dark circles under them. I liked him better with the shades on.

"So you came on at midnight?" Rick said.

"Yup."

"And?"

"And what?"

"Darren," Rick said. "An elephant is missing."

"Tole you. Didn't see nothin', didn't hear nothin'."

"Were you here the whole time?"

"That's the job."

Rick's voice rose. "Answer the question."

"Yeah, I was here."

"Awake?"

Darren nodded, the toothpick moving fast, like he was chewing on it hard.

"Let's hear a verbal answer."

"Yeah. Wide awake every goddamn minute. No one came in. No one went out."

Silence.

"Can I get my ID back now?"

Rick turned to Bernie. "Any thoughts?"

"Darren," Bernie said, "this is Chet."

My tail started up.

"So?" said Darren.

And went still, just like that.

"Chet's a great tracker," Bernie said.

"The best," said Rick.

That Rick! What a guy! My tail started right back up again, wagging hard.

"And," Bernie went on, "he's tracked the elephant from its cage over to here. The likely scenario is that the elephant was in some kind of trailer. Less likely would be the elephant being led on foot. Either way, a hard-to-miss sight for anyone who happened to be in the gatehouse."

"Unless that someone was asleep," Rick added.

"Or blind drunk," Bernie said.

Darren gave Bernie a hard stare. "Tole you what I tole you."

"But it doesn't add up," Bernie said.

"You believe a fuckin' dog over me?"

"Language," said Bernie.

"Huh?"

"His name's Chet."

"So?"

Now Bernie was giving Darren a hard stare back. Darren looked away, spat out his toothpick. We stood there, me, Bernie, and Rick, our eyes on Darren. No one spoke. Finally, Rick handed back the ID. "And here's my card," he said, his voice not friendly, "in case your story changes."

"Nothin's gonna change," Darren said and headed toward the gatehouse.

I wandered over to that toothpick, lying in the dirt, and gave it a sniff. Hey! Darren had done some puking, and pretty recently. Impossible to miss: I've smelled lots of puke in my time—alleys behind bars are prime spots, and so are the parking lots out front, and even right inside the bars, fancy ones, too. I barked a bit and pawed at the toothpick, but no one was paying attention. They were watching a long, white convertible approaching the gate on the road outside.

# FIVE

The long, white car stopped outside the gate. The driver, a big-headed dude with a dark tan and a cigar sticking straight out of his mouth, leaned on the horn, even though Darren P. Quigley, the gatekeeper, was already on his way. The sound of a car horn honking really hurts my ears. I gave my head a good shake and felt better. By that time, Darren had the gate open.

"Morning, colonel," he said.

Rick stepped up to the car. "Colonel Drummond?" he said.

The colonel took the cigar from his mouth. "Yes, sir."

"Owner of the Drummond Family Traveling Circus?"

"In conjunction with a bank or three," said the colonel. "What can I do you for?"

"Rick Torres, Missing Persons," Rick said. "I'm in charge of the investigation."

Colonel Drummond switched off the engine, stuck the cigar in his mouth, and talked around it. "Put me in the picture," he said. Or something like that: humans can be hard to understand even without cigars in the way.

"Mostly a mystery at this point," Rick said. "Your trainer, Uri

DeLeath, and the elephant are missing. This gentleman here is Bernie Little, private investigator."

The colonel's eyes shifted to Bernie. "Howdy," he said. "Don't recall hiring you."

Bernie smiled; maybe he was liking the colonel. "You didn't," he said. "I had tickets for today's show."

"They'll be good tomorrow," said the colonel. "Come on back. And here's a coupon, good for twenty dollars at any of our food concessions. I highly recommend the devil dogs, prizewinners in six states."

Devil dogs. Whoa. That was new.

"The point is," Rick was saying, maybe a little while later, what with my mind having a hard time letting go of the devil dogs, "Bernie works with Chet. Chet's probably the best tracker in the Valley, and he's followed the elephant's scent from the cage to right here, leading us to suspect they left through this gate, most likely by trailer."

The colonel glanced at me. "What a fine-looking pooch," he said. Hey! A horn honker maybe, but Colonel Drummond was fine by me; plus he wore one of those string ties, which were fun to chew on, although I'm sure that thought didn't even occur to me at the moment.

"The problem," said Rick, turning to Darren, "is that the guard can't corroborate the theory."

Colonel Drummond eyed Darren. "Meaning?"

"Didn't see nothin', colonel. Didn't hear nothin', neither."

"You're Quigley, right?"

Darren nodded.

"Official word is this big fella Chet's one fine tracker, and I got no reason to doubt it," the colonel said. The end of the cigar glowed hot. "Anything more to say, Quigley?"

Darren shook his head.

"That leaves one of two situations," said the colonel. "Either you fell asleep or you deserted your post."

Darren shook his head harder.

"Any situations I missed?" the colonel said.

Darren stopped shaking his head, let it hang down. We have the same thing in our world: it means you're beat.

Colonel Drummond took the cigar from his mouth, tapped a big chunk of ash over the edge of the door. It held its shape but quickly lost the glow. I went over and sniffed at the smoke curling up. Love cigar smoke!

"Take it on up to the office, Quigley," the colonel said. "Tell 'em to print out your last check, plus one week severance."

"You're firing me?" Darren said.

"Matter of principle," the colonel said. "Drummond Family Traveling Circus has a long tradition of full cooperation with law enforcement."

Darren backed away, got his lunch box from the gate-house—he had a peanut butter sandwich in there, the scent unmistakable—and slumped off toward the big top.

"Hate like hell doing that in this economy," the colonel said, "but there are lines you can't cross."

Rick nodded. "Any idea what's going on here, colonel?" he said. "Anything like this ever happen before?"

"Anything like my trainer making off with the star of the show?" the colonel said. "Of course not—DeLeath would have been out on his ass."

Bernie's eyebrows rose. Have I mentioned how expressive they are, kind of with a language of their own? "That's what you think happened?" he said. "He stole Peanut?"

"What other possibility is there?" said the colonel.

Bernie and Rick exchanged a look. "Kidnapping, for one," Rick said.

The colonel laughed. He had fat cheeks and they shook. I always like that in a human. "Kidnap an elephant? You guys are too much."

"Why is it out of the question?" Bernie asked.

"What would be the point?" said the colonel.

"Ransom," said Bernie.

"How much do you think an elephant costs?" said the colonel.

"No idea," Bernie said.

"As low as ten grand," the colonel said. "That's for an Asian—Africans are more, of course, just the females, I'm talking about. African males are too dangerous to work with. But the kicker is the cost of care and feeding: try three grand a month, minimum. So even if the ransom gets paid, this kidnapper of yours could easily wind up losing money on the deal. Nope, gentlemen—DeLeath stole Peanut, end of story."

"Why would he do that?" Rick said.

"Have to ask him," said the colonel. "Now if you'll excuse me, I've got a business to take care of, plus all the folks who work in it." He reached for the ignition. Bernie put both hands on the top of the door. A big car, but it sagged a bit; Bernie's strong, don't forget that.

"Two lives may be at risk, colonel," he said. "We need to know why you're so sure."

The colonel gazed down at Bernie's hands. Bernie has beautiful hands, but the colonel didn't seem to be appreciating them.

"Bernie's right," Rick said. "How come you're so sure?"

The colonel took a deep breath, let it out slowly. Don't know what that's all about, but I always watch for it. "No one, man or beast, is at risk, I assure you," he said. "Uri DeLeath has simply gone over to the other side."

"Other side?" Rick said.

"The animal rights fanatics," Colonel Drummond said. "What other side is there? All we want to do is entertain kids and their parents in an age-old way, but they won't rest until they drive us out of business."

"I thought DeLeath was known to be a humane trainer," Bernie said, stepping back a little from the car.

"The exact reason the fanatics have been trying to get their hooks into him," the colonel said. "The way cults go after the softheaded types. They're very clever. Trust me—we'll never see Peanut again."

Bernie looked like he was about to say something else, but before that happened Corporal Valdez drove up in her cruiser, Charlie beside her, lights flashing. Charlie's voice came over the PA: "Message for Dad—ready to go home."

Not long after, we were on our way out of the fairgrounds, Charlie riding shotgun, me on the shelf but handling it well.

"Me and Mindy were looking at mug shots," Charlie said.

"See anyone you know?"

Charlie laughed. Laughter: that's the best human sound, and kid laughter is the best of the best. Then Charlie stopped laughing and his face got serious. The serious look on a kid's face is always interesting.

"There sure are lots of bad guys, Dad," he said. "How come?"

Bernie glanced over at Charlie. "No one really knows," he said, "but I can tell you what I think."

"Okay."

"It's about conscience." Oops. I was lost already. "You know—a sense of right and wrong." Oh, that. "Everyone starts out with one, but the more you override it, the weaker it gets. Remember when the threads got stripped on the thing that attaches the propane tank to the barbecue?"

"Dad?"

"Yeah?"

"I'm hungry."

So was I, had felt a hunger pang the moment Bernie mentioned the barbecue.

"We'll pick up something on the way home."

Like what? I waited to hear, but Bernie didn't say. And were we even going home? We didn't take the freeway ramp, instead stayed on the road that ran around the fairgrounds fence. Soon we were on the back side, coming up to the gatehouse.

No sign of Colonel Drummond or his long, white car. The gate was closed, the gatehouse empty. Bernie stopped the car.

"What are we doing, Dad?"

"Just, ah, checking on something," Bernie said. "You can stay in the car."

"What kind of something?"

"Hard to say," Bernie said, opening the door. "Vague feelings."

I was already out and sniffing around. I picked up Peanut's scent, getting a little weaker now—time was passing—and followed it down the road in the direction we'd just come.

"Hey, slow down, big guy."

I tried to slow down, maybe did a bit. Soon we were at a stop sign. I lost the scent for a moment, sniffed in a little circle, and picked it up, no longer present on the road around the fairgrounds but headed toward a freeway ramp on the other side. I could hear freeway noise close by, kind of like a howling storm.

"Southbound ramp," Bernie said. "Good enough, Chet. C'mon back."

I turned and trotted over to Bernie. He gave me a nice long

pat. Ah. I could tell from the feel of his hand that he loved me. We're a good team, me and Bernie.

We walked back to the car, side by side. Charlie was standing on the driver's seat, turning the wheel and going, "Vroom vroom." That was so much fun to watch that I almost missed a strange sticklike thing lying in the ditch by the side of the road. I darted over and picked it up, a heavy wooden stick with a sharp metal point at one end, and not only a sharp metal point but also a sharp metal hook, ending up with two sharp things to watch out for.

"What you got there?" Bernie said.

I went up to Bernie and dropped the stick thing at his feet. He reached down, then paused and went back to the Porsche. He put on surgical gloves, returned, and picked up the stick thing.

"What's that?" Charlie called over from the car.

"No idea," Bernie said. "Looks like a weapon of some sort." His face brightened a bit; that sometimes happens when he has a good thought. "Have I ever mentioned General Beauregard?"

"A friend of Chet's, right, Dad?"

Actually one of my very best pals. General Beauregard lived down in Gila City with Otis DeWayne, our weapons expert. Gila City was somewhere in the Valley or maybe not, but the important thing was all that open country in the hills behind the house. Can't beat open country, of course, and guns often got fired out back for testing purposes, which was always fun, but the best part was General Beauregard, a real big dude—the biggest German shepherd I've ever seen—who likes to tussle.

The Porsche hadn't even come to a stop when the General bounded over, his big white teeth exposed. I leaped out of the car. He ran right into me, knocked me off my feet. I rolled over, ran right into him, knocked him off his feet. He rolled over, ran right into me, knocked me off my feet. I rolled over, ran right—

"What the hell is going on?" Otis came hurrying out the front door. He had hair down to his shoulders and a beard down to his chest. "Shoulda known it was you," he said. Did he mean me or Bernie? I had no time to figure that out, because at that moment the General gave me a nip. I gave him a nip back. For some reason that made him charge around the house. I charged after him. We charged around and around the house neck and neck, ears flat back. What was more fun than this? Dust clouds were rising, who knows why. We ran through them and ran through them again. I'd been in dust storms before, and believe me this was nothing compared to—

Crack! At first I thought it was a gun going off—nothing unusual at Otis's place, if I haven't mentioned that already—but then the sound came again and I saw Otis clap his hands. He was one of those real loud clappers. We came to a halt, me and the General, outside the front porch, panting side by side. Bernie, Charlie, and Otis were sitting at a table, drinking cold drinks— beer for the men, what smelled like lemonade for Charlie. Right away I was in the mood for a cold drink myself, preferably water, always my favorite.

Bernie laid the stick thing on the table, holding it with the edge of his shirt. "Know what this is?" he said. "Chet found it."

"Where?"

"In a ditch behind the fairgrounds."

"Circus in town, by any chance?" Otis said. Or something like that: he had so much beard it hid his mouth, and I do better when I can see the mouth moving.

"Yeah," said Bernie. "What makes you say that?"

Otis wasn't wearing a shirt. He had lots of hair on his chest, which met his beard hair in a sort of big hairy confusion, but that wasn't the point. The point was he didn't have an edge of shirt for picking up the stick thing, so he used a scrap of paper that happened to blow by. Otis picked up the stick thing and gave it a close look.

"Any elephants in this circus of yours?" he said.

"Come on, Otis," Bernie said, "spit it out."

Uh-oh. Spitting is something humans did from time to time—although not the women, for some reason—but they never looked their best doing it, no offense. I got ready for a glob to fly, but it didn't. Instead Otis set the stick thing down and said, "Ankus, Bernie. Also known as an elephant hook, elephant goad, or bull hook."

Charlie put down his lemonade. "It's not for hurting the elephants?"

"'Fraid so," said Otis DeWayne.

## SIX

We swung by Burger Heaven, picked up a quick snack. Back home, I went into the kitchen, lay down under the table, stretched my legs way out. All of a sudden, my paws did that quivering thing. Can't start it or stop it, but I like when it happens. When the quivering was over—ending just like that—I closed my eyes. In the mood for a nap, no question about it: that always happened after my visits with General Beauregard.

When I awoke it was night, maybe late at night, the house dark and quiet. Somewhere in the canyon coyotes were shrieking. I trotted to the back door, a plan forming in my mind, all about getting to the patio, checking the gate, maybe even leaping over, something I'd done in the past, kind of a secret. But the back door was closed.

I went down the hall, paused outside Charlie's door. He sounded restless, turning over in his bed, even muttering to himself, words I didn't understand. I stayed there, standing still, until he settled down, his breathing soft and regular. The coyote shrieking died away, but for some reason my ears remained stiff and straight up, listening hard. Do you ever get the feeling that something's going on? I had that feeling, but nothing happened, nothing went on. I moved into Bernie's room, stood by the bed. He was sleeping quietly, moonlight shining on his face, making it look like stone. The stony look made me uneasy, and I was already a bit uneasy to start with. I hopped up on the bed, lay beside him.

Bernie spoke in a sleepy voice, thick and slow. "Go to sleep, big guy. It's late."

I closed my eyes, but sleep wouldn't come. After a while, I got up and went into the front hall, lying down with my back to the door. The feel of the night leaked in through the crack at the bottom. I caught the scent of flowers, specifically those big yellow ones in old man Heydrich's garden. Sleep came.

"Dad," said Charlie the next day, "are we going to look for Peanut now?"

"Can't," Bernie said.

"How come?"

"We've got no standing in the case."

"What's standing?"

"Reason to be involved."

"Don't you care about Peanut?"

"I do."

"Then that's a reason."

Bernie reached over, mussed up Charlie's hair. Charlie jerked his head away, like he was angry or something. Bernie withdrew his hand. "We're not the same as the police," he said. "They get involved whenever there's a crime—that's their job. The Little Detective Agency is private. We can't operate without a client."

Of course not: who else would cut the checks?

"Could Colonel Drummond be the client?"

"Yeah, but he didn't exactly beat down our door."

And if he or anyone else ever tried that, they'd have me to deal with, count on it.

Charlie gazed down at the table. Bernie's hand moved. For a moment I thought more hair mussing was on the way, even though Charlie's hair was already messed up pretty good, sticking out all over the place, but instead his hand went still—hey, Charlie's hair was a lot like Bernie's except much lighter—and he said, "Tell you what. Why don't I show you how to change the oil on the Porsche?"

I could think of a reason right away—namely what had happened the last time Bernie changed the oil. Not too many women would have been as nice as Suzie about how her dress ended up. Suzie was a gem, always brought treats from Rover and Company. Was she coming over today? I listened for her car—one of those Volkswagen Beetles, an easy sound to pick up—and didn't hear it.

Soon we were in the garage, Bernie and Charlie dressed in old clothes, me in my brown collar; the black is for dress-up, when I went to court, for example. Once I was Exhibit A. The judge had me come up and sit beside him. He gave me one of those nice pats that let me know he liked me and my kind. Nothing wrong with judges, in my opinion. The perp's now up at Northern State, wearing an orange jumpsuit.

"First," Bernie said, sliding under the car, "always do this with a cold engine. Second, identify the oil pan—here—and the cap, which is—"

"What if you didn't change the oil?"

"It gets dirty—" Grunt. I stood back a bit. "All these moving parts, the engine could seize up and—" Bernie let out a cry, but not the kind that comes from pain; he would never do that. I didn't get splashed at all, a good thing, because once oil gets on my coat the smell stays for weeks, or months, or some other long long time.

After Bernie and Charlie finished with their showers, we had a little snack on the patio: blue skies, not too hot, nice breeze, tuna sandwiches for them, Milk-Bone for me.

"When can we do that again?" Charlie said.

"In five thousand miles."

"How far is that?"

"From here to New York and back."

"That's where Mom went this weekend."

"Yeah?"

"Her and Malcolm."

"Um."

"You ever been to New York, Dad?"

"Once."

"What's it like?"

"Don't remember," Bernie said. "I was on leave."

Charlie nodded like that made sense, but I couldn't figure it out.

"Uh," Bernie said, "how are—you know—things?"

"What things, Dad?"

"In general. Pretty good? Going all right? No big problems?"

"Well," said Charlie, "one big problem."

"Oh?" Bernie said, his voice normal, but his body growing still. "What's that?"

"Peanut," said Charlie.

"Besides that," Bernie said. "Everything okay at your mom's place?"

"At home, you mean?" Charlie said.

54

"Yeah," said Bernie. Sometimes a little twitch happens in his jaw; like now. "At home."

"Fine."

"How's, uh, um, well . . ."

"Malcolm?"

"Yeah, Malcolm."

"It's a Scottish name."

"Yeah?"

"They throw the caber."

"Sorry?"

"The Scottish. It's like a big pole they throw. For sports, Dad. Malcolm told me."

"Did he throw the thing? Cable, whatever the hell it is?"

"Caber, Dad. Nope. He's not strong like you. Mom had to open the pickles."

Bernie grunted, not one of those grunts humans do when they're changing the oil, or lifting something heavy, or getting hit in the gut; in my job I've heard that hit-in-the-gut one plenty of times. No, this was the kind of grunt where whatever's just been said clears things up. So, if all that—pickles, cabers, other stuff that had zipped right by—cleared things up for Bernie, great. As for me, I felt cleared up already.

Leda and Malcolm came to pick Charlie up a while later, Leda walking to the door, Malcolm waiting in the car. Leda threw her arms around Charlie, picked him up, and gave him a big kiss. She looked real happy, eyes and mouth smiling at the same time; I didn't remember much of that from before.

"Did you have fun?" she said.

"Yeah."

"What did you do?"

"Nothin'."

"Oh, I'm sure that's not true." She put Charlie down. "Where's your other shoe?"

"Don't know."

"Go find it, Mr. One Shoe Off One Shoe On Diddle Diddle Dumpling My Son John," Leda said.

"Huh?" said Charlie. His eyebrows were fair and hardly noticeable, but they rose just the way Bernie's did at that exact same moment.

Leda laughed. "Just go look," she said. "Pretty please."

Charlie went back into the house to look for his shoe, leaving me, Bernie, and Leda in the front hall. Bernie gave Leda a quick glance.

"Good trip, huh?" he said.

"A very good trip," Leda said. She looked him in the eye. "We're getting married."

Bernie's eyebrows rose again, even higher this time, and his mouth hung open for a moment. "Married? You and—"

"Malcolm, of course, who do you think?" She laughed again, and seemed about to elbow Bernie in the ribs, but then came Charlie's voice.

"Can't find it."

"Oh, Charlie," she said and went down the hall.

Bernie glanced down at me. "She's getting married to Malcolm?"

I wagged my tail; couldn't think of a reason not to.

Bernie turned toward the street. Malcolm sat in his car, that same dark sedan, thumbing some little device. Bernie walked toward him. I went with Bernie.

"Hey," Bernie said.

Malcolm glanced up. The car window slid down.

"Bernie?" Malcolm said. "Something wrong?"

"Wrong?" said Bernie.

Malcolm looked past us, toward the house. "With Charlie?"

"Can't find his shoe," Bernie said.

Malcolm checked his watch. "Still got a way to go on his organizational skills."

"Like every other six-year-old on the planet." Bernie and Malcolm exchanged a look. These guys didn't like each other; I could smell that in one sniff. "Congratulations," Bernie said.

"For what?"

"I hear you're getting married."

"Oh," Malcolm said, "yeah. Thanks, Bernie. Appreciate the sentiment."

"Got a date set?" Bernie said.

"Still working on that. We're not planning anything extravagant."

"No."

"Second marriage for both of us, after all. We're not kids anymore, none of us."

"You can say that again," Bernie said.

Malcolm blinked. "But still, very exciting and everything."

"Must be," Bernie said.

"A big step, is what I mean."

"Sure," said Bernie. "What made you decide now?"

"Decide what?" Malcolm said.

"To pull the trigger."

"Isn't it 'tie the knot'?" Malcolm said.

Triggers and knots: if this was making sense, please let me know how. Bernie didn't answer about the knot. Maybe he was going to, but at that moment Leda came out of the house, trailed by Charlie, now wearing shoes on both feet.

———

"Hi," Malcolm said. "Bernie was just asking how we decided to tie the knot."

"What did you tell him?"

"I was *about* to tell him," Malcolm said, still speaking to Leda but looking right at Bernie—humans could be tricky—"that sometimes you just know."

Leda smiled.

Then she and Charlie were getting in the car. As they drove off, I heard Charlie say, "What's 'tie the knot'?"

Donut Heaven is across the street from Burger Heaven. We met Rick Torres outside, parking beside his cruiser cop-style, driver's side door to driver's side door. He handed a bag through the window.

"Bear claws," Rick said. "Half price after four."

Bears I've seen plenty of on Animal Planet, never in real life—fine with me—and I'd watched what their claws could do, oh, brother, but how these delicious bear claws fit in was a mystery. We got busy with our bear claws, Rick and Bernie sipping coffee at the same time.

"Got anything?" Bernie said.

"Nope," Rick said. "An elephant disappears and no one saw zilch."

"Plus the trainer."

"Yeah, plus the trainer. We checked his bank account. Balance of a few thousand dollars, no recent withdrawals amounting to anything."

"But he could have stashed something somewhere," Bernie said.

"Thanks," Rick said. "That's a big help."

"There's also this," Bernie said, handing over the ankus, now wrapped in plastic.

Rick turned it in his hand. "Which is?"

"An ankus," Bernie said.

"Looks nasty."

"It's an ancient device from Asia, apparently. For training and managing elephants."

"They poke them with it?"

"More like goading them," Bernie said.

"Christ."

"Yeah. Chet found it in a ditch, not far from that back gate at the fairgrounds."

I thumped my tail, or at least thought about it. This was the best bear claw I'd ever had, no question.

"Someone dropped it?" Rick said.

"Or it fell off the back of a trailer," Bernie said. "Hard to imagine Peanut on foot and not even one lousy citizen calling in."

"I can imagine that easy," Rick said. He touched where the point of the ankus hook pushed at the plastic. "I thought DeLeath was supposed to be humane." Rick sipped his coffee for a bit. "I'm gonna have this dusted for prints," he said.

"See?" Bernie said, talking to who I didn't know. "That's the kind of thing that can't be taught."

Rick winged his coffee cup lid at Bernie. Bernie laughed. Humans can be impossible to understand, but I don't let it bother me.

Night was falling when we got home; that's the way humans put it, but to me night seems to rise up from the ground, the sky dimming last. Also night and day smell different, even indoors. But forget all that. The important thing was that someone in dark clothes—a thin someone with a thin face and dark hair, cut short—was standing at our front door, all shadowy. Bernie didn't notice at first, but I did. I leaped out of the Porsche, charged toward the—and then caught the scent, caught and recognized it. I slowed down. Bernie came up behind me.

"Looking for someone?" Bernie said.

"You. You and Chet."

"Do I know you?" Bernie said.

"This always happens," said Popo.

# SEVEN

"No one knows the real you?" Bernie said.

"I wouldn't quite put it that way," Popo said. "More like no one recognizes me out of costume."

"Isn't that a good thing?" Bernie said. "Might even be useful."

"What do you mean by that?" Popo said.

"To be unknown to people who think they know you," Bernie said.

"I'd have no use for that," Popo said.

Bernie's head tilted slightly, a look he sometimes gives people, why I'm not sure. Also, I had no idea what they were talking about. Plus, I was a bit thirsty; bear claws did that to me. So, time to go inside. I pressed against Bernie, just a little. Popo turned to me.

"Is it true what they say about Chet's tracking ability?"

"Why do you ask?" Bernie said.

"I want to hire you," said Popo.

"To do what?"

"Find Uri, of course. Bring him back safe."

"That's what the police are doing."

"Maybe."

Headlights appeared down the street. A car approached, then stopped, backed into a turn, and drove away. "Let's go inside," Bernie said.

We sat in the kitchen, me by the water bowl, all topped up with fresh water, the way I like, Bernie in his usual chair at the end of the table, Popo at the other end where Leda used to sit. No one sat there now: when Suzie came over, she pulled one of the side chairs up close to Bernie.

"What are your fees?" Popo said, reaching into his jacket the way men do when a checkbook is coming out.

"We'll get to that," Bernie said, the checkbook staying out of sight. Oh, Bernie, get to the fees now. Our finances were a mess. "First, we'd like to hear a bit more about your dissatisfaction with the police investigation." Did we, whatever that happened to mean? Why couldn't we just take on the job, hop in the car, get started?

"I didn't say I was dissatisfied," Popo said.

"Then let them handle it," Bernie said. "Sergeant Torres is highly competent."

"I don't sense any urgency in his approach."

"That's not his style."

Popo rubbed the side of his face. He had prominent cheek-bones, was maybe goodlooking for a human male, not anything like Bernie, of course. "I can't just sit on the sidelines. If you won't help me, I'd appreciate a recommendation of someone who will."

I hated hearing that one.

"What's your interest in this?" Bernie said.

Popo went still, except for his hands, which shook a little. "I thought that was obvious."

Bernie was silent for a moment. Take the case! "We'll take the case," he said. "The retainer's five hundred dollars."

And out came the checkbook! "Thank you," Popo said, starting to write. "I—"

Bernie interrupted. "But I hope you've thought this through."

The writing stopped. Popo looked up. "What do you mean?"

"Suppose Uri doesn't want to be found?"

"How could that be?"

"Colonel Drummond believes he's come under the influence of animal rights advocates."

"Impossible. Uri is and always has been the most humane of trainers, as I told you. He's also a circus person through and through."

"Sounds like that might be a source of tension," Bernie said.

I knew tension, was feeling it now, would keep feeling it until that pen moved again.

"Between whom?" said Popo.

"Internal tension is what I'm talking about," Bernie said. "Maybe it's not so easy to be humane and a circus person at the same time."

Popo's face tilted up in an aggressive kind of way. I got my paws underneath me, ready for anything. "Sounds like you're an animal rights activist yourself," he said.

I knew lots of human jobs, like prison guard and homicide detective, but animal rights activist was a new one on me. Bernie didn't say yes, didn't say no. Instead he said, "Describe Uri's ankus."

"Uri's ankus?"

"Bull hook, elephant goad—you must know the term."

"Uri doesn't own an ankus," Popo said. "He hasn't used one in years."

"How did he control Peanut?" Bernie said.

"Why are you using the past tense?"

"Sorry."

"Do you think he's dead?" There was a little quaver in Popo's voice, a sound you sometimes hear before humans start crying.

"No," Bernie said.

"Or have reason to think he's dead?"

"No," said Bernie. "It was a verbal slip. How does Uri control Peanut?"

"He talks to her."

"Saying what?"

"Little things," Popo said. "Like—foot up higher, there's a good girl. Or give your good buddy a ride—that's for when she uses her trunk to help Uri get up on her back. Plus there are hand signals for all the commands, and lots of treats."

Treats? I tried to piece together what they'd been talking about and couldn't quite do it. Was Bernie planning to go to the treat cupboard over the sink? I waited.

"What kind of treats?" Bernie said.

"Bananas and pretzels are the favorites," said Popo.

Bananas didn't do much for me, but I could always manage a pretzel. I waited.

"You have to remember," Popo said, "Uri's been working with Peanut since she was a baby."

"How valuable is Peanut?"

"In what way?"

"How much would it cost to buy her?"

"As a circus animal?" said Popo. "A lot, I suppose, but you'd have to buy Uri, too. Another trainer would have to start over, probably impossible with Peanut all grown up."

"Colonel Drummond said you can buy an elephant for ten grand."

"Colonel Drummond," said Popo, sitting back in his chair and crossing his arms over his chest, "is one of those people who knows the price of everything and the value of nothing."

The price of everything and the value of nothing? I turned that over in my mind. It turned over a couple of times and then went away.

"How long have you worked for him?" Bernie said.

"Six years," Popo said. "But I don't work for him. I work for the circus."

"Which he owns?"

"He inherited it."

"Was he in the military before that?"

"The military?" Popo laughed. This wasn't the usual human laugh, one of my favorite sounds, but something harsh and metallic. "Do Kentucky colonels count as military?"

"You don't seem to like him much."

"We have an acceptable working relationship."

"How's his relationship with Uri?"

"Businesslike."

"Did you and Uri start here together?"

Popo shook his head. "Uri owned a small circus that Drummond bought out about ten years ago."

"So Uri went from boss to employee?"

"Employee of the most skilled and indispensable kind."

"How did he handle that?"

"In his usual way—like an old-fashioned gentleman," Popo said. "I'm not sure where you're going with these questions."

"When someone disappears the first thing we check out is their enemies."

"Drummond is not an enemy."

"Who is?"

"Uri has no enemies."

"How does he get along with his family?"

"He has no family. Except for me. We're each other's family, if you can understand that."

Bernie is a great nodder, has different nods for different occasions. This one was just a tiny up-and-down movement, hardly anything at all. What did it mean? I wasn't sure, but Popo seemed to relax a little, his arms uncrossing.

"How about Peanut?" Bernie said. "Does she have any enemies?"

"Is that a serious question?"

"Not really," Bernie said. "But if she does, look out."

"Why is that?"

"Because an elephant never forgets."

Whoa right there. An elephant never forgets? Had I heard that before? Couldn't quite recall. What was Bernie saying? Not that elephants are in some way better than—? My mind dug in its heels, wouldn't go any further in that direction.

". . . hard to imagine a middle-aged man in a demanding job having no enemies," Bernie was saying.

Popo shrugged. I liked how he shrugged, in fact, liked watching all his movements. "Uri is special," he said. His eyes got a little misty. He looked down and—yes!—went back to writing the check. "Which is why I'd like you to get started."

"We've started," Bernie said, taking the check and tucking it away without looking at it. "How's the circus doing?"

"The kids still love us," Popo said.

"I meant financially," said Bernie.

"You'd have to ask Drummond." Popo rose. "Anything else?"

"We'll need the names of any animal rights people who've had contact with Uri."

"What makes you think any of them have?" Popo said.

66

"Am I wrong?"

Popo looked away. "Nadia Worth," he said.

"Who's she?"

"One of those fanatics who want to shut down animal shows completely. They follow us from town to town, picketing almost every night. Eventually Uri met with her and she backed off."

"How did he get her to do that?"

"He showed her his methods."

"Where do we find her?"

"She's got a website—Free All Animals Now," Popo said. "But you're barking up the wrong tree."

Huh? I'd barked under plenty of trees, but never picked a wrong one. No way to miss that squirrel smell.

"What's the right tree?" Bernie said.

"I don't know."

This was interesting. I'd seen Bernie bark once or twice—the party after we finally cleared the Junior Mendez case, for example, maybe a story for another time—but never up trees. Was that about to happen? I was ready.

"We'll also need a good picture of Uri," Bernie said. And then, "Easy, big guy." Oops. I was up on my hind legs, front paws on the table. How had that happened?

Popo reached into his jacket again, handed over a photo. Bernie got up and stuck it on the fridge: the smiling dude with the pencil mustache who we'd seen in the video, the one where he lay under Peanut's raised foot. In this picture he wore his tall, sparkly hat and had his arms raised.

"He always gets a standing ovation," Popo said.

Not long after that, we were on the job, Bernie at the wheel, me riding shotgun. We left the freeway, drove through a part of town

I didn't know, the streets dark and shiny, as though they were wet, but it hadn't rained and none was on the way: I sniffed the air, cool and dry, coming in off the desert. Things were different at night, muzzle flashes much brighter, for example. I'd seen muzzle flashes lot of times, although not at the moment. Not every case we took had gunfire, just my favorites.

"They're getting married," Bernie said, "and at the same time, the bastard is . . ." His voice trailed off. That happens with humans. Stuff never stops churning around in their heads and sometimes it leaks out. What was Bernie talking about? Bastard was some sort of bad guy, but exactly what sort I had no idea. I shifted in my seat, put my paw on Bernie's leg.

We turned down a street lined with brick buildings, some dark, some with lights showing here and there. "Warehouses from when the railroad first came through," Bernie said, "beginning of the end of the old West." We passed a café with a few people at outside tables, then stopped in front of a building with a man and a woman sitting on the front steps. "Now the artists are moving in, or maybe they're already moving out and the hipsters are moving in." No problem. We'd dealt with artists and hipsters before, none of whom ever seemed to be gunplay types.

We got out of the car, approached the steps. The man and woman gazed down at us. They both had Mohawk haircuts. Was that hipster or artist? I couldn't remember. Mohawk was a kind of Indian. We knew Indians, Sheriff Tom Flint down in Ocotillo County, for example, but his hair was more like Bernie's, with a tendency to stick up all over the place.

"Looking for someone?" said the man.

"We are," said Bernie.

"We?" said the man.

"Yeah," said Bernie, "Chet and I."

"And Chet, I suppose is your quote unquote dog?" the man said.

"Wouldn't put it that way," Bernie said.

"No?" the man said. "How would you put it?"

I'm the type who likes just about every human I've ever met, even some of the perps and gangbangers, but this dude was rubbing me the wrong way, an expression I've never understood since my coat's been rubbed lots of times but no one's ever found a wrong way of doing it.

"I'd put it in a way you'd really like and then we'd be good buddies forever after," Bernie said, "but there's no time for all that." He turned to the woman. "We're looking for Nadia Worth."

The woman kept gazing down at Bernie, saying nothing. No expression on her face, but she was nervous; hard to keep that a secret from me.

"Nadia doesn't deal with animal exploiters," the man said.

"Good to know," said Bernie, "unless she makes an exception when it comes to harming them."

"What are you talking about?" said the woman.

"You're Nadia?"

The woman nodded.

Bernie showed her our license. The dude leaned over so he could see it, too. "We'd like to talk to you in private," Bernie said.

"What about?"

"It's for your ears alone," Bernie said. I checked out Nadia's ears: flat to her head and kind of big for a human—which I always liked, hard to say why—with some studs in one and nothing in the other.

The man rose. "If you imagine that breeding animals in such

a way that they can't help fawning all over us is somehow admirable, then you're a menace as well as a fool," he said.

What was that all about? No idea, but for some reason I really wanted to bite the guy.

"You'd prefer to socialize only with members of your own species?" Bernie said.

"I'm not saying that," the guy said. "The human race is the cancer of the earth." He turned, hurried up the steps and through the door, slamming it shut.

"Your friend's not happy," Bernie said.

"He has a strong sense of justice," said Nadia.

"Me, too," Bernie said. "Which is why we're here. Do you know Uri DeLeath?"

Her gaze shifted away from Bernie, landed on me. Lots of times the expression in people's eyes changes when they see me, like maybe they're thinking of giving me a pat. My tail started wagging, not hard, just a little. The expression in Nadia's eyes didn't change. She turned back to Bernie. "I wouldn't say I know him," she said. "Very slightly at the most."

"How do you know him?" Bernie said.

"I chair our committee on circus outreach," Nadia said.

"And?"

"And I met him a few times in the context of that work."

"Meaning when you were picketing the circus?"

"I have every right."

"No argument there," Bernie said. "What did you talk about?"

"Our position," Nadia said, "meaning the position of FAAN, on circus animals."

"DeLeath has the reputation of being a humane trainer."

"Irrelevant," said Nadia. "The whole concept of animal training is an abomination."

"Seems to me there's a difference between a trainer who uses an ankus and one like DeLeath who doesn't."

"If he told you he doesn't use a hook, he's a liar—they all do."

"Did you try to persuade him to stop?"

"I tried to persuade him to give up the whole so-called profession."

"How did that go?"

Nadia snorted. I can do that, too, and so can horses, horses in general being a big subject, better for some other time, but the human snort is different, means something not good.

"Did things get heated?" Bernie said.

"I wouldn't say that," said Nadia. "Not like some conversations I've had with circus people."

"When was the last time you saw him?"

"Six months ago or so," said Nadia. "They come to the fairgrounds twice a year."

"They're here now."

"I'm aware of that. Some of us are actually headed out there tomorrow."

"I have a witness who says DeLeath showed you his methods and got you to stop picketing."

"Your witness is wrong."

"Planning on seeing DeLeath tomorrow?"

"I'll certainly try. We never stop applying the pressure. The stakes are too high."

"What kind of pressure are you talking about?"

"Whatever it takes." Nadia gazed down at Bernie, eyes hard.

"Including violence?"

"No comment."

"I'm not a reporter," Bernie said. "I'm a private detective, investigating a crime, and 'no comment' doesn't cut it."

"What crime?"

"Any chance you've seen DeLeath more recently than six months ago, like last night, for example?"

"Absolutely not."

"Or maybe not you," Bernie said. "Maybe your unhappy friend, or others in your group."

"No," said Nadia. "What are you getting at?"

"Is it possible your powers of persuasion are stronger than you let on?"

"What do you mean?"

"Maybe you were able to persuade DeLeath to come over to your side."

"I wish."

Bernie glanced up at the building. "Or you could be in the act of persuading him now."

"You're making no sense."

"I'd like to have a look inside your place."

"Out of the question."

"I can get Metro PD down here with a warrant if I have to."

"But why? What's going on?"

"Uri DeLeath is missing," Bernie said.

Nadia laughed, the second unpleasant laugh I'd heard today. What was going on? "You think I have something to do with that?" she said. "Search away."

"Peanut's missing, too," Bernie said.

Nadia stopped laughing. One of those faraway looks came into her eyes. We always watch for that, me and Bernie.

# EIGHT

We went into the building. Nadia had an apartment on the top floor, a small apartment with lots of plants, the smell of food cooking, but not any food I liked—had that ever happened before?—and—the most important thing—no Uri DeLeath.

"Aren't you going to peek under the bed?" Nadia said. "What about lifting the floorboards?"

"If he was here, Chet would know," Bernie said.

Nadia turned to me. We were in her kitchen. "Does it bother you that you're exploiting this animal?"

"I don't think Chet feels exploited," Bernie said.

"You flatter yourself," Nadia said. "And isn't that the whole point of pet dogs—to flatter humans?"

What was this all about? I had no idea, didn't find it interesting. We were supposed to be on the job. Where was DeLeath? I took a sniff or two, smelled Nadia and her nervousness, mouse droppings, whatever was in the pot on the stove, not much else.

". . . discuss some other time," Bernie was saying, "but right now we need your help."

"I've got nothing else to tell you," Nadia said. "I had nothing to do with his disappearance and know nothing about it."

Bernie moved over to the stove, glanced in the pot. "What's cooking?" he said. Tiny bright blue flames flickered under the pot; always liked watching those.

"Chili," Nadia said. I knew chili, but the chili I knew had a different smell, the kind of smell that made you want to stick your nose in right away. Nadia's chili was different.

"Vegetarian?" Bernie said.

"Of course," said Nadia.

Bernie turned to her. "Maybe you don't care that DeLeath is in danger, but what about Peanut?"

Nadia twisted a dial on the stove. The bright blue flames disappeared. "You've had your look around."

"Is it possible," Bernie said, "that you're not worried about Peanut because you know exactly where she is?"

Nadia took the pot off the stove, stuck it in the fridge. "No," she said, "it's not possible."

"Therefore, you must be worried about Peanut."

Nadia closed the fridge door, but not before I spotted a whole big row of eggs. Love eggs—Bernie always mixes them into my kibble.

"I've got nothing more to say," Nadia said.

"If you want Peanut brought back safe and sound, we're your best hope, me and Chet."

"Safe and sound? That's far from the life of a circus elephant."

Bernie's mouth opened like he was about to say something, but he didn't. I'd seen other humans do that, but never Bernie. We headed to the door, Nadia following. She opened it and we stepped into the hall, Bernie first, then me. Nadia closed the door behind us, but not before I felt a pat—very light, very quick—on my back.

\*     \*     \*

Back in the Porsche, Bernie was quiet for a long time. Then he said, "Scenario one—Nadia gets DeLeath on her side and they spirit Peanut away somewhere. If that's the case, DeLeath will probably reappear with some cockamamie story." Uh-oh. Cockamamie had come up in the past, always on our toughest cases. "Scenario two—it's a kidnapping, engineered by Nadia, in which case . . ." Bernie's voice trailed off. I curled up on the shotgun seat, got comfortable. Passing headlights shone on Bernie's face. His eyes were dark, the lines on his forehead deep. "Scenario three— it's a kidnapping, but engineered by—"

And just like that, I was in dreamland. Did Bernie say: "Exploitation? But what about the love?" Or was that part of the dream?

When I woke up I saw an amazing sight: the giant Ferris wheel at the fairgrounds, all lit up, and then, just as my eyes opened, going dark. What a world! I looked around, saw we were on the ring road, approaching the back gate. It was open and cars were coming out. We started driving in. The guard stepped out of the gatehouse, hand raised.

Not our guard, Darren Quigley, the little guy with bloodshot eyes and a toothpick; this guard was big and the whites of his eyes looked very white. "Closing down," he said.

"That's all right," said Bernie. "We're looking for Darren Quigley."

"Don't work here no more."

"No?" said Bernie. "Need an address, someplace to send the reward."

"Reward?"

"Lost my watch here the other day. He found it. I told him next paycheck, I'd drop by with a reward."

The guard's gaze went to the watch on Bernie's wrist—the everyday watch, not Bernie's grandfather's watch, our most valuable possession—then to me, then to the car, which at that moment started shaking, the way it did sometimes.

"A modest reward," Bernie said.

The guard held out his hand. "I can get it to him."

"Thanks," said Bernie. "Wouldn't want to inconvenience you."

"Uh," said the guard. He blinked a few times. I've seen lots of human blinking. Does it happen because something gets screwed up inside, the same way the car was shaking? Hey! Where did that thought come from? Did it mean that . . . I lost whatever might have been coming next, a kind of distant shadow. Meanwhile, the guard had gone into the gatehouse. He came out, handed Bernie a scrap of paper.

Bernie glanced at it, then said, "Here's for your trouble," and gave the guard a dollar, at least I hoped it was only a dollar; I'm not too good at telling the bills apart, even close-up. Who are those dudes in the pictures? Scary-looking, each and every one; perps, most likely.

The guard touched the stick-out part of his cap. We drove away. I turned back, no reason why. The guard was in the gatehouse, picking up the phone.

The Valley goes on just about forever in all directions. At night the sky turns dark pink, with a few stars sometimes peeking through. We hit the freeway, drove all the way past the downtown towers and took the exit into South Pedroia. I always know we're in South Pedroia from the high smokestack that never stops spewing a kind of smoke that smells like eggs left out in the sun; sometimes at night there are sudden bursts of fire way up there, too. There was one: like a muzzle flash in the sky.

Bernie gave me a pat. "Nice night, big guy."

Yeah, a nice dark-pink rotten-egg night with giant muzzle flashes and us on the job. Who could ask for more? Not this dude, amigo.

We went down a street that looked like it was paved with cracks, little run-down houses on both sides, some of them boarded up. Bernie stopped in front of one of the houses, a brown or maybe yellow cement-block box, a blue TV light showing in the front window. Scraps of paper and plastic lay on the tiny hard-packed dirt yard, shifting around in the breeze. Bernie turned to me, put one finger across his lips. That meant we were being quiet.

We got out of the car, me landing without a sound, Bernie banging something, possibly a trash can, as he opened the door. A face appeared in a window across the street, and quickly withdrew. We walked up to the front window of the cement-block house. Curtains were drawn inside but not all the way, and we could see Darren Quigley. He sat in an easy chair, wearing only boxers, beer can in one hand, cigarette in the other, blue TV light flickering on his slack face and bare, scrawny chest. The TV itself I couldn't see, but I knew from the sound that Darren was watching NASCAR. We watched NASCAR sometimes, too, me and Bernie, but never long in my case on account of how sleepy I always got. We moved to the door. Bernie knocked. Car sounds came from inside. He knocked again, harder. The cars went silent.

"Someone there?"

"Friends," said Bernie.

I heard footsteps inside. They approached the door and stop-ped. "Friends?"

"Everybody has some," Bernie said.

"Jocko? Don't sound like you, Jocko."

"Even better friends than Jocko."

"Don't got no better friends than Jocko."

Bernie was silent. He was always the smartest human in the room, in case I haven't mentioned that already, so silence had to be the right move. The door opened—just a bit, on account of the chain. Darren peered out, eyes glassy, breath strong and beery.

"I don't know you," he said.

"Sure you do," Bernie said. "You must remember Chet."

Darren looked at me, then back to Bernie. "You're the bastard that cost me my job."

"That's what we want to talk to you about."

"Feelin' guilty? Ain't it a little late for that?"

"I wouldn't say feeling guilty, exactly," Bernie said. "But it's never too late to make amends."

"What are those?"

"To patch things up."

"Think the colonel'll give me my goddamn job back? You don't know him."

"True," Bernie said. "But maybe you can fill us in."

Darren's eyes narrowed. Glassy and narrow at the same time: not a pleasant sight. "What's your angle?"

"No angle," Bernie said. "We just want things to come out right."

"I remember now," Darren said. "You're a private dick."

"I like private eye better."

"How come?"

"Figure it out."

Darren's eyes shifted. I could feel him thinking, sort of. "Can't," he said at last. "Fact is, that's it for chitchat, far as I'm concerned." He started to close the door. Bernie stuck his toe in the gap, one of his best moves. I just loved when he did that.

"What the fuck?" said Darren.

"Sorry about the private dick thing," Bernie said. "Call me whatever you want and don't worry about it—in fact, don't worry about anything. Can we come in from the cold?"

"Cold? What are you talking about? Hasn't gone below eighty in weeks." Darren stuck his hand out to feel the air. I let Bernie grab Darren's wrist: he was closer. Darren struggled some, but he was a scrawny little guy and Bernie was Bernie, plus I might have growled a bit, letting impatience get the best of me. Soon we were inside Darren's crib.

Not much of a crib: a front room that felt too small for me, made me want to get out, a hallway leading back into shadows, and also—hey! The smell of Cheetos. So: it could have been worse. We sat down, Darren in the easy chair, Bernie on the arm of a sagging couch, me on the floor. The Cheetos were also on the floor, in a bag by the base of the easy chair, next to some empty beer cans. Some of the Cheetos had actually spilled out already, all by themselves. Lots of good things happen to me.

"How about we lose the TV?" Bernie said.

"Huh? That's a flat screen, cost me a bundle."

"I meant just turn it off, so we can hear ourselves."

"These are NASCAR highlights, man," Darren said, but he switched off the TV. It got quiet, but also the whole room went dark.

"And maybe turn on the lights," Bernie said.

"Lights don't work."

We ended up with the TV back on but the sound off. The tiny cars went round and round. Bernie gave Darren a nice smile, his teeth blue in the TV light.

"How're things, Darren?" he said.

"Not too good."

"But at least you've got a friend in Jocko."

"That's right."

"Any chance he's an animal rights activist?"

"Huh?"

"What does Jocko do for a living?"

"Jocko? He gets by. No worries with Jocko."

"How about you? Are you an animal rights activist?"

"What's that?"

"Someone who thinks animals shouldn't be in the circus, for example."

"Huh? What's a circus without animals?"

I knew this was an interrogation, had sat through plenty in my time. Was it going well? Hard to say. I inched closer to the Cheetos.

"Do you know Nadia Worth?"

"Never heard of her."

"How about FAAN—Free All Animals Now?"

"How about it?"

"Ever had any dealings with that group?"

"Never heard of them, neither." Darren reached for a beer can, took a long drink, head tilted up, throat exposed. That throat-exposed thing is always interesting to me, can't tell you why.

"Here's the problem, Darren," Bernie said. "Your story just doesn't add up, and when that happens we keep going over and over it until it does, me and Chet. So if you'd like to make this our last conversation, you'll have to come across."

"With what?"

"The truth about Peanut and DeLeath," Bernie said. "Or at least some lie we can't shoot holes in."

"Didn't lie about nothin'," Darren said. He took another long swig, or at least it looked like it was going to be a long swig, but all of a sudden Bernie leaned across the small space between them and batted the can away with the back of his hand. It spun through the blue light trailing sparkling blue beer drops, a beautiful sight.

"What the hell?" said Darren, starting to rise. I rose, too. He sat right back down. Since I was on my feet anyway, I scarfed up a Cheeto or two. Cheetos: even better than I remembered.

"What you're missing—maybe because you're not thinking your clearest—is that we're on your side," Bernie said.

"Yeah, I'm missing that."

"Unlike the colonel, who's obviously not on your side. How could he be, thinking the way he does that either you fell asleep on the job or deserted your post. We know you're better than that."

"Goddamn right," said Darren.

"So all that's left is for you to tell us about the better you."

"The better me?"

"The you that didn't fall asleep or desert," Bernie said. "The stand-up you. What's that guy's story?"

Darren licked his lips. "The stand-up me," he said. Sometimes humans get a look in their eyes that tells you they like the sound of what they're saying; this was one of those times. "Goddamn right," he said. "They say he's not even a real colonel, can you believe that?"

"Easily," Bernie said. "Getting back to the stand-up you."

"The stand-up me." Darren turned to Bernie and met his gaze, at least for a moment. "The stand-up me don't fall asleep on no job, don't desert no post—you can take that to the bank."

Meaning we were putting money in at last? That was good news. This case was looking up already.

"You got me convinced," Bernie said. "But something unexpected happens to the stand-up guy last night—that's my guess."

Darren gave Bernie a quick glance. "You're a good guesser."

Bernie shrugged his shoulders. Sometimes he also said, "Shucks," while he was doing that, but not now. Instead he said, "Fill us in."

Darren took a deep breath, let it out slow. This was usually a sign; of what, I couldn't quite remember at the moment. "God-damn JB, every time," he said.

"Who's he?" Bernie said.

"JB? Son of a bitch Jim Beam. Never heard of Jim Beam?"

"Heard of him," Bernie said.

"Truth is, I got a bit of a weakness where JB is concerned."

"You're not alone," Bernie said.

Darren looked surprised. "No?"

"No."

Darren leaned a little closer to Bernie, like they were buddies now. "Thing is, I never drink on the job."

"Got you."

"Hardly ever."

"Nobody's perfect."

"And then beer only."

"Wise choice."

"But last night what happens?"

"Some kind of bad luck."

"You can say that again. Just doin' my shift, quiet night, a few hours to go. And then I get a visit."

"Yeah?"

"Yeah." Darren went silent, took a few more deep breaths, shook his head from side to side.

Bernie checked his watch. "A visit from who, you don't mind my asking?"

"My man Jocko."

"Your pal."

"Best pal. Sometimes he drops by, you know, when it gets slow. His job, I'm talkin' about."

"Which is?"

"Troubleshooter."

"What kind of trouble?"

"You name it."

"Who does he troubleshoot for?"

"Whoever's payin', I guess. Jocko's what you'd call a consultant."

"A troubleshooting consultant?"

"Yeah."

"And last night there were no troubles, so Jocko dropped by with a bottle of JB," Bernie said.

Darren sat back a little, no longer quite so close to Bernie. "You're one hell of a guesser."

"Not really," Bernie said. "You and Jocko shared a drink or two?"

"Yup."

"Or maybe three or four?"

"Musta been more than that."

"How come?"

"Or else I ate something bad, 'cause the next thing I know I'm wakin' up down on the floor of the gatehouse, pukin' my guts out."

"Jocko still around?"

"Nope. All by my lonesome. Not for long—by the time I get it all cleaned up, the place is swarmin' with cops. And I told them God's own truth—didn't see nothin', didn't hear nothin'."

"No arguing with that. Did they ask if you'd had a pop or two?"

"Nope."

"Well, there you go."

"Yup."

"Been in touch with Jocko since then?"

"Nope. But he's got my back."

"How do you know that?"

"Christ, I thought you were smart." Darren wagged his finger at Bernie. The last guy who did that? Flatfoot Bardiccio, now breaking rocks in the hot sun. "Because no one knows about the JB is why," Darren said. "Jocko's no snitch."

"Sounds like a helluva guy," Bernie said. "He got a last name?"

# NINE

Jocko's last name turned out to be something I forgot right away. But I hung on to the fact that he slept in his pickup, though where that was also got away from me. We drove out of South Pedroia, took one freeway, then another, soon put the downtown towers behind us. The rotten-egg smell lingered in my nose. I tried snorting it out, making a funny little sound I liked, so I did it again.

"Tired, big guy?"

Tired? I was full of pep, rarin' to go, feeling tip-top.

Bernie gave me a pat. "I know it's late, but got to strike while the iron is hot."

Please, no, not the iron. Most of the time the iron stayed in the closet, but when it came out—like when Bernie decided his pants were too wrinkled for going to court—look out; although the firemen turned out to be great guys, with a big bag of treats in their truck. I kept a close watch on Bernie for the rest of the ride. Was *he* tired? I didn't think so: not from the sparkle in his eye.

We took an off-ramp, drove through some quiet streets—in the headlights I spotted a cat gliding up onto a trash can, hate the way they glide around like that—and the next thing I knew we were back on the ring road behind the fairgrounds. The gatehouse appeared—I saw the guard, feet up on the desk—but we didn't stop, instead continued over a little rise with the fairgrounds fence on one side and a bare hillside on the other. Bernie slowed down, gazing at the base of the hillside. "Should be somewhere around . . . there we go."

We turned onto a rough track that slanted up across the hillside, rounded a big rock, and headed the other way. Almost at once, we saw a pickup, parked off to the side, the front facing us. Bernie stopped the car, cut the engine. We sat there, real quiet. I heard little metallic pings coming from our engine, plus the hum of traffic and other city sounds, but nothing from the pickup. Bernie was squinting in its direction. The way his eyes worked at night always surprised me. Long about now he would often make a remark about adjusting them.

He spoke in a low voice. "Better let my eyes adjust." Letting Bernie's eyes adjust meant just sitting there. We just sat there for a while and then he said, "Okay. Quiet as a mouse."

Say what? I paused, then leaped silently out of the car. What made Bernie think mice were quiet? What made him want me to be like mice in any way? Meanwhile, he was getting out of the car, almost at once stepping on a twig that cracked like a gunshot in the night. At times like that we always froze, so we froze. The pickup sat still and silent. Does the taste of something you ate earlier sometimes come back up into your mouth? That happened to me as I waited for Bernie's signal that frozen time was over, and the taste was Cheetos. I wanted more.

Bernie made a little chopping motion and we got started, moving toward the pickup, not side by side but spread out a bit, a new thing we'd been working on recently. We came to the pickup.

Bernie took out the pencil flash, shone it through the windows, then into the cargo bed.

"Nobody home," he said. He went behind the pickup, aimed the beam at the license plate, bent down. "An easy one to remember—JOCKO 1." Bernie rose. He gazed up the hill. "Any reason not to call it a night?"

Not that I could think of. We headed down the track toward the Porsche. I sniffed at a bush. A coyote had been this way, but not recently. I raised my leg, marked the bush, at the same time gazing up at the dark pink sky which a plane with flashing lights was slowly crossing. An interesting sight, and maybe it distracted me, because I almost missed the crunching sound of a hard shoe in the dirt. I turned—oh, no, maybe too late!—and a guy was coming out from behind the big rock, a huge guy sneaking up on Bernie real fast. I charged. Bernie must have heard me, because he turned, turned at the very moment when the huge guy was raising some kind of club, maybe a baseball bat. Bernie got his arm up just as the huge guy swung. Yes, a baseball bat, only partly deflected by Bernie's arm. It cracked against the side of his head, a horrible sound. Bernie sank to the ground. The huge guy lifted the bat again, high in both hands, like he was about to chop wood. I sprang.

And hit him hard, right square in the back. But what was this? He didn't go down? Everyone went down when I hit them like that. But this guy didn't fall. He only staggered, then whirled around and swung the bat at me. And he got me in the shoulder, got me pretty good. I lost my balance, rolled in the dirt. Meanwhile, the guy was turning toward Bernie, like he was going to club him again. I rose, leaped at him once more, maybe not my strongest leap, on account of the way one of my front legs had gone weak on me. But I hit him again, from the side this time, and managed to get my mouth on his arm. I bit, hard and with no hesitation. Most humans scream at a time like that, and this guy did, too, although maybe more the angry kind of scream than the pain one. Also, the arm I had hold of wasn't the bat arm. The huge guy tried to twist away. I hung on, biting deep, tasting blood. He cocked the bat, one-handed. Our faces were close. I got a real good look at him. He wore a polka-dot bandanna, had sideburns, a big crooked nose, furious eyes. I gazed right into those furious eyes, and maybe because of that didn't see the bat swinging down on me until too late.

The next thing I knew I was lying on the ground and the huge guy was running toward the pickup, holding his arm, the bat left behind. I got up, kind of dizzy, and ran after him, not my normal running on account of what he'd done to my shoulder. He opened the door, climbed inside just as I got there. I dove for his leg, clamped down on—but no. Just as I was about to clamp down on his leg, he yanked the door against me, whacking the same shoulder he'd whacked before. I tumbled to the ground. The door slammed shut. The engine roared, the pickup swung around in a tight skidding turn, raising dark pink dust clouds, and shot away, back down the track. I took off after him, more of a trot and maybe limping a little, but I can trot all night if I have to. And that's what I would have done, except when I came to where Bernie lay beside the track, I stopped.

Bernie lay on his back, not moving. His eyes were closed. I smelled blood, saw some glistening on the side of his head, but not much. I stood beside him. After a while I barked, a high-sounding bark that just came out on its own. I did that a few more times, then poked my muzzle against Bernie's chest. I could feel his heart beating. That was good; I'd felt human chests with no heartbeat on a case or two in the past. I licked Bernie's face.

*Come on, Bernie. Wake up. Wake up, big guy.* I stopped licking and panted for a bit. What was that? A groan, a very soft one. *Come on, big guy.* I gave his face another lick.

Bernie groaned again, louder this time. And then his eyelids trembled open in a way that made me think of butterflies. His eyes scared me. They were like the eyes of humans with no heartbeat I'd seen, like poor Adelina di Borghese, for example. But then they changed in a way that's hard to describe, as though a light had switched on, even though they didn't get any lighter, and he was Bernie again.

"Hey," he said, his voice so soft I could hardly hear. "Chet."

Yeah, me, Chet, pure and simple.

"You okay?" he said.

Me? I was fine, if not tip-top, then pretty close. I gave his face another lick. He made another sound, maybe a groan, but with a bit of a laugh mixed in, and his face scrunched up, the way human faces scrunch up when you lick them.

"Ow," he said.

Ow? Had I hurt him somehow? Oh, no. I backed away.

"Not you, fella," he said. "Sudden movement. Not a good idea at the . . ." He raised his head. Pain crossed his face; I could see it, like everything twisted up. But he kept going, raising himself onto his elbows. He looked around. "Son of a bitch got away."

I barked. I knew the son of a bitch and would never forget him.

Bernie sat up. Pain started to cross his face again, but he stopped it somehow. He put his hand on my shoulder, bracing himself to rise. But it was the wrong shoulder, and I shrank back, couldn't help it.

"Chet? Something wrong?" He felt around my shoulder, very gentle, hardly touching at all. A new look appeared on his face, powerful and scary, like pain, but this was anger, something I hardly ever saw from Bernie. "His days are numbered," Bernie said. "Don't you worry."

Me? I wasn't worried, not the least bit. I trusted Bernie.

He rose, all by himself. Maybe that hurt, but he didn't show it. His face seemed very white, except for deep shadows under his eyes. He swayed slightly, then hunched forward, hands on his knees, and puked.

*Oh, Bernie.* I'd never seen him puke before. All at once I had to puke myself. For some reason, I didn't want Bernie to see, so I went behind the big rock. Up came a pool of stuff that smelled of Cheetos. I was tempted to scarf it all up again, but I didn't, not sure why. Instead I came out from behind the rock, and on my way back to Bernie spotted the baseball bat lying in the track. I went to it, hardly limping at all now, and barked.

Bernie came over, walking real slow, kind of like old man Heydrich, our neighbor who shuffles around his lawn in bedroom slippers. I'm always on the lookout for bedroom slippers, maybe something we can get into another time—or did we already? Bernie reached down, his hand not quite steady, and picked up the bat. He shone the pencil flash on the barrel.

"Louisville Slugger, Willie McCovey model—may actually be worth something," Bernie said, which I didn't get at all. He looked at me. "Hope the bastard didn't use this on you." Bernie stroked my head. "But I think he did." I got that.

We walked toward the Porsche, neither of us moving at our best. On the way, I spotted a scrap of cloth lying in the dirt. I went over and sniffed. Hey! The enormous dude's polka-dot bandanna—his smell was all over it, not a nice smell like Bernie's. This was nasty and stale; and mixed in was another scent I'd picked up recently. Where was that? Oh, yes—strong and unforgettable: the smell in Peanut's cage. I picked up the bandanna.

"What you got there?" Bernie said.

I dropped it at his feet. "Nice work," Bernie said. He took a plastic bag from his pocket, sealed the bandanna inside, held it in the beam of the pencil flash. "A blood smear?" he said. "Did you do some damage, Chet?"

A light breeze sprang up behind me. In a matter of moments, I realized it was my tail. Yeah, I'd done some damage. We headed for the car, side by side, with a little spring returning to our step.

Were we headed for home? That was what I thought until I saw the big wooden cowboy outside the Dry Gulch Steak House and Saloon going by. Loved the Dry Gulch—and loved the wooden cowboy with his lasso and his six-guns, you can see him for miles, whatever those are—but that wasn't the point. The point was we always took the ramp right before the sign when we went home, and now we didn't. Why not? There was hardly any traffic on the freeway, meaning it had to be real late, and Bernie looked tired, tired and green in the light from the dash. Plus there was a zigzag line in his forehead that I'd never seen before.

"Lie down, boy," he said. "Take a nap."

A nap sounded good, but I stayed where I was, sitting straight in the shotgun seat. This was the kind of job where sometimes you had to stay up late.

When I woke up we were back on that street paved with cracks, Darren Quigley's street. His house was dark, no blue TV light showing. We parked outside, walked to the door, Bernie making no effort to be quiet, me being quiet anyway. Not actually sure how I'd go about moving noisily, but no time for sorting that out at the moment. This time we didn't knock on Darren's door. Instead Bernie raised his leg and kicked the thing open. CRACK!

SPLINTER! I loved when we did that, hadn't done it in way too long. We went in fast, Bernie stabbing the light here and there. No sign of Darren in the front room. We hurried down the hall and searched the rest of the crummy crib. No Darren.

Back in the front room, Bernie shone the light at the beer cans on the floor, the cigarette butts all over the place, dirty plates, scattered clothes. "No signs of violence," Bernie said, "but how the hell would you know?" He aimed the flash at the big flat-screen TV. But what was this? There was nothing but a cable dangling from the wall. The TV was gone.

"Do you have a headache, Chet? I have a headache."

Nope. I had a shoulder ache, but not bad, not bad at all. I moved closer to Bernie, pressed my head against his leg.

# TEN

My eyes snapped open. I was lying with my back to the door, our front hall full of sunshine. I gave myself a good stretch, sticking my legs way way out, and felt a funny—not pain, really, more of a tug—yes, a funny tug in my shoulder, and everything came back to me, and if not everything, then at least some of it. Like that huge guy, and the baseball bat, and what else? Cheetos. I rose and went into the kitchen.

Food bowl: empty. I licked it anyway. Water bowl: full. I lapped some up. Not fresh, even a bit dusty on the surface, but I found I was real thirsty and drank and drank, splashing some of it here and there. While that was happening, the phone on the counter rang. A voice came through the answering machine: "Bernie Little? Marvin Winkleman here." Marvin Winkleman? I recognized the voice but . . . and then it came to me: divorce work, ticket guy, comb-over. "That jerk, the one my wife is cheating with? I've changed my mind—I want you to check into him after all. Get back to me as soon as you can." Click.

Then the house was quiet again, except for the faint sound of Bernie's snores. Bernie's snores are nice, kind of like ocean waves on a beach, a sound I'd heard once in my life, that time we went to San Diego. We surfed, me and Bernie! I'll get to that another time. Right now I was on my way down the hall to take a look at him.

He lay on the bed, still dressed from last night, even down to his shoes, with one arm thrown back over his head. I moved to the bedside. His chest rose and fell. I could see dried blood on his head above one ear, not much. I climbed up on the bed and settled down. Bernie snored.

Sometime later the phone rang again, not Bernie's cell phone, which lay on the bedside table, but the phone in the kitchen. Bernie grunted, reached out for the cell phone, eyes still closed, had some trouble with the buttons, finally said, "Hello? Hello?" Meanwhile, I could hear Winkleman's voice again on the answering machine in the kitchen. A thought about humans and machines started to take shape in my mind.

"What, uh?" Bernie said. The phone slipped from his hand, fell on the floor. His eyes opened, but not quite at the same time, one a bit ahead of the other; that bothered me, can't say why. He sat up, that zigzag groove suddenly appearing on his forehead, and said, "Who's that?" at the same moment Winkleman stopped talking. He looked at me. "Hey, Chet." He gave me a pat. "How are you doing?" I thumped my tail on the blanket. "Good boy." He glanced around. "Broad daylight. That's no good." He rubbed his face, got up, went into the bathroom. "Still in my goddamn . . ."

Then came pill bottle sounds, tooth-brushing sounds, showering sounds. Wisps of steam leaked out from under the bathroom door. After a while, he started singing. I recognized the song: "He Stopped Loving Her Today." We'd been listening to it in the car a lot lately, but I couldn't say it was one of my favorites, like "It Hurts Me Too" with Elmore James's slide guitar that did things deep inside my ears, hard to describe. I got up, went into the kitchen, sat down; near the food bowl, but that was just by accident.

Bernie came into the kitchen looking great, all back to normal. No dried blood, no zigzag groove. "Any chance someone's hungry?" he said. Bernie was a good guesser. Who'd said that recently? I tried to remember, soon gave up. "Any of that salami left?" Bernie opened the fridge. Salami? You bet there was some left, and I knew right away, but it took him a while to find it. "Thought, I'd . . . ah, here we go." Soon Bernie was slicing a nice fat salami. He put some slices in my bowl, mixed them in with kibble. Then he heated up coffee from yesterday or maybe the day before, sliced some more salami for himself, and sat at the table. I poked through my bowl, gobbling up all traces of salami before I even took one bit of kibble. We had a nice breakfast.

Bernie finished his coffee, sat back, rubbed his hands together. Always a good sign, meaning soon we'd be in action. "C'mon over here, big guy. Let's see how you're moving." I walked over to Bernie, moving just fine. He took my head in his arms, gave me a big hug. "You're something, you know that?" he said. Not sure what he was getting at, but nothing wrong with that hug. "I've got a strong suspicion you saved my bacon last night."

Bacon? There'd been bacon last night? Cheetos, yes, but that was it. Had I somehow missed out on bacon?

"Hey," said Bernie, "something the matter?" He felt my shoulder.

What a question! Of course something was the matter—did bacon happen every day? Nowhere close. Why was that, anyway? I tried to think of one good reason and couldn't.

Bernie noticed the message light blinking, jabbed the button as he went by. "Bernie Little? Marvin Winkleman—" Bernie hit the button again. "Later, Marv." He wrapped the baseball bat in plastic, grabbed the plastic bag with the bandanna inside, and we hopped in the Porsche. Iggy, watching from his window, jumped up and down as we drove away.

We met Rick Torres at Donut Heaven, parking cop-style.

"Cruller?" said Rick.

Bernie shook his head. "Just ate. We—"

"How about Chet?"

"He just ate, too."

Yes, but very late and really not all that much, considering that yesterday amounted to a few Cheetos and hardly anything else. And can I mention something, even though I love Cheetos? They're mostly air. I'm a hundred-plus-pounder, can't live on air.

"Also got a bacon croissant I can't finish," Rick said.

Bacon? Bacon coming up again, and so soon?

"Chet! Down!"

Oops. I slid back onto my seat.

"I get the impression he wants it," Rick said.

Bernie sighed, a real good sign at a moment like that. "Oh, what the hell," he said.

The next little while I was too busy to take in much of what they were talking about. That whole package, croissant with bacon inside? What can I tell you? I licked every last crumb and flake off my lips and then sat up straight and still, a pro, on the job.

"We're nowhere, really," Rick was saying, "and I'm not sure there's anywhere much to go."

"What's that supposed to mean?" Bernie said. "Don't we have a missing person and a missing elephant?"

"Yes and no," said Rick. He handed Bernie a sheet of paper. "Came about an hour ago—this is a copy."

Bernie read the letter out loud. "'Dear Sergeant Torres, I can no longer be complicit in the exploitation of this magnificent creature. I have taken Peanut to a place where she will be safe for the rest of her life. You will never find us and I do not believe you have any cause to search. Peanut is the property of no one. Sincerely, Uri DeLeath.'" Bernie looked up. "Checked the handwriting?"

"His, uh, friend, the guy who plays the clown—"

"Popo?"

"Yeah, Popo. He had some samples, grocery lists, that kind of thing. Handwriting guy says it's a match." Rick's phone rang. He spoke into it. "Torres. Uh-huh. Yup." He clicked off. "Forensics—they got two clear prints on the original, thumb and index finger, both DeLeath's."

Bernie was silent for a moment or two. Then he said, "What does Popo think?"

"We're gonna let a clown run the investigation?" Rick said. He started laughing, couldn't stop. That happens to humans sometimes, always ends up making me anxious. Rick gasped for air, wiped away tears with the back of his sleeve.

"Feel better now?" Bernie said.

"Aw, come on, Bernie—where's your sense of humor?"

"Lost it last night."

"What happened last night?"

"Doesn't matter," Bernie said. "The point is that if DeLeath has really taken off, then he took off on Popo, too."

"Yeah," said Rick, "making him an unreliable interpreter of events."

"What's his interpretation?"

"Like you'd think."

"Meaning he doesn't believe the letter?"

"Correct. But he has no alternate theory."

"And you?"

"We're in a wait-and-see mode, Bernie. The case is open, but the department's not going to devote a lot of resources to this, absent some new information."

"How about the colonel? Doesn't he want his elephant back?"

"He was headed out to the golf course—didn't have much to say."

"Is Peanut insured?"

"I can check," Rick said. "Think it's an insurance scam?"

Bernie thought for a moment. "Not really," he said. "Did you get any prints off that ankus?"

"Yeah," said Rick. "But not DeLeath's."

"Whose?"

"Nobody in the system."

Bernie gave the bat to Rick.

"Cool," Rick said. "Willie McCovey model. Five bucks if you can tell me his nickname."

"Stretch," said Bernie. "See what Forensics can find on the bat—a match to prints from the ankus would be nice."

"Why?" Rick said, handing over some money, for what reason I didn't know.

"Even if the letter's kosher," Bernie said, "there's no way DeLeath did it alone."

Kosher? I knew all about kosher, a kind of chicken, in fact the best chicken I'd ever tasted, at the celebration dinner after the final stakeout in the Teitelbaum divorce. The Teitelbaum divorce: a nightmare. Mrs. Teitelbaum riding a bulldozer straight through the wall of the garage where Mr. Teitelbaum kept his antique car collection—hard to forget a sight like that. My mind stayed with the memory a little too long, and if Bernie mentioned how chickens were coming into the case, I missed it, looking up only in time to see him handing over the plastic bag with the bandanna.

"And how about running a couple names," he was saying, "Darren Quigley—"

"The guard?" Rick said. "Ran him first thing. Think I don't know how to do my job?"

"Hey, easy. You know I don't think anything like that."

"Sorry," Rick said. "These goddamn budget cuts—everybody's on edge. As for Quigley, one DUI a few years back."

"That's it?"

"Yup. What's the other name?"

"Jocko Cochrane."

Rick turned to his computer, tapped at the keyboard.

"Could be Jack," Bernie said, "or possibly John."

Rick gave Bernie a look. "Bernie?"

"Sorry."

"I'm your defender—you realize that?"

"Defender against what?" Bernie said.

"Some people in the department aren't fans of yours," Rick said. "I hope that's not news."

Someone wasn't a fan of Bernie? I didn't get it.

"That was all a long time ago," Bernie said.

"You stuck it to the big guys, Bernie. Big guys have long memories."

Wow! I'd never known that. Bernie was bigger than Rick, so he had a longer memory. And that huge guy with the bandanna? His memory would be even longer. What about Cedric Booker, the Valley DA? He'd starred on the Valley College basketball team, might have gone pro, Bernie said, except he couldn't play with his back to the basket, whatever that meant. The truth is, I've never had much interest in basketball, on account of the ball being impossible for me, but the point is . . . gone right now, but maybe it will come back.

Meanwhile, Rick was checking his computer. "No hits," he said, "not for Cochrane—Jocko, Jack, or John. Who is he?"

"Someone you'd expect to have hits," said Bernie.

"The smartest ones never do," Rick said.

"This guy's not that smart," Bernie said.

"Maybe he has a brainy boss."

A look came into Bernie's eyes, like he was watching something far, far away. Always interesting when that happens, but what it meant I couldn't tell you.

Rick drove away. We sat there in the Donut Heaven lot, Bernie sipping what was left of his coffee, me eyeing the traffic going by on the street, just in case any of my guys—the guys from what Bernie calls the nation within the nation—went riding by. Didn't see any of my guys, but then a car I knew pulled into the lot. I'm not too good on cars, but this one—a yellow Beetle—was easy. It zipped up on my side and Suzie Sanchez got out. Suzie's a reporter for the *Valley Tribune*. I'm pretty sure she likes Bernie and he likes her, but it hasn't been smooth, partly on account of her old boyfriend Dylan McKnight, possibly a perp of some kind, and partly I don't know why.

"Hi, guys," she said.

"Uh, hey," said Bernie. "Hi. Hello."

"And hi hello to you, too," Suzie said. She has shiny black eyes like the countertops in our kitchen. "Someone's been eating bacon."

How did she know that? It was gone, every last morsel.

"How do you know that?" Bernie said.

"From the smell—what do you think?" Suzie said.

Suzie's a gem. If I already mentioned that, I'm mentioning it again. She gave me a quick pat and moved around to Bernie's side of the car.

"Um," said Bernie, looking up at her, "didn't expect to see you here."

"But *I* expected to see *you* here," Suzie said. "Hoped, actually."

"Yeah?" Bernie said. "Want a cruller?"

"No," Suzie said. "I want to interview you."

Uh-oh. Suzie had interviewed Bernie once before, which was how they'd met. It hadn't gone well: she'd described Bernie as shambling. Can't remember what that means now, but Bernie hadn't liked it.

"What about?" he said.

"This story you're sitting on," Suzie said. "The missing elephant."

"There's not much to tell."

"Liar," said Suzie, flipping through a notebook. "Let's start with the trainer, DeLeath—does that rhyme with death, by the way?"

"Wreath," Bernie said, losing me completely.

"And he's missing, too?"

"I can't really say. I've got a client."

"Who?"

Bernie laughed, wincing slightly at the end.

"Bernie? Are you all right?"

"Yeah."

"You look like you have a headache or something."

"I'm fine."

Suzie put her hand on Bernie's forehead. A very nice expression appeared on his face. "No fever," she said, taking her hand away. "Is the client Popo the clown?"

"Why him?" Bernie said.

"Because he and DeLeath are a couple."

"How do you know that?"

"Sometimes I actually do research, Bernie. They went to

Massachusetts and got married a few years ago. The AP wrote it up."

Bernie said nothing, just sat there, that faraway look in his eyes again.

"What are you thinking?" Suzie said.

"Not every couple splits up," said Bernie.

"True," said Suzie. "And therefore?"

"Chet and I have to get going."

"You're not being very helpful."

"Should know more tonight. How about the Dry Gulch at seven?"

Couldn't be better.

# ELEVEN

We met Popo under the big top, just me, Bernie, and Popo—the two of them seated on a bench, me in the aisle. The benches were all worn, with paint flaking off, and the tent itself had lots of little holes and tears in it, some not so little. High above, the Fearless Filipoffs, First Family of the Flying Trapeze, were practicing their tricks. I have a few tricks myself, catching Frisbees, for example, but they're nothing like what the Fearless Filipoffs were doing. All those Filipoff tricks going on made whatever Bernie and Popo were talking about a little hard to follow.

"I'd like to clear up this question of the ankus," Bernie was saying, or something like that. "You claimed that DeLeath never used one, but we've heard that all animal trainers do, no exceptions."

Popo sat hunched forward, forearms on his knees, head down. He wore jeans and a T-shirt; his forearms were skinny and bone-colored. "Who told you that?"

"A source."

"A source?" said Popo. "I'm the client and that's the best you can do?"

"Nadia Worth," Bernie said.

"Didn't I tell you she's not to be trusted?"

"You didn't quite put it that way," Bernie said.

"What are you getting at?"

But I missed whatever Bernie was getting at because at that moment one of the Fearless Filipoffs, a little dude with long hair and huge arms, oh, no!—let go of Fil Filipoff, who spun through the air and began falling a horrible long fall when suddenly another little dude with long hair and huge arms came swinging in from the side and caught her by one hand, and then they were swinging back, and what was this? Now he was somehow upside down and Fil was dangling from a rubbery-looking thing he had between his teeth, the other end between her teeth? I hardly had a chance to wonder what that rubbery-thing tasted like, when she was flying through the air again, twirling right into the grasp of the first little dude, and the next thing I knew, they were all standing together on a platform and Fil was saying to the little dude with the rubbery-looking thing, "If you don't start brushing your teeth you're out of the show."

"So what are you telling us?" Bernie was saying. "The handwriting matches and Forensics found two of his prints, but he didn't write the letter?"

"It's just not Uri," Popo said.

"In what way?" said Bernie. "Whether he used a hook or not—"

"He didn't."

"—he was known as a humane trainer. Isn't it possible he took one more step in that direction?"

Popo didn't answer. He raised his head, glanced up. Fil was spinning through the air again, hands crossed over her chest, ponytail sticking straight out, muscles bulging in her legs. One of the little dudes came swinging in, reached out and—missed her! Fil stayed still in midair for the longest time, like—like she really was a bird—and then she fell.

"Chet! Easy."

Fell and fell and then landed in a net, which sprang her back up, kind of the same as a trampoline. I made the mistake of getting on a trampoline once. Never again: can't beat solid ground, as far as I'm concerned. Fil bounced up and down a few times, and called up to the little dude who'd missed her, "Hung over again, you stupid jerk?"

"Who's that?" Bernie said.

"Her brother Ollie," said Popo.

"He's a boozer?"

"Not for me to say," said Popo.

"Your circus seems to have some problems," Bernie said.

Popo turned to Bernie. "Are you going to keep looking for Uri? That's all I want to know."

Bernie took out the letter. "'You will never find us and I do not believe you have any cause to search.' Sounds like he doesn't want to be found."

Popo looked away, but not before I saw tears in his eyes.

"Uh," Bernie said. "Um." He smoothed out the letter, looked at it again. "Are there any secrets in here?"

"Secrets?"

"Hidden messages," Bernie said.

"Like invisible ink?"

"Forensics probably checked for that, but I'll remind them. What I meant was any meanings that would reveal themselves only to someone who knew him really well."

"Like me."

"Yeah."

"There's nothing like that," Popo said.

Bernie handed him the letter. "Take another look."

Popo held the letter up. His eyes moved back and forth. He shook his head. "No hidden messages in your sense," he said.

"Then in what sense?"

"The whole thing is one hidden message," Popo said. "Uri would never do something like this." Bernie's mouth opened, but before he could say anything, Popo went on. "I know what you're thinking—I'm just a pathetic aging reject who can't face the truth."

What did that mean? Couldn't tell you, but from the quick sideways movement of Bernie's eyes—real quick, easy to miss, a look I'd seen often in discussions between Bernie and Leda—I was pretty sure that Popo had in fact known what Bernie was thinking.

"Far from it," Bernie said. "Not my thought at all. But now that you raise the, uh, relationship aspect, we should explore a few obvious avenues, a formality, more or less."

"I don't understand."

"Was Uri interested in someone else?"

Popo was silent for a long time. He seemed to be watching the Fearless Filipoffs as one by one they climbed down a long ladder from their platform to the dirt floor. "You never know, do you?" he said at last.

"Yeah," Bernie said, "lots of times you do know. So if you've got a name, let's have it."

Popo rose. He was shaking. "There is no name."

"But you suspect someone?"

"No, and I don't think you do, either."

"Why not?"

"Because, although it turns out you're not very likable, you're not stupid, either. Therefore you've already asked yourself why, if Uri was only running off with someone new, would he go to all the trouble of taking Peanut, too?"

Whoa. Bernie not likable? Where did that come from? And then, another surprise: Popo took out his checkbook. "Is fifteen hundred enough for now?" That had to mean we were still on the case, whatever it was. Things were happening fast.

"More than enough," Bernie said.

Oh, Bernie.

We left the big top, went past the ticket booth, and took a little walk around the fairgrounds, me and Bernie. Were we going anyplace special? I didn't know, but I never turned down the chance for a walk. Soon we came to one of those places for throwing baseballs at milk bottles. We'd been to one before, me, Bernie, Suzie. The guy running it—tattoos all over his face, I never like that in a human—told us to get the hell out of there and never come back. By that time Bernie had won too many stuffed animals to carry, but why anyone would want even one was beyond me. Bernie showed no interest in this particular booth even though the woman at the counter with the baseballs in her hand said, "Try your luck, big guy?" Instead we kept going, stopped at a little outdoor bar at the end of the row of booths. The only customer was one of those little Filipoff dudes, sitting at a corner table with a mug of beer.

"Once in a while," Bernie said, "you've just got to roll the dice."

Oh, no, not the dice. The last time—in some late-night dive after the Police Athletic League fund-raiser—we'd had to pawn Bernie's grandfather's watch, our most valuable possession, with Mr. Singh, our go-to move in financial emergencies.

No dice appeared. We walked around the railing, entered the bar, and stopped in front of the little dude. Bernie looked down at him and smiled, a nice big friendly smile, and Bernie has the best smile going. "Ollie Filipoff?" he said.

The little dude glanced up. "Sorry, bud," he said. "Off duty."

"Off duty?" Bernie said.

"No autographs."

Bernie pulled up a chair and sat down. "Wouldn't dream of it," he said. I sat beside him. Under the table I saw that Ollie Filipoff was wearing flip-flops. His feet had an interesting smell—leather, sweat, toe-jam. I was all set to like him.

"Huh?" said Ollie. "I'm kinda—"

The waitress arrived. "Same as my friend here," Bernie said, "and why not another one for him while you're at it? Plus a bowl of water for Chet."

"He's adorable," the waitress said. One thing about this job—you meet great people. "We've got an order of short ribs a customer just left, hardly touched," she went on. "Is he allowed to—?" Some of the greatest people on earth. Short ribs were new to me, but even if they weren't as long as the kind I was used to, no complaints.

Bernie gave Ollie another smile. "Saw your practice session," he said. "Fantastic."

"Uh-huh," Ollie said.

"It's all one family?"

"Yup."

"That must be fun."

"Why?"

"One big happy family."

Ollie snorted. I was always on the lookout for that. It's not about clearing their nose because nothing ever comes out, and often meant we were about to get somewhere.

"Your part looks difficult," Bernie said.

"Catcher? Goddamn difficult." Ollie took a long swig of beer. "And that's putting it . . . you know."

"Mildly?"

"Yeah, mildly."

The waitress came with two more mugs of beer and a paper plate, and on that paper plate: ribs, and they didn't look short to me, not one bit. She put the plate on the floor and patted my back; she was a good patter, but I was in a rush. I wagged my tail one quick back-and-forth and lowered my head to give the short ribs a try. What can I tell you? If you've had short ribs, you know.

"Oh, and miss?" said Bernie. "How about a couple shots of JD, just to celebrate." He raised his mug, clinked it against Ollie's.

"Celebrate what?" said Ollie.

"The artistry of the trapeze," Bernie said.

"Artistry my ass," said Ollie. He drained his first mug, started on the new one. "Know how long I've been doing this?"

"No."

"Long as I can remember. I was the flyer for years."

The waitress came with the shots. Ollie knocked his back in one throw; Bernie left his alone.

"What do you like more," Bernie said. "Flyer or catcher?"

"What do you think?" said Ollie. "Flyer's the star of the goddamn show."

"Wouldn't have guessed that," said Bernie, "seeing how strong and quick the catcher's got to be."

"Frickin' right," said Ollie, giving one of his upper arms a little rub; I glimpsed that through the glass table top in mid-bite. "But does anyone appreciate it?"

"Tough break," Bernie said. "Who decided to make the switch?"

"Gramps, of course," Ollie said. "Who else? That old scumbag decides everything."

"Maybe he was thinking since Fil's the smallest—" Bernie began.

"She's as strong as an ox. Gramps always liked her better, simple as that. And I was practically an Olympic gymnast." His legs started trembling under the table. I've seen a lot of that, mostly from perps. Hey! Was Ollie a perp? I glanced at his pant leg: our cases usually end with me grabbing the perp by the pant leg. Ollie's pant leg was in easy striking distance.

"Didn't know that," Bernie said, sliding his shot glass closer to Ollie.

"I had a screen test at Universal," Ollie said.

"I'm not surprised."

Ollie's hand moved toward the shot glass. "Still waiting to hear on that."

"It can take time."

"That's what I tell Gramps, but he says after five years there's no chance. See the kind of support I get? And on top of that, Fil's a drill sergeant."

"So you're under a lot of pressure," Bernie said.

"Tell me about it."

Ollie downed the second shot. While he was doing that, Bernie made a quick motion to the waitress.

"Don't know about you," Bernie said, "but when I'm under pressure my sleeping patterns go all to hell."

Ollie raised the shot glass, found it empty, switched to the beer. "Can't sleep for shit," he said. "I'm up every goddamn night."

"Without exception?"

"Huh?"

"Meaning each and every."

"Didn't I just get finished saying every?"

"Yes, sir," said Bernie. Bernie calling someone sir? Always a sign we were winning. "My mistake. I'm a little surprised that's all."

"Why?"

"Because it means that the other night when Uri DeLeath and Peanut disappeared and no one saw or heard anything, there's a real good chance that you did."

Ollie sat back.

"So you must have had a good reason for keeping your mouth shut," Bernie said.

"You a cop?" Ollie said.

"No."

"You look like a cop."

"Ex-military," Bernie said.

"Yeah?" said Ollie. "I was thinking of joining up with the SEALs myself."

"You'd have been great."

Ollie drank more beer. "Thing is," he said, "I've never been comfortable in the water."

"They can work around that," Bernie said.

Ollie gave Bernie a long look. By that time I was all done with the short ribs, also done with licking the plate clean, and was just getting comfortable in a shady patch. "Know what kind of guy you are?" Ollie said.

"Tell me," said Bernie.

"A glass is half-full guy," Ollie said. "All I deal with is the half-empties."

The shots came. "Cheers," Bernie said.

They threw down the shots. Ollie wiped his mouth with the back of his hand. "Yeah, I saw some shit that night, but I'm no fool—I keep things to myself."

"Don't blame you," Bernie said. "Like what kind of things?"

"Like this big old eighteen-wheeler going out the back gate," Ollie said. "I was just coming in from this after-hours joint I hit sometimes."

"Uncle Rio's?" Bernie said.

"How'd you know that?"

"It's nearby," Bernie said. "What can you tell me about the eighteen-wheeler? Or were you seeing two of them?"

Ollie paused for a moment. Then he laughed, a squeaky little laugh. "So right," he said. "Maybe even four. Four times four red roses—that makes sixteen."

"Not quite following you," Bernie said.

"That's what was on the side of the trailer," Ollie said. "Four red roses."

# TWELVE

We drove home. Bernie's face had this still and quiet kind of look it gets when he's thinking. I was thinking, too, in my case about short ribs. After a while, he said, "The whole universe is just one huge clock. But keeping time for what? That's what I'd like to know." So what if short ribs turned out to be shorter than the longer kind—they still tasted great.

A car was parked in front of our place. The door opened and a man got out as we pulled into the driveway. I recognized him from the comb-over: Marvin Winkleman. "What the hell is he doing here?" Bernie said.

Winkleman walked over to us, one of those human walkers whose knees go in and whose feet go out. Getting around on two legs: you have to wonder.

"Hey, Marvin," Bernie said. I wagged my tail. I had nothing against Marvin. His checks had cleared, no problem. Not sure what check clearing was all about, but we'd had trouble when they didn't—take the DeMarco case, for example, where we'd ended up getting paid with a gift certificate at a hair-cutting place, useless to us since Janie's Pet Grooming Service—We Pick Up and

Deliver took care of my hair, and Bernie always went to Horace the Barber on the Rio Seco strip, where you could still get a haircut for a reasonable price, Bernie says, like eight dollars, or maybe seven, I can't remember, the low prices having something to do with the back room at Horace's, a bookie joint where Bernie once bet a whole retainer fee on a horse named Scooter Girl. That was a bad day.

"You don't answer your calls?" Winkleman said.

"We've been on the road."

"I tried your cell."

"Beyond the coverage area, Marvin. What's up?"

"I've changed my mind. I want you to look into him."

"Who?" said Bernie.

"The asshole who's dicking my wife, who else?" said Winkleman.

"I thought you were getting divorced."

"I am."

"Then what's the point?"

"Bobbi Jo won't tell me his name."

"Does it matter?"

"Yeah, it matters."

"Why?"

"Why?" Marvin waved his arms around, a human thing that happens sometimes when they're getting worked up. "Because why should I take this lying down, is why."

Bernie reached out, put his hand on Winkleman's bony shoulder. "We see a lot of divorce in this job," he said. Way too much. "The people who do best are the ones who put it behind them."

Winkleman jerked away. "Why should I be the putz?"

On, no. Putz had come up before, late one night when a mob guy named Sid Siegel asked the exact same question and then pulled a .44 out of his pocket; he's now wearing an orange jumpsuit up at Northern State Correctional. I shifted closer to Winkleman, got my legs under me. Sid Siegel had squeezed out a round or two; I wasn't going to let that happen again. Winkleman waved his hands around some more, but they didn't go near his pockets; if he had a .44, it stayed tucked away.

"You're not the putz," Bernie said.

"Then who is?"

"Does there have to a putz?"

"When it comes to someone dicking your wife?" said Winkleman. "Damn right."

A funny look crossed Bernie's face, like something wasn't comfortable. Hey! I came close to making—what would you call it? A connection? Or not.

"Maybe," Bernie was saying, "but that just makes it more important to move on."

"I'll move on when I'm good and ready," Winkleman said. "Right now I want the dirt on that son of a bitch."

"What if there isn't any?" Bernie said.

"Doesn't have to be dirt dirt. Just some facts, that's all."

"Like?"

"Like is he married, for example?"

"Why would you want to know that?" Bernie said.

"Think about it," Winkleman said, and at that moment another look crossed Bernie's face, a look he gets when he tastes anchovies, which he doesn't like; me, neither. "What if he's married and what if she's living in the dark," Winkleman continued, "just like I was? What if there's a kid or two? Maybe it's my duty to enlighten her."

"He's not married," Bernie said.

"No? What else do you know about him?"

"Not much."

"What's his name?"

"We never got that."

"You never got that?"

"Weren't the pictures enough?" Bernie said. "You seemed to think so at the time."

"I've changed my mind."

"Why?"

"Didn't I explain? I don't want to be the putz."

I moved closer, kept my eyes on Winkleman's hands.

"What's your dog doing?"

"Chet? Just hanging out."

"His teeth are huge."

"Come over here, big guy."

I went over to Bernie and sat beside him.

"How come you know he's not married, but you don't even know his name?" Winkleman said.

"Information flow is unpredictable in this business," Bernie said.

I had no idea what that meant, but it seemed to make sense to Winkleman. He nodded and said, "This guy—does he have a girlfriend, maybe? A fiancée?"

"Can't say," Bernie said.

"I'm hiring you to find out. What do you want for a retainer? A grand? Two?"

"We're pretty busy right now," Bernie said.

"Fine," said Winkleman. "I'll take my business elsewhere. I hear the Mirabelli brothers are pretty good."

The Mirabelli brothers down in Sunshine City? Who said they were any good? What about that time when both the brothers got themselves stuck in the same chimney and we had to rescue them, me and Bernie?

One thing about Bernie: he hardly ever gets angry. Another thing: sometimes when he doesn't get angry there's anger going on inside him. When that happens a little muscle bulges in his jaw. It bulged now, real quick and then gone.

"All right, we'll take the case," he said.

Winkleman reached for his checkbook. Now was the kind of moment when Bernie often said something about paying later, but not this time. "Make it twenty-five hundred."

Winkleman gave him a glance and wrote the check. As he handed it over, he said, "Enjoy the circus?"

"The trainer and his elephant are missing."

"So I heard. I had a minority stake until last year."

"In what?"

"Drummond's circus. He bought me out, paid cash. Surprised me."

"How so?"

"Where's he coming up with swag like that? His circus has been hemorrhaging money for years."

"Why?"

"Lots of reasons. Drummond's a big spender, been married four or five times, pays alimony out the wazoo. But mainly it's the competition."

"Other circuses?"

"Nah. Other forms of entertainment, mostly involving screens. Screen addicts, practically the whole goddamn country." Winkleman turned, moved toward his car. As he got in, he paused and said, "When am I gonna hear from you?"

"When we've got something to say," Bernie said. Winkleman drove away. Bernie watched until he was out of sight. "Christ," he said, "what are we going to do?"

Funny, but I thought of something right away. We have three

trees out front, my favorite being a big shady one just perfect for napping under, but there's also a soft spot in the earth on the other side of the trunk, ideal for burying things. I ran right over and dug up my lacrosse ball. You don't see lacrosse balls that often, but they're fine bouncers and chewing on them makes your teeth feel great.

I dropped the lacrosse ball at Bernie's feet. At first he didn't seem to see it; his eyes were all cloudy. I picked up the ball and dropped it at his feet again. His eyes cleared.

"Wanna play a little fetch?" he said.

Exactly.

Bernie picked up the ball, reared back, and fired it up Mesquite Road. Bernie pitched for Army until his arm blew out, if I haven't mentioned that already, but it's still a great arm, if you're asking me. The ball soared away, finally touching down and making a bunch of those huge lacrosse ball bounces. It was still bouncing when I snatched it out of the air with one quick head lunge, wheeled around—my claws actually ripping into the pavement!—and tore off, back to Bernie, airborne almost the whole time. I dropped it at his feet.

"That was quick," Bernie said.

We did it again. And again. And once more. And a few more times after that. And again. And once more. And a few more—

"Chet! My arm's falling off."

Uh-oh. Didn't want to see that. We went into the house and drank some water, me from my bowl, Bernie from the tap. He raised his head.

"One thing's for sure—Winkleman and Leda can never be in the same room."

We went into the office. Have I described the office yet? It's a little room next door to Charlie's bedroom, at the side of the house facing old man Heydrich's fence. A basket of kid's blocks lay in one corner—the room was meant for a little sister or brother that never came along; sometimes I played with the blocks myself. The rest of the office was mostly Bernie's books—on shelves, in stacks here and there, sometimes scattered on the floor; plus the desk; the two client chairs; the wall safe, hidden behind the picture of Niagara Falls, and a nice soft rug with—and this was the part that got my attention now—a pattern of circus elephants. The rug had been there forever, so I was very used to that circus elephant pattern. Normally I lie down on the rug, but all of a sudden I didn't want to, something about a real circus elephant now being in our lives, couldn't quite figure it out. I lay under the desk instead.

Bernie tapped away at the keys, a calming sound. I snuggled up against his feet; they smelled nice.

"What we're looking for," Bernie said, "is some hauling company with red roses on their trucks."

My eyes closed. That often happens after fetch.

I felt a nudge in my side, a gentle nudge I knew well. I opened my eyes and there was Bernie looking down.

"Sorry to yank you out of dreamland, big guy." I'd been dreaming all right, but what? I came close to remembering. "We got work to do."

The next thing I knew we were in the Porsche, Bernie at the wheel, me riding shotgun. The sun was low in the sky, big and orange, and we were headed right into it. Bernie took his shades from behind the visor and put them on.

"Chet! You do that every time."

Do what? The barking? That was me?

"They're just sunglasses, for God's sake."

Sure, just sunglasses, but I didn't like when he wore them, couldn't help it. I shifted back over to my seat, turned my head to look out the window, which was always down because it wasn't working these days, and neither was the top, not a problem because the monsoons had come and gone, what there was of them which had been hardly any—a big problem for Bernie on account of how much he worried about the aquifer—and so there was no chance of getting wet, not that I minded getting wet. I've never laid eyes on the aquifer and it's a big mystery to me. All I know is there's only one of them and back in Indian times the arroyos ran with water all year. But if they didn't now, was it a problem? We went by a golf course, water spraying all over the place, making beautiful rainbows, and then another golf course, and another. We had water out the yingyang.

We got off the freeway, went through a rough part of town with boarded-up houses and lots of dudes sitting around doing nothing. Some of them looked like okay kinds of dudes; some watched us go by with hard eyes. We'd taken down a lot of hard-eyed dudes, me and Bernie. Then I thought of Jocko, a hard-eyed dude for sure, and the taking-down had been done by him.

"What's that growling about?" Bernie said. "You see something?" He glanced around. "I don't." He gave me a pat. We crossed some train tracks. I settled down.

On the other side of the tracks everything was warehouses, chain-link fences, loading bays. We turned down a dusty street, passed a lumber yard, and stopped in front of a low brick building with some pallets stacked by the door. Over the door, a sign: "Cuatro Rosas Trucking," Bernie said. "Know what that means?" I did not. "Four roses." Four roses? I remembered something about that.

We went inside. I'd been in lots of offices but never seen one quite like this, so empty. There was a desk, a phone, and a chair. A round-faced guy with a black handlebar mustache sat in the chair, reading a newspaper, his feet on the desk. He wore cowboy boots of shiny snakeskin—that got my attention—and a cowboy hat. He gave us a look, first Bernie, then me, then back to Bernie.

"Cuatro Rosas Trucking?" Bernie said.

"That's what it says over the door, last time I checked."

"We're looking for some information on one of your trucks."

"Yeah?"

"Specifically a truck that left the fairgrounds early Saturday morning."

"Just curious?" said the guy.

"No," Bernie said. He stepped forward and handed over our card.

The guy gazed at it. "Little Detective Agency," he said. "Cute."

"I'm Bernie Little. This is Chet."

"Uh-huh."

"And you're . . ."

"Tex Rosa," said the guy.

"The owner?"

"That's right. Which is how come you can take it to the bank that ain't none of our drivers been anywhere near the fairgrounds this month."

"Then it looks like one of them has misled you, or maybe got a little off course, because an eighteen-wheeler with four roses on the side was seen leaving by the back gate."

"'Fraid not, pal," said Tex Rosa. "We're only runnin' half a dozen eighteen-wheelers right now. Two's in Arkansas, three's in California, one's down in Sonora—makes six."

"But where were they on Saturday?"

"What I just said—Arkansas, California, Sonora."

"Maybe one of your drivers made an unscheduled detour."

"Ain't no such thing no more, not with GPS. I know where every one of my trucks is every goddamn minute of every goddamn day." Tex Rosa raised his finger, a big fat finger. He wagged it at Bernie, something I knew Bernie hated. "And every goddamn driver knows I know—you can take that to the bank, too."

# THIRTEEN

We got back in the car. Where were we with the case? Were we going to the bank? And if so, taking what, again? I didn't know. The sky was dark orange now, all the low, square buildings and telephone wires black against it.

"They call this part of town the Roads," Bernie said. "First time I worked with Stine was right around here." Hey. Lieutenant Stine. That meant Bernie was talking about his days with Metro PD, which he hardly ever did. "Turned into a bad night." I waited for more, but no more came.

We headed out on the dusty road toward the train tracks but just before we got there, Bernie swung down a narrow alley with dark brick buildings on both sides, the kind with painted-over windows. The alley led to another alley, even narrower and darker. We climbed a bit, made a few more turns, and stopped behind a bunch of rusty barrels. Between them we could see down to a fenced-in yard with a low building at one end.

"The back side of Cuatro Rosas Trucking," Bernie said.

I saw a gas pump and next to it a truck with roses on the side. Not an eighteen-wheeler: this was more like the UPS truck that sometimes came down Mesquite Road. Love UPS! The driver always tosses me a biscuit as she zips by.

Time passed. The sky lost its fiery color and went dim, shadows deepening over the yard. A light went on in the Cuatro Rosas office. "Sometimes it's what they don't say," Bernie said. I thought about thinking about that. After a while, Bernie said, "In this case, not one single question from Tex Rosa about what we were working on. Suppose we were investigating an accident, for example, with potential liability, even criminal charges. Wouldn't you expect him to be curious? So either he's a total incompetent or he already knew."

Already knew what? Was Bernie still talking about Tex Rosa? I remembered Tex Rosa perfectly, especially those snakeskin boots. The combination of the snakeskin boots and his handlebar mustache suddenly made me nervous, no idea why. Nervousness often leads to gnawing, no idea about the why on that, either. I glanced around; nothing to gnaw on but the dashboard, never a good idea. The problem was that when the gnawing bug hits me, it's just about impossible to con—

"Here we go," Bernie said, his voice low.

A door opened at the back of the Cuatro Rosas building. Two men walked out, illuminated by light spilling from the doorway. One was Tex Rosa; standing up now, he was bigger than I'd thought, but not as big as the other man. The other man was huge, had long sideburns and a crooked nose, wore a bandanna: Jocko Cochrane.

"Shh," said Bernie, just as I felt the growling urge.

Tex Rosa and Jocko Cochrane moved out of the light and into the shadows but were still easy to follow, although I was aware of Bernie leaning forward and squinting. Humans never looked their best squinting, not even Bernie. But no problem, I saw the whole thing: the two men walking to the truck, Jocko getting in, them talking through the open window—I even picked up a bit of what they were saying, like "next time blow his head off," and "any bonus for that?" and "how's five hundred bucks?" Then the truck was turning in the yard and Tex Rosa was on his way back to the office. We turned, too, no lights, Bernie driving fast, and came to a street just as the Cuatro Rosas truck was going by. I got a real good look at Jocko, laughing into a cell phone. Also I smelled bananas, kind of strange. We pulled out and followed.

First came some deserted streets I didn't know, and then we were on a freeway with lots of traffic; Bernie switched on the lights. "Thought I heard them talking down there by the truck," Bernie said. "I'd give plenty to know what they were saying." I took a quick glance at Bernie's ear, the one I could see. Nicely shaped and good sized for a human ear: what was it for, exactly?

We came to the big interchange near the downtown towers— "the stupidest traffic plan in the whole country," Bernie said every time, including now—and changed freeways. Jocko drove in the middle lane; we tailed him on the inside, always with other cars in between. We were real good at this, me and Bernie.

After a long long time we left the Valley, which goes on for- ever in all directions, and entered open country. The sky turned from dark pink to black and the stars came out. "A hundred bil- lion stars in the Milky Way," Bernie said, "maybe even twice that number. And a hundred billion galaxies in the universe. So what are we doing?"

What were we doing? We were tailing a real bad guy who'd hurt us with a baseball bat and we were going to bring him down. Bernie had to know that, right?

We crossed the desert, dark and empty, except for occasional distant towns, like baskets of lights. Why I mention baskets of lights is because once when Leda was decorating the Christmas tree—always an exciting time for me, and I end up outside—the lights were all coiled up in a basket and Bernie plugged them in for a test. This was back when Bernie and Leda were still sort of getting along, before that breakfast where she took a sip of coffee and said, "This isn't working for me." At first I thought it was something about the coffee, and so did Bernie.

Jocko left the freeway for a two-lane highway with not much traffic. We followed at a pretty long distance, through one of those light basket towns and then onto another road that wound up into hilly country. Jocko's taillights kept disappearing and twinkling back into view as he took the curves. He topped a rise, dropped out of view again. By the time we got up there, the Cuatro Rosas truck was partway down the other side, but no longer on the road; instead Jocko had turned onto an unpaved desert track.

"Heading south," Bernie said. From up on the rise we could see a flat plain extending into the distance, the truck's headlight beams cutting slowly through the night. "Getting pretty close to the border," Bernie said, and just then the truck's lights went out. The truck kept going—I could still see it in the starlight. "Christ," said Bernie, "where the hell?" And then: "I think I see him." He cut our own lights, fishtailed onto the dirt track.

We followed the truck—a sharp-edged shadow—across the plain, followed close enough so the dust Jocko raised coated our windshield and got in my nose. "Might even be in Mexico already." Uh-oh. Mexico. We'd worked down there before, the Salazar kidnapping and another case I couldn't remember, except for part of a pork taco I'd scarfed up behind a cantina. My guys, not all but some, are different in Mexico—real tough customers, red-eyed dudes, lean and mean. Got into some scraps down in Mexico, and so did Bernie. The Mexican vet had to stitch me up;

she stitched up Bernie, too. She was nice, kind of fell for Bernie, which led to complications on account of she forgot to mention her husband. But he turned out to be a real bad shot, so it ended up okay.

I glanced around, saw a pair of glowing eyes in the night, and then another. My guys, of the Mexican type? I sniffed the air. No, this was something else, something closer to cat. There were big cats out in the desert, as I knew all too well.

The track grew fainter and fainter and finally vanished. We slowed down, picking our way around rocks and bushes. Up ahead, the sharp-edged shadow was approaching a long line of low hills. I lost sight of it.

"Where'd he go?" Bernie said.

We reached the hills, steeper than they'd looked from a distance. Was there a way in? We drove back and forth along the base of the hills, saw a few gullies leading up, but narrow and rocky. Bernie stopped the car, took the big flashlight from under the seat. We got out.

Bernie put a hand to his ear. "Don't hear him," he said softly. No surprise there, but I didn't hear anything, either, except for a faraway coyote cry.

"I don't get it." Bernie shone the light around. "No tread marks leading up and it's way too steep anyway." We walked around, Bernie shining the light here and there. "So where the hell did he go?" I didn't know, but the truck's exhaust fumes were easy to pick up. I followed them to some tall spiky bushes that grew in front of where the hills rose practically straight up; from there the fume scent led back toward the plain. "He turned around?" Bernie said. "How could we have missed him?"

I went to the spiky bushes—ocotillo, was that the name?— and sniffed at them again. Hey! They smelled like bananas. Bernie came over, shone the light. Nothing to see but the bushes, their long stems with spines sticking out, and the rocky wall behind them.

We stood there, Bernie thinking, me smelling exhaust fumes and banana scents as they faded slowly away. It was nice being under the stars, the air so clear, the night beautiful. "How about we go up top," Bernie said, "see what we can see?"

Sounded good to me. We walked along the face of the hills until we came to one of those gullies and started up. The flashlight picked out little cacti, lots of rocks, an old wagon wheel. No water visible, but I could smell it, practically under our feet. Bernie gave the wagon wheel a look as we went by. "Could be a mine around here." Bernie was interested in abandoned mines in the desert; that had led to problems in the past.

We climbed higher. The gully narrowed, twisted around, then disappeared into a fold in the hillside. After that, the climbing got harder, at least for Bernie. He grunted; he panted; the flashlight beam wobbled; little landslides got started. But not by me. Pretty soon I came to a huge saguaro, the biggest I'd ever seen, and found myself at the top. So close to the stars! What a life we had, me and Bernie. And in the distance, another broad plain with a town, not very lit up, in the distance. Were we going down there? I was ready.

Bernie drew up, stood beside me, huffing and puffing. "Got to get in shape, big guy," he said. Had to be talking about him, not me, right? He switched off the light, gazed across he plain. "Yeah," he said, "Mexico for sure—that's got to be the El Gato pueblo. You know what I'm thinking?" Most of the time I don't, but now I was pretty sure it had to be that Mexican vet. Wrong. "We've had two big things disappear on us, Peanut and Jocko's truck," Bernie said. "Can that be a coincidence?"

I tried to understand. Peanut was in Jocko's truck? No way that truck was big enough for Peanut. I sniffed around, found no trace of Peanut's smell. But what was this? Very faint, but in the air: a scent close to frog or toad except fishier, the fishy part sharper and more thinned out than the scent of an actual fish. I'm talking fresh fish, of course; rotten fish is another story. This particular smell—froggy, toady, fishy—meant just one thing: snake. Snakes scare the hell out of me. I'm not ashamed to admit it.

"Let's poke around a bit," Bernie said.

Were we still looking for the truck? How could it be way up here? I didn't know, but if Bernie said poke around, we poked around. I like poking around and there's a lot of it in this job.

We wandered over the hilltop. Bernie kicked at a rock, as he often did during poking-around sessions. The flashlight beam followed the rock, which bounced down a side slope and dropped into a little dip, out of sight. We started down the slope ourselves. That fishy-toady smell was still in the air, but now mixed with another smell I knew from K-9 school. The fur rose on the back of my neck.

"Chet—what is it?"

I hurried to the little dip, gazed down and saw only darkness; but I already knew what was there. Bernie caught up, aimed the flashlight. At the bottom of the dip lay a man, facedown, one arm stretched out to the side. He wasn't all twisted and broken, the way you sometimes see, even looked like he could be sleeping, although of course he wasn't.

"Goddamn it," Bernie said.

We moved down into the dip, took a closer look. The man wore loose-fitting dark-colored pajamas and had slippers on his feet. Bernie shone the light on his face, a face I'd seen before, smiling in the video with Peanut, also smiling in the picture on our fridge. His mouth was closed now but his eye, the one I could see, was open. An ant crawled across its surface.

"Uri DeLeath," Bernie said.

He knelt down, slowly ran the beam over the body, examining it inch by inch, but not touching.

"No obvious cause of death," he said. "No blood, no bullet holes, nothing looks broken, I just don't . . ." The circle of light paused on DeLeath's outstretched hand. "Although this hand looks swollen, and what's this?" He leaned closer. I saw what he was talking about: two punctures in the back of DeLeath's hand, not big, bruised and purple around the edges.

We were concentrating so hard on those punctures that I almost didn't see a quick ruffling movement happening somewhere inside that pajama top and the next thing I knew a snake slithered out of the silky material, not a long snake but thick, and with a real big head and angry eyes. It reared up—so quick—its mouth gaping wide and showing huge fangs, and struck at Bernie.

Bernie made a startled kind of noise I'd never heard from him before and sprang back, just out of reach. I lunged at the snake's tail—as far from those fangs as I could get—and trapped the very end under my paws, digging my claws in, but the front whipped around and the snake rose up, eyes right on me, mouth opening, and—and then Bernie clobbered the back of that big head with the flashlight, clobbered it hard. The snake sank twitching down to the ground. Bernie stomped on its head, more than once; in fact, way more. The snake lay still. Bernie's face looked wild.

# FOURTEEN

Look like a diamondback to you?" said a guy in a uniform, what kind of uniform I didn't know. The sun was turning a milky kind of color—milk's not my drink at all—and lots of different uniformed guys were around—Metro PD, state troopers, Border Patrol, maybe some others. "Looks like a diamondback to me."

"I'm no expert," Bernie said. "Isn't there supposed to be a clear-cut diamond pattern?"

"Don't know about clear-cut, but right there, see? Looks like diamonds."

"Sort of."

"Or maybe it's a goddamn sidewinder. But what's the difference? Poor son of a bitch—what a way to die."

By that time, they'd taken Uri DeLeath's body away, gotten busy with cameras, asked Bernie questions. I was pretty tired and not really listening. All I knew was that the more they asked him the less he said. Bernie had dark patches under his eyes: he was tired, too. A curved sliver of the sun topped the rise, and Bernie's face went all sorts of hot colors, and with the tiredness at the same time it kind of scared me. Then the sky turned blue and everything was all right. I lay down, my back against a rock that still felt cool from the night, that huge saguaro towering above me. Another conversation started up, maybe about what to do with the snake. It was still going on when we left, me and Bernie.

The motion of the car was nice. I curled up on the shotgun seat. Bernie was quiet for a long time. Then he said, "What could we have done differently?" About what? I wasn't sure, and no ideas came. Bernie rested his hand on my back. Hadn't we done well? We'd killed that horrible snake without getting bitten. My eyes closed, but right away I saw those two puncture wounds in DeLeath's swollen hand. I opened my eyes, watched the side of Bernie's face. My eyes closed again. This time I saw nothing bad, just lots of clouds rolling in.

"You look like shit," said Rick Torres, "but Chet looks great."

And felt great, pretty much tip-top. I gave myself a nice shake, the kind that ends with a ripple all the way to the tip of my tail. Can't tell you how good that feels. I'd slept the whole way.

We were outside Metro PD, central station. It's downtown, not far from the tall buildings, and has some comfortable benches in front where friends and family of perps sit and wait. They were doing that now, but not on our bench—and not on the benches near us, either, for some reason—which had Rick at one end and Bernie at the other, with me climbing up on the middle as soon as the rippling shake was all done. Sometimes it's nice to sit up high.

"Want to know what I think?" Rick said.

"Probably not," Bernie said.

"That's because you're a conspiracy theorist."

"The hell I am."

"No? Are you ready to accept that the guy went a little crazy, saw himself as this great elephant liberator, ended up wandering in the desert, probably with no food or water, and ran into the kind of trouble that's waiting out there?"

"No."

Rick laughed. "Here we go."

"Let's start with Peanut," Bernie said.

"Whatever you say."

"Where is she?"

"Couldn't tell you, but so what?"

"So what? If they were wandering around the desert together like you said, there'd be signs."

"What kind of signs?"

"Ever heard of elephant dung, Rick?"

All this talk had been flowing back and forth over my head in a pleasant way, but elephant dung: that got my attention.

"Not hard to spot," Bernie was saying. "And I looked. Even if I hadn't, do you think Chet would have missed something like that?"

"Got a point there," said Rick, giving me a quick pat.

Damn right, Bernie had a point. I'd never overlooked dung of any kind, not once in my whole career.

"But," said Rick, "that could just show they got separated earlier, like before they reached the border."

"You think it's a coincidence," Bernie said, "two Cuatro Rosas trucks showing up in the same case?"

"Spoke to that guy, Tex Rosa—absolutely clean, by the way, not even—"

"Don't say it."

"Don't say what?" Rick said.

"'Not even a parking ticket,'" Bernie said. "It's one of those cop clichés that drive me crazy."

"Okay," Rick said, "I won't say it. Am I allowed to say he

denies that any of his trucks were anywhere near the fairgrounds the night of the disappearance?"

"I've got a witness who contradicts that."

"Name of?"

"Ollie Filipoff—one of the acrobats."

Rick wrote in his notebook. "I'll check him out."

"Do that," Bernie said. "And then ask yourself what the second truck was doing down there."

"The so-called second truck's back in the yard," Rick said. "Saw it myself this morning. According to Rosa, it was headed to Santa Fe with some engine parts last night, but developed an oil leak at spaghetti junction and turned back." Rick paused, cleared his throat. I always listen for the throat-clearing thing, in case I haven't mentioned that already. "Bernie?"

"Don't want to hear it."

"I'll say it anyway—spaghetti junction's a goddamn nightmare, plus it was nighttime, and anyone could go in tailing truck A and come out tailing truck B."

The muscle in Bernie's jaw jumped. "That didn't happen."

"Suit yourself," Rick said. "But big picture—what we're left with is a missing elephant and the body of the guy who stole it. Not much rationale for a big commitment of Metro resources." Rick got up. "But if something new comes up, let me know."

"That'll be my number one priority," Bernie said.

They didn't shake hands.


The door to Popo's trailer was open. We went in, found him sitting in front of a mirror, putting on his clown face. He had the white stuff on already, and the thick red lips, but he hadn't started on the eyes or the nose.

"Hi," he said, turning; his eyes looked very small. "What brings you here?"

"Uh." I felt Bernie steel himself. That's what he does at tough times—stands straighter, makes himself hard like steel. "We've got news," he said. "Not good."

"Oh, no," Popo said. He put one hand to his mouth, smearing the red lip stuff over his face.

"I'm sorry," Bernie said.

Popo sucked in air, real fast, making a rasping sound. He turned his face away from us. Popo was wearing a sleeveless T-shirt, one of those wife beaters, I think they're called, not sure why. The one wife beater we'd come across wore a leather jacket. We broke down his door and caught him in action. Bernie made him pay. But that's another story. Right now I was watching Popo's shoulders, skinny shoulders, not at all like Bernie's, and his neck was skinny, too. Something about the back of his head was very nice, hard to explain. He was trembling, just the tiniest bit. I went around and sat down in front of him, at his feet. Maybe he didn't see me right away, on account of his eyes being so damp and cloudy. But then he did, and reached out. I gave his hand a lick. It tasted of lipstick, a taste I knew from having chewed up one of Leda's lipsticks in the old days, or possibly more than one, even lots.

Popo's eyes, overflowing now although he didn't make a sound, stayed on me. His face was very strange, part clown, part man, and all smeared with red and tears, but I wasn't afraid. I moved closer, pressed against his leg. Popo was the kind of human I really liked, don't know why. He put his hand on my shoulder and pulled me closer. I let myself be pulled.

Bernie told Popo the whole story about what had happened out in the desert. Popo asked some questions and Bernie explained again. Then came more questions and more answers from Bernie. I ended up almost understanding the whole thing myself.

Popo wiped what was left of the makeup off his face. "I want you to keep looking," he said.

"For what?" said Bernie.

"For Peanut, of course. That's what Uri would have wanted."

"Um," said Bernie, "I'm not sure that—"

Popo's voice rose, got real loud, in fact. "Name the price."

Bernie nodded. "The normal rate—four hundred a day plus expenses."

Four hundred a day? Wasn't our normal rate five hundred? Which was more? That was the one I wanted.

Popo opened a drawer and took out his checkbook.

"That can wait," Bernie said. Oh, Bernie.

Popo glanced at a wall clock—and, yes, gave himself a little shake. Then he turned to the mirror, and began spreading white stuff from a jar onto his face.

"What, uh . . ." said Bernie.

"Showtime," Popo said. From the set of his skinny shoulders I knew he was steeling himself, too, the best he could.

We left Popo's trailer. Outside were a bunch of circus people, some I knew, like Fil and Ollie Filipoff, and lots I didn't, like a bare-chested strongman, a woman in motorcycle leathers, a man with one of those single-wheeled bikes in his hand. They all started filing inside.

We drove out of the fairgrounds. The patches under Bernie's eyes were even darker now. He made some calls. I kept a close watch on the car in front of us, specifically a car with a cat lying on the rear-window shelf, as cats often do. What's wrong with the shot-

gun seat? This cat was watching me, too, watching me in a way I didn't like one little bit.

"Chet! Knock it off."

I tried to knock it off.

"Chet! What's gotten into you?"

Bernie didn't know? The cat was practically right in his face, yawning and stretching in a way that made me want to . . . but then we turned onto an exit ramp and the cat was gone. I settled down, no problem, quiet, alert, professional.

Pretty soon we were going by a golf course. Lots of golf courses in the Valley, always the greenest land around. That bothered Bernie, on account of—hey! We weren't actually going by this one, but turning in and following a curving driveway lined with flowers. In the lot at the end we parked beside a long, white car that seemed familiar.

Nice smells in the golf course air: flowers, fresh-cut grass, and water, lots of it, even though I couldn't see any. We walked over to the practice tees—I knew practice tees from the Dalton case, where it turned out Mrs. Dalton was having an affair with her golf pro, although at the same time her game improved so much she and Mr. Dalton won a local husband-and-wife tournament just before the divorce, so everything ended up okay—where only one person was taking swings, a tanned, big-headed, cigar-smoking guy wearing yellow pants, a pink shirt, and a straw hat: Colonel Drummond. He took a short, choppy backswing and jerked his club down at the ball with surprising force. Was that called topping it, when the ball hit the ground almost right away, bounced a few times, and rolled to a stop close by?

Colonel Drummond glanced up. "Mind not moving when a player's addressing the ball?" he said. He looked more closely. "Oh, it's you."

"Your office said you'd be here," Bernie said.

Drummond reached into the basket, placed another ball on the tee. "This about DeLeath? I already heard." He shook his head. "Terrible, terrible news," he said, talking around his cigar. "I'm devastated, don't mind telling you." He waggled the club, took another swing, a lot like the last, but this time he didn't top the ball. Instead it darted rapidly to one side and dinged off a golf cart. "See?" the colonel said. "Can't hardly think about anything else. Our little world—the circus world, I'm talking about—has lost one of its best." He teed up another ball.

"What do you want to do about it?" Bernie said.

Drummond, already into his waggle, stopped. "Do about what?"

"Getting to the bottom of what happened."

"The animal rights assholes got into DeLeath's head and he went off the deep end, that's what happened," Drummond said. "Unless you have a different story."

"I don't," Bernie said. "I only have questions."

Drummond checked his watch. "Tee time's in five minutes," he said, "so there's time to hear just one."

"Okay," said Bernie. "Do you know Tex Rosa?"

"Never heard of him." Drummond started his waggle again, took the club back, and swung. This time the ball rose off the ground a bit and went down the fairway, although not far.

"More like it," Drummond said. "What would you say—two twenty?"

"Tex Rosa owns a shipping line called Cuatro Rosas," Bernie said.

Drummond took the cigar from his mouth, tapped off the ash, smiled. "That's pretty damn close to a second question," he said. "The answer's still no."

Bernie gave him a long look. "Your stance is too wide," he said. "Messes up your rotation."

"Huh?" said the colonel. "You know the game?"

"Not really," Bernie said. "I caddied a bit when I was a kid."

Hey! That was new. Bernie could still surprise me, always in a good way. No one comes close to him, if you want my true opinion.

Drummond lined up before another ball. "Like this?"

"Even more."

Drummond brought his feet closer together, swung again. This was his best by far, not what you'd call soaring, but well off the ground and past some bushes, rolling up to the edge of a sand trap. "Well, well," said Drummond. "Much obliged."

"What about Peanut?" Bernie said.

"What about her?"

"Don't you want her back?"

"How can you even ask me that?" Drummond said. "But we've got to face facts—elephants aren't built for desert survival."

"Meaning she's dead?"

"Wish to God I could be more hopeful."

"Is she insured?"

Drummond laughed. "Can't buy life insurance for circus animals," he said.

"So that's it?"

A golf cart came bumping up with a guy dressed a lot like Drummond and also smoking a cigar at the wheel. "Sneaking in some practice?" the new guy said. "You sly son of a bitch."

Drummond picked up his bag, turned to Bernie. "It's business, son. I'm interviewing for a trainer next week and we'll have a new elephant act up and running by spring at the latest. The show must go on." He got in the cart. "Thanks for the tip."

As the cart drove off, I heard the other guy say, "What tip?"

"Gonna cost you to find out," said Drummond. They both laughed. Cigar clouds lingered in the air behind them.

Bernie watched until the cart was out of sight. "Two twenty, my ass," he said. Someone's bag of clubs stood waiting on the next tee. Bernie grabbed a club, toed a ball into place and whacked it. CRACK! ZING! Wow! So high and zooming—that ball just took off, soaring straight, way over the bushes and the sand trap, and a pond and the green with its flag, and some trees and the fence beyond, and over the road on the other side, where I finally lost it.

We went home. I took a ball with me, actually more than one. Golf balls aren't big—you can fit a surprising number of them in your mouth at the same time.

# FIFTEEN

Back home, Bernie filled my water bowl and went into the bedroom. I lapped some up and followed him. "Hate sleeping in the daytime," he said, lying on the bed, still in his clothes. He rolled over and fiddled with the alarm clock. "One hour, tops." He lay back, closed his eyes. I wasn't really in the mood for this, felt like a hike in the canyon out back, or a game of fetch, or even a quick walk up and down the street. But Bernie looked so tired, and that strange zigzag line was showing on his forehead again, like maybe he was in some kind of pain. I backed out of the bedroom, went into the hall, looked out the side window, and there was Iggy, in *his* side window. He jumped up, front paws on the glass, excited to see me—Iggy was a good pal. I got up on my hind legs, too. Iggy went yip-yip-yip, that high-pitched bark that annoyed all the neighbors, except for us, of course. I started to bark back, but then swallowed it—or most of it, or at least some of it—thinking of Bernie. Then old Mr. Parsons appeared behind Iggy and said something that I could tell was all about knocking it off and getting away from that damned window. Iggy kept yipping and jumping up and down and wagging his stubby tail.

Mr. Parsons went away, then came back with—hey! with a chew strip, a real big one. He waved it in front of Iggy's nose and walked away. That was the end of all the yipping, jumping, and wagging; Iggy turned from the window and scuttled after old Mr. Parsons. I wanted that chew strip real bad.

"Chet!" Bernie called from the bedroom. "Cool it."

I caught the faint echo of barking in the air. Me? Oops.

I moved toward the front door, circled around a bit, lay down. Then I got up, looked out the side window again. No Iggy. He was probably working on that chew strip. I came close to barking again, very very close, maybe even too close. I went still, listening for Bernie. He was breathing, slow and regular. I went down the hall, peeked in the bedroom. He lay on his back, forearm over his eyes, chest rising and falling. I watched him for a while. He was sleeping. That was nice, watching Bernie sleep. Soon he'd be up and we'd be hiking in the canyon or playing fetch, or doing that other activity I'd thought of before but couldn't think of now.

I went into the office, gazed at the elephants on the rug, and was still gazing at them when the phone rang. The machine picked up.

"Still not taking your calls? The retainer I put down doesn't entitle me to more . . . Christ. Listen, it's Marvin. Marvin Winkleman. Give me a call at your, quote, earliest convenience." Click.

I like most humans I've met, even some perps and gangbangers. Take Boodles Calhoun, for example, now breaking rocks in the hot sun, but once he'd scratched between my ears— this was just before he realized Bernie and I actually didn't have a trunkful of gold coins for him—and he'd been very good at it. But forget Boodles Calhoun. The point was Marvin Winkleman seemed to be turning into one of those few humans I didn't much like.

I went into the kitchen, lapped up more water. Water's my drink, although I've tried others, like beer from a hubcap, that time with the bikers. Loved those bikers! For a while I thought about all the fun we'd had and then I went sniffing under the table and found a few crumbs and after that I returned to the front hall and gazed through the tall window beside the door. Oh, no: a squirrel on the front lawn, just standing there! I growled. Maybe he heard me, because he scampered off, although not that desperate scamper squirrels do when they're running for their lives, and that's the scamper I like to see.

Sometime later, old man Heydrich appeared on the sidewalk with a broom. He glanced over at our place, saw me, and made one of those nasty faces humans can make—I think that one's called a smirk—and then started sweeping all the dirt from his part of the sidewalk over to our part, something Bernie hated. If only I'd been out there, I'd have—

Old man Heydrich went away. A moment or two after that, a dusty pickup drove by. We get lots of dusty pickups in the Valley and I wasn't watching very carefully until the driver's head turned and he looked at our house. He got a real good look at the house and I got a real good look at him: his crooked nose, his long sideburns, his bandanna. I started barking my head off.

"Hey, Chet, what's happening?" Bernie came into the front hall, not looking so tired now, the zigzag line gone. I barked and barked. "Heydrich sweeping the damn sidewalk again?" Bernie peered out the long window, gazing in the direction of Heydrich's strip of sidewalk. Down at the other end of the street, Jocko rounded a turn and disappeared from view; Bernie looked that way, too late. I barked a few more times, but what could I do? "Come on, boy, how about a snack?"

*   *   *

We had a nice snack—salsa and chips for Bernie, king-sized biscuit for me—and then Bernie took a shower, hanging his bathrobe over the bathroom door. This was the robe Leda had always called Bernie's ratty robe, although I didn't know why, since the pattern didn't have a single rat on it, was all about martini glasses with long-legged women in them. Bernie loved his robe, an old robe he'd had a long time, and that used to belong to a buddy from army days named Tanner who Bernie never talked about except for one night when we were camping out in the desert and he'd been staring into the fire. "Poor Tanner." That was all he said.

But now, in the shower, he was in a good mood. I could tell from his singing. He went through some of his favorites: "Lonesome 77203," "Born To Lose," "A Tear Fell," "Sea of Heartbreak"; yes, a very good mood. Steam came pouring through the doorway and I went closer; love the feel of steam. And what was this? Maybe Bernie didn't have the shower curtain quite right, because water was pooling on the floor. I tasted it: a little too warm and soapy, but not bad, not bad at all.

Soon Bernie was all dressed—khakis, sneakers, T-shirt—and fresh coffee was dripping into the pot. "Love that smell," he said; Bernie was capable of smelling coffee, I knew that for a fact. We went out to the patio, Bernie sipping from his mug, me checking under the barbecue and finding zip.

"Kind of odd," Bernie said. "Haven't heard from Suzie in a—oh, my God!" He hurried into the office, got on the phone. "Suzie? Pick up if you're there. I just, um, realized about our, like, date—you know, the Dry Gulch. Something came up, work, this case, developments. Uh. But I should have called. So, um, sorry. Please call. Or I'll call you, maybe that's the best way to . . ." He hung up, looked at me. "I'm an idiot," he said. No way. Bernie was always the smartest human in the room.

"Maybe I should send flowers," he said. "Or buy her a present. But it's so hard to . . . She never wears those earrings I gave her, for example." Earrings. I tried to remember. Was he talking about the ones that glowed at night?

His gaze fell on the blinking message machine. He pressed a button.

"Still not taking your calls? The retainer I—"

Bernie pressed the button, shut him up. "Winkleman's trouble, Chet. Big trouble." That little guy with skinny legs and a comb-over was trouble? I didn't see it. Jocko—*he* was trouble.

"Hey—what are you barking about?"

Jocko had cased our house, that was what.

"Easy, big guy. Want a Milk-Bone?"

Life can be funny. Milk-Bones had been the farthest thing from my mind, but now I wanted one more than anything. And soon I had it.

"Let's try to be smart about this," Bernie said. I had no idea what he was talking about. We hopped in the car, me downing the last bite.

Pretty soon we turned into High Chaparral Estates, one of the nicest developments in the whole Valley, as Leda often mentioned. She and Malcolm had a big house there, and that was where Charlie lived now, except when he was back home, which wasn't often.

We parked in front of their house. It had columns, big windows, balconies, and a bright green lawn that went on and on. "There's only one aquifer," Bernie said as we left the car and walked up the winding, flower-lined path to the door. "Why don't people get that?" He pressed the buzzer.

The door opened and there was Leda, talking on a cell phone. Her eyebrows went up in surprise at the sight of us, not that she has much in the way of eyebrows, on account of how she'd go at them with tweezers, at least back when we were all together. "A hundred and ninety a head and you're telling me we don't get the sabayon?" she was saying. She listened to a squeaky voice on the other end, but not for long. "Stop, stop, stop, stop," she said, her voice rising in a way I remembered well. "Run those numbers again and call me back—with a different answer this time." She clicked off. "Caterers are going under all over the goddamn Valley, and still they try to pull this shit."

"What's sabayon?" Bernie said.

"Sabayon? You don't know sabayon?" She blinked. "What are you doing here anyway?" She checked her watch, a beautiful glittering thing that reminded me of an unfortunate incident involving me and her leather jewelry box, not long before the split. "Charlie's not home yet, and it's not the weekend, and even if it were it's not your weekend."

"True," said Bernie. "Uh, the fact is, we were in the neighborhood, and I thought, well, why not stop by and see how you're doing?"

"See how I'm doing? Are you feverish?"

"Ha ha," Bernie said. "There's that sense of humor."

"Bernie. Do I look like I've got time for your sarcasm?"

"No sarcasm," Bernie said. "I always, uh, admired your sense of humor."

"You hid that so well."

"Ha ha—there it is again."

A silence fell. I got ready for the door to slam in our face, wouldn't have been the first time. Their eyes met, Bernie's and Leda's. And then, big surprise: Leda was laughing—and so was Bernie. When was the last time I'd seen that, if ever?

"So," Bernie said. "How are you doing, really? Must be a lot of stress, planning the wedding and all."

"Understatement of the century."

"I'm sure it will be great."

"Thank you. Oh, Christ, don't tell me you're angling for an invitation."

"No, no, no. Not in my wildest—"

"Because even though Malcolm's doing so well—you wouldn't believe what's coming in even if I told you—we're still trying to keep the guest list manageable. There's such a thing as overdoing it. In terms of taste, if nothing else, what with the economy and all."

"I agree. Remind me what Malcolm does again."

"Software."

"But more specifically."

"It's complicated—licensing, China, integrated apps."

"Integrated apps?"

"No time to explain. Is this good mood of yours all about the alimony?"

"Alimony?"

"After the wedding you won't have to pay alimony anymore."

"Hadn't thought of that," Bernie said.

"You hadn't?"

"Nope."

"You know something, Bernie? You're changing."

"How?"

"I'll put it this way," Leda said. "If things hadn't worked out so well with Malcolm, crazy as it might seem, I could almost even toy with the idea of . . . dot dot dot."

Dot dot dot? What the hell was she talking about? Did Bernie know? I couldn't tell. He was looking down at his feet, doing a strange little shuffling thing.

"Crazy," he said. "I mean great, just great the way everything's, you know, you and Malcolm. He's, uh, excited about this, too?"

"What a question! He's head over heels. Haven't you seen the engagement ring?" She thrust her hand out at Bernie before I had chance to think about that head over heels thing.

"Wow," he said.

"Forty grand," Leda said. "Took it to the appraiser first thing."

"Wow," Bernie said again.

What was going on? I had no idea. A phone started ringing in the house, and Leda said, "That'll be him right now."

"The appraiser?"

"Of course not," Leda said. "Malcolm—he's away on business."

"Well, then, we'll just—"

"Bye," Leda said. "And Bernie? Thanks."

"—be on our—"

The door closed in our face, but not in a slamming sort of way. We got in the car. Bernie rummaged around in the glove box, found a bent cigarette way in the back. He lit up, breathed in, blew out a big smoke cloud. I knew he was trying to quit, but that smell—I couldn't help liking it. I breathed in, too.

"That wedding has to happen," he said, turning the key. "And not just that—the goddamn marriage has to last. In fact, it has to be great, like . . . like—I don't know, think of some great marriage, Chet."

Missed that, whatever it was. We drove out of the Valley and into the desert, and not long after on account of how we were passing everything in sight although I didn't know what the hurry was, we entered a little town I recognized, the one that Bernie had called flea-bitten. I started scratching, first behind my ear, soon along my side, then both at once, really digging in with my claws, faster and—

"Chet, for God's sake."

We parked behind the palm tree on the street in front of the horseshoe-shaped motel. Two cars in the lot: one a red convertible, the other a dark sedan.

"Oh, boy," Bernie said, and almost right away a motel room door opened and out came Marvin Winkleman's wife—unless the divorce had already happened, couldn't recall the details on that—short, blond, and curvy, possibly named Bobbi Jo, followed by Malcolm, knotting his tie. "I want to strangle him with it," Bernie said. I got ready, but no strangling happened. We sped off while they were still getting in their cars, the strangling of Malcolm maybe being something to look forward to in the future.

# SIXTEEN

The heel is down at the foot: I was pretty sure of that, because when Bernie says heel, which he really never has to, I walk along right beside his feet. The head is the head, at the top. So head over heels means what? The head is always over the heels, except in an upside-down situation, for example when a perp by the name of Nuggets Bolliterri tried to escape on us from an upstairs window and ended up dangling headfirst in a tangle of tied-together sheets. Leda had just said Malcolm was head over heels. Meaning what? He was tangled in tied-together sheets? I couldn't take it any further.

We got stuck in traffic, not moving at all, the kind of getting stuck where drivers climb out of their cars and stare into the distance. Bernie called Suzie. "Hi, it's me. Are you there? Did you get my message, uh, the one about being sorry about the Dry Gulch thing? Hope you didn't hang around there too long, and also, um—"

Suzie picked up. Her voice came over the speakers. "Three hours," she said.

"Oh," said Bernie.

"But I'll never do that again." Suzie's voice over the speakers, yes, except I'd never heard her sound like this. Suzie has one of my favorite voices, like she's having fun just being there—can't help listening whenever Suzie speaks, letting the sound flow over me—but there was no fun in her voice now. Instead it was flat, and also kind of cold.

"Like I said," Bernie said, "I'm sorry."

"I know you are," Suzie said. "And I also know how it is when you're on a case. But I'm starting to think you may not be ready for this."

"For what?" Bernie said. Someone honked behind us; traffic was moving again. Bernie shifted into gear, but not in the usual way: there was a nasty grinding.

"See, right there," Suzie said. "I'm talking about being ready for whatever this is we've got going on between us."

"Oh," said Bernie again. This wasn't easy to follow, but I knew from experience that whenever Bernie kept saying "oh" things weren't going well.

"How would you define it, Bernie?"

More honking. Bernie pressed on the gas, maybe too hard. We jerked forward. "Define what?" he said.

Suzie's voice got colder. "What we have."

"What we have?" said Bernie. "It's like, you know, a good thing."

"A good thing," Suzie said.

"Yeah."

"Can you elaborate?"

"Elaborate? Well, a very good thing. Very, very good."

"Have to go into a meeting," Suzie said. "When you come up with a better definition, feel free to give me a call."

"But—"

Click.

"Christ," Bernie said. "What was that about?"

I couldn't help him.

"I mean," Bernie said, rummaging in the glove box, this time coming out empty-handed, "it's very, very good. What's better than that? When I'm with her I feel great, every single minute. She doesn't even have to say a word, but I love when she does. Christ Almighty. Just her presence makes me want to be my best self." He tried fishing under his seat, found a pen, a broken CD case, and a coffee cup lid, but no cigarettes. "So what the hell does she want me to say?"

I had no idea. In my world, the nation within the nation, we do things differently. Take this one night, for example, when I heard some distant she-barking, and in fact it didn't turn out to be so distant after all—I was there in no time! She was in a fenced-in backyard, kind of a high fence, but not quite high enough. No, sir. I've always loved leaping and that night I loved it even more, taking this all-out sprint—she was standing still watching me the whole time through chain-link—and getting my paws underneath me and—

The phone buzzed. "Suzie?" said Bernie, just before hitting the button.

Not Suzie; the voice over the speakers was Rick's. "Update for you," he said. "Autopsy came in on DeLeath. Cause of death—" Paper rustled in the background. "—necrotic blah blah, here we go—shock, induced by cytotoxic venom resultant from a snakebite to the dorsal yada yada of the right hand."

"You're saying he died of snakebite?"

"Haven't lost your quick, Bernie."

"Any other signs of violence?"

"Isn't that enough?" Rick said. Bernie didn't answer. "Nothing else," Rick said. "Snakebite, period."

"Thanks."

"Any time. Talked to that little trapeze guy, by the way, Ollie Filipoff. Do you know if they use a net?"

"Yeah, they do. Why?"

"Just wondering."

"Why?"

"It makes a difference, don't you think?" Rick said. "Like say the difference between kissing and the old boom-boom."

"Have to think about that," Bernie said. Not me. I didn't get any of this, so far. "Is that what you talked to Ollie about—sex and the flying trapeze?"

"Nope," said Rick. "We discussed his retraction."

"Of what?"

"That tale he fed you—the eighteen-wheeler with four roses on the side, leaving the fairgrounds by the back gate."

"Tale? What are you talking about?"

"Fiction, Bernie. He made it up."

"Why the hell would he do that?"

"Says he was scared."

"Of what?"

"Of you. You and Chet."

"Bullshit."

"He says you came on strong—don't tell me that never happens. Plus he has a fear of dogs."

Whoa. Rick was saying Ollie was afraid of me? No way. Not that he'd patted me or anything like that, but when a human had fears of me and my kind I always knew, and Ollie didn't.

"He sensed rough treatment just around the corner," Rick was saying, "so he gave you what he thought you wanted."

"It's just around the corner now," Bernie said.

"I'll pretend I didn't hear that."

"And how could he have known what I wanted? I never mentioned a truck of any kind, let alone with four roses on the side."

"Ah," said Rick. "The roses. They were for verisimilitude."

That one was brand new, sounded very bad.

"Meaning?"

"Verisimilitude? I'm surprised you're not familiar—"

"Cut the crap," Bernie said.

Rick laughed. "Apparently you were plying him with JD."

"Plying? We had a friendly drink."

"And, in search of the telling detail that sells the story—he's that kind of witness, basically a sneak—he happened to think of another bourbon."

"Four Roses?"

"Haven't lost your quick, Bernie. Or did I already say that?"

The next day—or was it the one after? or maybe the same one?—we parked in a lot outside a cemetery gate, away from all the other cars. The gate was open, but we didn't go in. A burial was happening inside—we could see people in dark clothes standing around—and Bernie tries to stay away from burials, not always easy in our job. About cemeteries, all I know is that they probably smell different to me than they do to you. A big black bird flew in slow circles high above but no one was watching it, except me. I admit I've got a thing about birds, bad-tempered critters, and I don't just mean the one that followed me and a tiny show dog named Princess across the desert, something wicked on its mind. But that's another story. The point is, would I be bad-tempered if I could drift around in the bright blue sky all day? I ask you.

After a while the people started coming out and getting in their cars. I recognized some of them—Popo, Colonel Drummond, Fil, and others I'd seen around the circus. They got in

their cars and drove away. We sat where we were until Ollie Filipoff walked through the gate, just about the very last person.
He headed toward a motorcycle in the far corner of the lot, took
off his jacket and tie, and then his shirt, balled them all up and
shoved them into a saddlebag. A little guy, but with big pop-up
muscles. He took a T-shirt from the saddlebag, put it on, and
carefully rolled the sleeves up a little higher over his arm muscles.

"At least somebody loves Ollie," Bernie said. I waited to find
out who, but Bernie didn't say.

We walked across the lot. Ollie was swinging one leg over the
motorcycle when he saw us. He paused, then sat slowly on the
seat.

"Got a moment?" Bernie said.

"Pressed for time, tell you the truth," Ollie said.

"The truth is always a nice change of pace," Bernie said.

"Huh?" said Ollie.

Bernie smiled, the kind that's only about showing teeth.
"Cool bike," he said, putting his hand on it.

Ollie gave Bernie's hand a look—he didn't like his bike getting
touched, hard to miss that—but all he said was, "Yeah. Thanks."

"Came to express our condolences," Bernie said.

"For what?"

"The circus's recent loss."

"What was that?"

"Uri DeLeath," Bernie said. "Unless we've got the wrong
funeral."

"Nope, it's the right one. He passed on."

"One way of putting it."

"Like, to the other side," Ollie said.

"How do you feel about that, Ollie?"

"The other side, you mean?"

"Sure, why not?"

Ollie squeezed his eyes shut for a moment. A certain kind of dude, the kind we always bring down, does that when he's trying to have a thought. "I don't know," he said, eyes opening. "Is there a hell, too? Or just heaven."

Bernie smiled again, this time the actually-having-fun type. "What if there's hell and hell only? Ever think of that, Ollie?"

"Damn. You think that's possible?"

"Depends on the point of all this," Bernie said, "assuming there is one." Ollie glanced around the way humans do when they're trying to figure out where they are. "But what we really wanted to know," Bernie went on, "is how you feel about DeLeath's death."

"How I feel?" Ollie licked his lips; I watch for that—usually a good sign. "Tough break, I guess," he said.

"Hear about what killed him?"

"Oh, yeah. Snakes scare the shit out of me. Ironic, huh?"

"Didn't quite follow you," Bernie said.

"The animal guy getting offed by an animal."

"Where did you hear that?" Bernie said. "About the irony."

"The colonel mentioned it."

"Did he?"

"On the way out of the church." Ollie leaned forward, put his hands on the controls. "Well, better get goin'."

"No problem," Bernie said. "We'll just clear up one little discrepancy and you can ride this baby into the wild blue yonder."

"Discrepancy?"

"On the four roses story. You're on the record as telling two different versions, one to Sergeant Torres and one to us."

"Who's us?"

"Chet and I."

Ollie gave me a look, his face kind of pinched—like . . . like how could I be part of the team, or something. I made up my mind about him. My teeth got this funny feeling, a sort of wanting to bite.

"Aw, c'mon, man," Ollie said, "what difference does it make now? Gonna indict a snake?" He laughed, a haw-haw-haw that went on way too long for me.

"We killed the snake," Bernie said. "Chet and I."

"Yeah?" said Ollie, giving me another look, not so pinched this time.

"And that still leaves us with a missing elephant," Bernie said. "So we're going to have to straighten out your testimony."

Ollie's eyes went to the key in the ignition. Bernie removed it in one smooth motion that didn't look particularly quick, but by the time Ollie said, "Hey!" the key was in Bernie's pocket. That Bernie! I remembered once when he told me you don't bring a spoon to a fork fight, or something like that.

"Think, Ollie."

"About what?"

"What you saw the night you came back from Uncle Rio's."

"Didn't see nothin', man."

"So you lied to us."

"Sorry."

"The eighteen-wheeler with the four red roses on the side?"

"Made it all up," Ollie said, "like out of whole, um, whatever it is."

"Cloth."

"Yeah."

"Why did you lie?"

"More like a fib. And I already said I was sorry."

"You told Sergeant Torres you were afraid of us."

"Yeah. Never been comfortable around dogs." Uh-uh, buddy;

I wasn't getting that, not one whiff. "And you're kind of threatening yourself, no offense."

"Me?" said Bernie.

"You took my key."

"Not nice."

"No."

"But the thing is, Ollie, you're an acrobat, and I just can't buy an acrobat scaring so easily. You're brave by definition."

"Thanks," Ollie said.

"So what's going on?" Bernie said.

Ollie's mouth opened and closed.

"You're afraid of something," Bernie said, "but it's not us. So let's hear the name."

Ollie stared straight ahead. "There's no name, man. Don't know what you're talking about."

Bernie took out the key, stuck it back in the ignition.

"You're free to go," he said.

"Uh, nice talkin' to you," Ollie said.

"Drive safe."

"Always do."

Bernie turned to go. "Oh, and one more thing—you know Darren Quigley?"

"Security guard? We've had a few drinks together."

"At Uncle Rio's?"

"Matter of fact, yeah." Ollie kicked the starter, vroom vroom. I've been on a Harley before, let me tell you. But some other time.

Back on the road, Bernie said, "Shot in the dark, Chet. Boozers working in close proximity—they tend to find each other."

A shot? Hadn't heard one, not at the cemetery, not since the Chang case, in fact. The Chang case: a nightmare, but the food!

Another story for later. I yawned a nice big yawn, the kind that sometimes catches my lip over a tooth, and by the time I got everything straightened out, whatever I'd been worrying about was gone. Why worry anyway? I had Bernie.

A green car with a gold star on the side was parked in front of our place. A bald guy in a green uniform climbed out as we pulled into the driveway.

"Bernie Little?" he said, as we left the Porsche, Bernie through the door on his side, me over the one on mine.

"Yeah," said Bernie.

The guy came closer. "What a great-looking dog," he said.

"Chet," said Bernie.

"Nice name," the man said. "Okay to give him a treat?"

What a question! The next thing I knew I had a biscuit in my mouth, not big but very very tasty.

"Mathers—Game and Fish," said the man. Mathers: he had a nice name, too. I liked him from the get-go. "You're the one who killed the snake?" he said.

"For God's sake—you came to write me up for that?" Bernie said. "It was self-defense."

"No, no, nothing like that," Mathers said. "I've got a map of the area here, southeast section of the Sangre Hills. If you can point me to the spot where this happened, I'll go out there and take a look."

He spread the map on the hood of the Porsche. They huddled over it. Bernie pointed. "Right about there, more or less. What are you hoping to see?"

"Hard to specify," said Mathers. "The remains of a crate, maybe, or a cage. Even a canvas sack."

"There was nothing like that."

"No?" Mathers said. "Nothing at all to indicate the snake wasn't just out there on its own volition?"

"On its own volition?" Bernie said. "Must be thousands of diamondbacks wandering the desert on their own volition."

"True," said Mathers. "But your snake was a puff adder."

"So?"

"So puff adders aren't native to our desert, aren't native to the Americas, in fact. This particular kind comes from sub-Saharan Africa—Gabon, Congo, places like that."

"I don't get it," Bernie said.

"Meaning the only puff adders in this state come in with a permit," Mathers said. "A permit to keep, not to release into the wild."

"I'm surprised you let them in at all."

"Completely insane," Mathers said. "But this is the land of the free."

Bernie laughed.

"We don't get puff adder applications very often," Mathers went on. "Three since I've been with the department—going on ten years now—all to licensed vendors and all accounted for, as of this morning."

"Meaning our snake was illegal?"

"Looks that way," Mathers said. "Could be some idiot sneaking it in through an airport and releasing it when he got tired of providing live mice for dinner. That, or it was an escapee from something bigger."

"Something bigger?"

"Illegal animal trafficking's a multibillion-dollar business. You didn't know that?"

"All new to me," Bernie said.

"Second only to drug smuggling in terms of illegal international business, but doesn't get much press," Mathers said. "And as usual, Mexico makes an ideal staging point." He folded the map. "Did you know the puff adder's responsible for more deaths than any other snake? I'm talking about within Africa, of course. Happening over here—that's unbelievably bad luck."

"Just what I was thinking," Bernie said.

Were they still talking about snakes? No snakes around: I'd have been the first to know, certainly in this crowd. But there was no question that more biscuits lurked in Mathers's pocket: the smell was overpowering. I moved a little closer to Mathers, wagging my tail.

# SEVENTEEN

U ncle Rio's," said Bernie, backing into a little parking
  space in one move, smooth and easy. Driving with Bernie: always a pleasure, unless the tools had to come out. "You'll
like this."

I was liking it already. Me and Bernie together—what was
not to like?

Uncle Rio's was on a dark street not far from the fairgrounds.
The only bright lights around were the top of the Ferris wheel,
spinning slowly in the night, and the neon signs in Uncle Rio's
window. It was a bar, of course: I can smell them from miles
away, miles away being kind of far unless I've missed something. What do bars smell like? Stale beer, burned grease, puke.
Hey! They go together! A strange thought, not my usual . . . I
wondered . . .

And was still wondering when we went into Uncle Rio's. It
turned out to be one of those dark skinny joints, a long bar on one
side, a row of tables on the other, a little dance floor at the end. No
dancing happening at the moment, probably a good thing, since
dancing sometimes gets me going. There was only one woman

in the place, drinking down at the end of the bar. A few big guys sat by the beer taps, big guys with cut-off denim jackets, maybe bikers. The bartender serving them had a tattoo on the side of his neck; a cigarette dangled from his mouth even though I was pretty sure there was no smoking in Valley bars. He looked at us, saw Bernie, and said, "You son of a bitch."

The big guys turned and gave us tough-guy stares. The biggest said, "Want us to take care of this dude, Rio?"

The bartender laughed, one of those booming laughs that came from deep inside. Women don't have that laugh and neither do most men, but no time for that now. I got ready for trouble, but no trouble happened. The bartender said, "Why'd I want you to do that? Bernie here would mop the floor with you assholes and then the cops would come and make me put out my smoke." The big guys looked confused. The bartender hurried around the bar and threw his arms around Bernie. They banged each other on the back real hard.

"Rio."

"Bernie."

More banging. "Bastard never comes in here," Rio said. "Too snooty now for a dump like mine?"

"You know the answer to that," Bernie said.

Rio stepped back. "You're in shape."

"Nah."

"Want to stay in shape, here's my advice—never run a bar," Rio said.

"Got ya."

"Imagine you running a bar."

"What's so odd about that?"

Rio didn't answer, just laughed another one of those boomers. He had a big belly and it shook; I always like the sight of that.

And maybe because I was watching him, he suddenly noticed me, an interesting thing that happens sometimes with critters of all kinds.

"Hey," he said. "Is this Chet?"

"How do you know about Chet?"

"Ratko Savic was in here last week."

Ratko Savic? Hard to forget old Ratko, with his long drippy nose and his fondness for knife play.

"What's he doing out?" Bernie said.

"Early parole," said Rio. "Have to ask yourself what the world's coming to when a menace like Ratko scores early parole. But nothing for you to worry about—he's got a healthy respect for Chet, better believe it."

"Did those skin grafts take?"

"Actually improved his appearance." Rio gazed at me for a moment, eye to eye. Some of my guys—General Beauregard, for example—don't like that one bit, but I don't mind. "He looks like a big sweetheart to me," Rio said. "Got some Slim Jims behind the bar—he allowed a Slim Jim? Hey, down, big guy!"

"Chet!"

Uh-oh. Was I embarrassing Bernie? Never want that. I sat down, alert, quiet, professional.

"Knows Slim Jims, that's for sure," Rio said. "I bet he understands a lot of things."

"His understanding can be selective at times," Bernie said, "in a convenient sort of way."

Lost me there.

"Sounds like my fourth wife," Rio said.

"There's a fourth?"

"Was. A stripper like number two, but less intellectual."

Soon we were at one of the side tables, Bernie and Rio with

glasses of beer, me underneath with a Slim Jim. The Slim Jim had pretty much my whole attention, so I missed a lot of what they were talking about, too bad, because the war was part of it, a desert war, but not our desert, somewhere far away, a war Bernie didn't talk about.

"I'll never fuckin' forget that," Rio was saying.

"It wasn't thought out," Bernie said. "Just dumb reaction, that's all."

"Makes it even better."

"Nah," said Bernie. He sipped his beer. "A guy named Jocko Cochrane ever come around? Sizeable, wears a bandanna?"

"Don't ring a bell."

"How about Darren Quigley? He's supposed to be a regular."

"Wouldn't call him a regular," Rio said. "He's in here from time to time."

"We're looking for him."

"What's he done?"

"Maybe nothing. He's more of a witness."

"Guys who run a tab I keep their addresses," Rio said. "Little creep like that I don't run a tab."

"Darren's actually in the wind right now," Bernie said. "Does he ever bring friends?"

"Sure—there's that drinking acrobat. Least he's supposed to be an acrobat. But a drinker for sure."

"Any others?"

"Isn't there a lady friend?" Rio looked up, called down to the woman at the end of the bar. "Hey, Delores, you know Darren Quigley?"

"Not in any meaningful way."

"C'mon over here a sec."

"I'm happy where I am," Delores said. "Deliriously."

The bikers all turned toward her. She ignored them, took a tiny sip of her drink, a greenish-colored drink in a tall glass.

"Maybe we could go join her," Bernie said in a low voice.

Rio called down again. "Mind if my friend Bernie here joins you?"

Delores gave us a long look. "If he brings the dog," she said.

We went down to the end of the bar, me and Bernie.

"I had one like this once," Delores said, "maybe not quite so handsome. What's his name?"

"Chet."

She reached out to scratch between my ears. "I suppose they call you Chet the Jet," she said. Hey. Delores was smart. Plus she turned out to be a real good scratcher, with long fingernails that dug in deep but not too deep, just the way I like.

"Can I buy you another one of those?" Bernie said, nodding toward her drink.

"Only if you've got an ulterior motive," Delores said.

Bernie laughed. "Bernie Little, Little Detective Agency. We—"

Delores raised her hands. "You won't take me alive, copper," she said. Then, in a quieter voice—up until then her voice had reminded me of Bernie's mom, and in fact she reminded me of Bernie's mom in other ways, including how the longer you looked at her the older she got—she added, "You're about ten years too late for that."

Losing me completely, but maybe not Bernie who said, "Don't believe that for a second—you're the liveliest thing I've seen all day."

"Aren't you sweet?" said Delores. "A transparent liar, but sweet."

"Bernie, sweet?" said Rio, now back behind the bar, appearing with another green drink for Delores and a beer for Bernie.

Bernie took out his wallet.

"Don't insult me," Rio said. "Your money's no good here."

"Free drinks at Uncle Rio's?" Delores said. "I'm hallucinating." She raised her glass. "To sweetness," she said. She and Bernie clinked glasses; love that sound.

"Darren Quigley has a lady friend?" Bernie said.

"The ulterior motive," said Delores, "but not the right one. Darren had a lady friend, past tense. The Darrens of the world don't keep lady friends for long."

"Why not?"

"Have you met him?"

"Yes."

"Then what's the question? As for the ex-lady friend, she's really just a girl, one of those small-town girls who still keep coming west, in search of I can't remember what. Her name's Bonnie Hicks, she works at a nails place in that strip across from the East Central Mall, and she lives in the trailer park behind the strip."

"Thanks," said Bernie.

"Any time," said Delores. "What else can I do for you?"

Trailer parks turn up in our job from time to time. Some are in the middle of nowhere—like that nudist one where we once had to go on a case I never understood involving a stolen oil rig, but I learned one thing for sure: humans look better with their clothes on. No offense.

Other trailer parks can turn up right in town. We parked in front of a strip mall, our headlights shining on the darkened store fronts. "Nails by Diva," Bernie read, as we got out of the car. "What's that all about?" he said, "women and their nails? Growing them longer, for one thing, and how come men don't . . ." His voice trailed off.

We walked around the strip mall into scrubland at the back,

came to a gate with two posts but no gate in between. Beyond that stood some trailers, low rounded shadows under the pink night sky, none of them showing any lights, and also a tent. A fire burned in front of the tent, and a dude sat beside it, smoking a joint. Bernie sniffed the air: pot's an easy scent for just about anyone.

"Evenin'," said the dude.

"Hi," said Bernie.

"You a cop?"

"No."

"Look a bit like a cop."

"Is that a crime?"

The dude started laughing, then stopped abruptly. "That's kind of a puzzler, stop to think about it," he said. "Like *The Matrix*." He took a long drag, noticed me. "Out walkin' your dog?"

"That's right."

"I had a dog once. He ran away."

"Too bad, at least for you," Bernie said. "We're looking for Bonnie Hicks."

The dude took a quick glance at one of the trailers, a small silver one up on blocks. He turned back to Bernie and said, "I might know how to find her."

"We're all ears."

We were? I looked at his ears, not small for a human, but how well did they hear? For example, was he picking up that sound—pretty faint, it's true—of a woman crying somewhere in the trailer park? If so, he showed no sign.

"Like they say," the dude was telling Bernie, "it's the information age."

"Yeah?" said Bernie. The firelight shone in his eyes, a beautiful sight.

The dude took another hit—that's drug lingo—and held his

breath. You see that pot-smoking breath-holding combo from time to time in this job, after which things usually go downhill pretty fast.

A big smoke cloud exploded out of the dude's mouth. "Put it to you this way," he said, "simple as I can. Once upon a time it was the age of things, and people paid money for them. A Pontiac Firebird, say—that's a thing. Now it's the age of information."

"You're saying you'll tell us where the girl is for money?" Bernie asked. The firelight suddenly looked different in his eyes, different in a way that would have scared some people, maybe most.

But not this dude. "Well, well," he said. "Pretty quick on the uptake for a visitor from the land of the bland."

Bernie stepped forward and took the joint from the dude's hand; didn't rush, didn't snatch it, just took the thing. He tossed it in the fire.

"What the hell?" the dude said, starting to rise. Bernie put his hand on the dude's shoulder, sat him back down. The dude tried to squirm free, then said, "Ow," and went still.

Bernie removed his hand. The dude stayed exactly where he was. "I'm going to give you five bucks for the information," Bernie said. "Know why?"

The dude shook his head.

"Because it's marginally less trouble than beating it out of you," Bernie said.

The dude raised his arm and pointed, real fast. "Third on the left," he said. "The Airstream up on blocks."

Bernie handed him money. "And here's a memo from the information age, absolutely free—we don't need to see you on our way out."

"I was just leaving," the dude said.

\* \* \*

The crying was coming from inside the Airstream. That was clear to Bernie by the time we reached the door; I could tell from the expression on his face. He knocked and the crying stopped abruptly. No one inside came to the door or made a sound.

"Bonnie Hicks?" Bernie called.

Silence.

"Is Darren in there?" He raised his voice. "Darren, it's Bernie Little. I think you need some help."

A woman spoke. "Darren's not here."

"Bonnie?"

No answer.

"Maybe you need some help yourself," Bernie said.

A long silence. Bernie waited. I waited beside him. I could feel how alert he was; I was pretty alert, too. At last the woman said, "Who are you, again?"

"Bernie Little. We're trying to get Darren out of a jam."

"He never mentioned you."

"No?" said Bernie. "When was the last time you saw him?"

"A few days ago, maybe?"

"How about the last time you spoke to him?" Bernie said.

"This morning. He called just when I was leaving for work."

"Bonnie?"

"Yes?"

"Can we come in?"

"We?"

I barked, not sure why.

"Is that a dog? I'm scared of dogs."

"Chet's not scary."

I barked again, louder this time.

"Yeah," she said. "Right."

"Okay, Bonnie," Bernie said, wagging his finger at me. That

hardly ever happened but I always liked it; I wagged my tail back. "We don't have to come in. Tell me about Darren's call."

"It lasted like a minute. He got cut off."

"What did he say?"

"It was kind of hard to hear, all staticky. He was actually being nice."

"In what way?"

"You know. Sorry about how he treated me, and if he ever got back he'd make it all up. I thought maybe he was crying."

"Back from where?" Bernie said.

"Mexico," said Bonnie. "That's why it was so staticky."

"Where in Mexico?"

"San something or other. Anselmo, maybe? Or was it Quentin? That's when he got cut off."

"Cut off how?"

"Like when the line goes dead."

"Did you hear anyone in the background?"

"I don't think so." Bonnie had one of those small voices, high and soft. She sounded a lot like a kid to me.

"What are you afraid of, Bonnie?"

"Besides dogs, you mean?"

My tail drooped a bit.

"Yeah, besides dogs."

"I'm not sure."

"Do you know Jocko?"

"I don't like him."

"Why not?"

"He looks at me funny."

"In what way?"

"At my body. Right in front of Darren."

"Has Jocko been around lately?"

"Not since I broke up with Darren."

"Why did you break up with him?"

"Do we have to talk about that?"

"Was it why you were crying when we came up?"

Another long silence. "I don't like it here anymore."

"Where are you from?"

"Schenectady."

"That's a long way from here."

Bonnie started crying again.

"Do you have any friends or relatives back there?"

"Maybe Jeanine."

"Who's she?"

"My half-sister."

"Do you get along?"

"Not really. Except for when we were kids. We were close when we were kids."

"You should go see her."

"That costs money."

"How much have you got?"

"Eleven dollars."

"When's your next payday?"

"I don't know."

"Aren't you working at the nails place?"

"The owner's mother came over from Korea. I got fired today."

Bernie reached for his wallet, counted out some bills. "I'm going to slide some money under your door," Bernie said. "On one condition—you use it to get back to Schenectady."

"What do you want from me?"

"I want you to go home," Bernie said. "Tomorrow at the latest."

"That's all?" she said. More crying, but growing quieter now. Bernie slid the money under the door.

---

# EIGHTEEN

B ack in the office, Bernie got busy with some maps. "San Anselmo, maybe," he said. "Or possibly San Quentin. Not uncommon south of the border, big guy, those Sans." Didn't I know San Quentin, a faraway jail where we'd put a perp or two, maybe including Crock Mullican? What a great guy—a real fan of my kind, gave off a huge scent of aftershave—and we were getting along great until Bernie brought up the matter of the missing stamp collection, and then his mood changed and the AR-15 came whipping out. We've still got Crock's AR-15, locked in the safe with all our other guns. The safe's right here in the office, hidden behind this picture of Niagara Falls, but that's just between me and Bernie. Bernie likes waterfall pictures—we've got lots at our place.

"Tenuous," Bernie said, a completely new one on me, "but except for Darren and that phone call, what else have we got?" I waited to hear. "Maybe we could go the puff adder route, or . . ." He went silent. The puff adder route? Anything but that.

Bernie turned to the computer, started tapping at the keys. I went to lie down on the rug, caught sight of those elephants, and moved out of the office and into the hall. I've always loved lying on the rug, but now, for some reason, I didn't.

"Chet? Everything all right?"

I just stood there, doing nothing. That happens sometimes.

The phone rang, and I heard Rick's voice on the speakerphone. "That baseball bat and the elephant hook?" he said. "We got a match."

"Who?" said Bernie.

"Didn't say we had an ID," Rick said, "just a match. Whoever it is isn't in the system."

"That's still helpful," Bernie said.

"Yeah?"

"It means something's not right."

"Like what?"

"Probably a lot of things, but the most important is DeLeath wasn't acting on his own."

"Don't see the connection," Rick said.

Bernie started explaining. Rick kept interrupting. Their voices rose. I lay down in the hall, back against the wall, got comfortable. Maybe the puff adder came into the conversation. Rick might have said something about the puff adder getting brought into the country by a reptile nut. Bernie might have said that all the reptile nuts were accounted for. Rick might have said so what? After a while, I got up, gave myself a good shake, and went into the office.

Bernie was at the whiteboard writing, drawing boxes, making arrows and other shapes I didn't know the names of. I know arrows on account of having one shot at me by a bow-hunting survivalist whose name isn't coming at the moment. Those survivalists— maybe later. In the meantime, it was fun watching the whiteboard turn black. "Round about now," Bernie said, "it'd be nice to have a theory of the case. Know what I'm saying?"

Of course. Bernie was talking about the case. How were we doing? Pretty well, I thought.

"But I can't come up with a theory," Bernie said, "so how about we do some digging?"

Love digging: one of my very best skills.

"San Anselmo's closer—we'll start there."

Fine with me. There's the front-paws method and also the all-paws method, for big jobs. I was ready either way. Bernie took down the Niagara Falls painting, spun the dial on the safe, brought out the .38 Special. A breeze sprang up. In no time at all I realized that was me, wagging my tail. The .38 Special plus digging—your tail would be wagging, too.

Whatever San Anselmo was, we didn't get there right away, because as soon as we stepped outside Suzie drove up in her yellow Beetle.

"Suzie?" Bernie said as she climbed out of the car and walked toward us. The streetlight shone on her in a funny way, leaving her eyes in shadow, making me uneasy. "I'm not, uh, quite ready," Bernie went on. "I mean, I've been thinking, of course, but I want to put it just right, and, well . . ."

"Bernie? What are you talking about?"

Bernie looked surprised. "What you said before, putting it into words, relationship et cetera and how it means to you. Me. I mean, means to me." Was this making any sense at all?

"Maybe some other time," Suzie said. "Right now I'm working on the DeLeath story."

"Oh," said Bernie. He has a way of saying just oh sometimes when he's talking to women, maybe a thing I've mentioned already. If I did, did I also point out it's never a good sign?

"Do you have time to answer a couple of questions?" Suzie said.

"Like?" said Bernie.

Suzie took out a notebook. "I'm trying to nail down the motive," she said. "What made him do it?"

"Do what?" Bernie said.

"Take off with Peanut, of course," Suzie said. "Unless you know something else he did?"

"Nope," Bernie said.

Suzie moved closer to our garage light, turned a page. "I'm getting conflicting accounts," she said. "Colonel Drummond seems convinced that the animal rights people made some sort of successful appeal to DeLeath's conscience. Nadia Worth of FAAN acknowledges speaking to DeLeath on several occasions but denies getting any sort of positive response." Suzie brought the notebook a little nearer to her eyes. "In fact, she didn't show much sympathy for what happened to him, gave me this quote, re that diamondback—'not an unfitting ending for an exploiter of animals.' And there are no red flags in his personal life. He and John Poppechevski—is that how you say it?—"

"Everyone calls him Popo."

"—appear to live—make that used to—a cozy, domestic existence. So—what am I missing?"

"I don't know," Bernie said.

"Do you agree that something is missing?"

"Yes," Bernie said. "Here's something I can tell you, but not for publication—the snake was a puff adder, not a diamondback."

"Thanks for the correction," Suzie said, "but not-for-publication corrections are unusual in my business, maybe even unique."

Bernie laughed. "See?" he said. "Right there is why I want—"

But whatever Bernie wanted didn't get said, because at that moment another car came barreling down Mesquite Road, made a squealing turn into our driveway and braked to a rocking stop. Out jumped Leda. She hurried up to Bernie—not looking at Suzie or me at all, maybe not even seeing us—grabbed his hand in both of hers and said, "Thank God you're here, Bernie. I need you."

"Well," said Bernie. "Uh." Have I gotten to his eyebrows yet? Very good-looking eyebrows, nice and thick, and also expressive, with a language of their own—a language I know, and right now it was a language all about surprise, confusion, and being real real uncomfortable.

Meanwhile Suzie, who has nice eyebrows, too, although not as thick or expressive as Bernie's, was looking at Leda, then Bernie, then Leda again, and her eyebrows were doing the same things as Bernie's, although in smaller ways. Bernie seemed to be trying to back away from Leda, or at least get his hand free, but Leda was hanging on. He turned to Suzie, his mouth opening like he wanted to say something, but nothing came out.

Suzie's eyes hardened. "I was just leaving," she said.

"No, no," Bernie, "I, uh . . ."

But by that time, Suzie was walking fast toward her car. She got in, closed the door, maybe more of a slamming, actually, and tore off.

Leda blinked. "Who was that?" she said.

"Christ," Bernie said, "what do you want?"

"You won't tell me?"

Bernie's voice rose in a way I hadn't heard since just before the divorce. "It's none of your business, Leda. Why are you here?"

Leda let go of Bernie's hand, let go real quick, like she'd had hold of something way too hot. That happened to me once, at a picnic when I spotted a blackened hot dog—what a strange name, totally beyond me what that's about—at the edge of the fire and went for it.

But back to Leda, who was saying, "You don't care at all, do you?"

"Huh?" said Bernie. He has a beautiful face, but for an instant it looked almost ugly.

"In that case, let's keep this on a professional basis."

"What the hell are you talking about?"

"Fifty percent of the Little Detective Agency belongs to me," Leda said; they were talking quicker and quicker and louder and louder. "It's in the agreement, in case you've forgotten."

"And you get your share of the profits every—"

"Profits? There's a concept. Did it—"

"You want more money? That's why you drove up uninvited and inter—"

"—ever occur to you that the name Little Detective Agency might be a turnoff marketing-wise?"

"What was I supposed to do? Change my name to Big?"

No time to think about that even though I wanted to—Bernie Big? Big Bernie?—because a light went on in an upstairs window next door and Mrs. Parsons peeked through the curtains. Hadn't seen Mrs. Parsons in a while—something the matter with her, couldn't remember what—and she was wearing a strange pointy cap and looked kind of scary. Bernie and Leda both glanced up at her and went quiet, the kind of real quiet that comes after lots of noise.

Leda lowered her voice almost down to a whisper. "What I came for—mistakenly, that's obvious—was your professional help."

"Professional?" Bernie lowered his voice, too.

"I think I'm being stalked, not that you give a good goddamn."

Bernie took a deep breath. "What makes you think you're being stalked?"

"You never believe me, do you?"

"Leda," Bernie began, voice rising again. He paused, got it back down. "If you're being stalked, I need the facts."

"Facts? How about this pickup that stayed right on my bumper for twenty miles on the Cross Valley Freeway yesterday, and then tonight when I left a meeting downtown, there it was again? Enough facts? I saw your exit and jumped off, didn't signal, didn't even slow down."

Bernie looked up and down the street: quiet, dark, no pickups in sight, no traffic at all. "Sure it's the same one?" he said.

"Of course I'm sure."

"What color is it?"

"Some dark color, blue, black, I don't know. But there's an antenna on the roof and it's crooked."

"Can you describe the driver?"

"I never got a good look at him. He was wearing sunglasses and had the visor down the whole time."

Bernie had a thought; I could tell from his eyes. The thought made his body tense up, changed his voice, too. "Was he wearing a bandanna?"

"Maybe. I don't know."

"Where's Charlie?"

"Right now?"

"Yes, right now."

"At home."

"With Malcolm?"

"With the sitter."

"Where's Malcolm?"

"Away on business."

That muscle in the side of Bernie's face that sometimes jumps jumped now. "Who's the sitter?"

"Kennedy."

"Who's Kennedy?"

"A neighbor kid."

"How old?"

"She's very responsible."

"How old?"

"Almost twelve."

"Call her," Bernie said.

There was a pause. Then Leda said, "Oh my God, you don't really think . . . ?" She dug out her cell phone. "Kennedy? Is everything all right?" She listened for a moment, then nodded to Bernie.

"Where's Charlie?" Bernie said.

Leda spoke into the phone. "What's Charlie up to?" She listened again. This time I heard the voice on the other end—a young girl's voice—saying something about TV. "No, that's fine," Leda said. "I'm on the way home." She clicked off.

"We'll follow you," Bernie said.

Soon we were in High Chaparral Estates, parked down the street from Leda and Malcolm's big house with the columns, in fact parked in front of another one a lot like it, maybe bigger and with taller columns. Leda had already run inside her place, called to say everything was fine. After that, a car left a driveway down the street, stopped in front of Leda's. A girl came out of the house, a small girl, not much bigger than Charlie, and got in the car. The car turned around, went back to the driveway down the street. The garage door opened. The car drove in. The door closed.

We sat. Sitting's a big part of this job. We're good at it, me and Bernie. After a while, he said, "If she's really getting stalked and it turns out to be Jocko, then . . ." Then what? I waited to hear. Time passed. Bernie said, "He's probably watching way too much

TV." Jocko was watching too much TV? Was that our problem with him? I thought it was all about how he'd gone over us both pretty good with that baseball bat and we still hadn't paid him back. Then came thoughts of smashing up Jocko's TV. After that, no more thoughts. We sat.

I heard an approaching car, looked down the street but didn't see it at first, on account of the headlights were off. It passed under a street lamp—not a car, but a pickup with a crooked antenna on the roof. I glanced at Bernie. His eyes were closed. I have different kinds of growls. One's real low and quiet, stays deep in my throat, just right for a time like this.

Bernie's eyes snapped open. "Chet? What's—"

The pickup with the crooked antenna slowed down and stopped, right in front of Leda's house. The driver, too far away for me to tell whether it was Jocko or not, pointed something out the window. All of a sudden the .38 Special was in Bernie's hand. But then I caught the tiny blue screen glow of the thing in the guy's hand, and so did Bernie. "Cell phone," he said. I knew cell phones weren't just for talking—they could take pictures, too, for example. Humans love gadgets, maybe way too much, but there was no time to think about that. The pickup started moving again, drove past us, headlights still off, meaning we weren't blinded and got a good look at the driver.

"I'm going to break his goddamn neck," Bernie said.

It was Marvin Winkleman.

# NINETEEN

This is like one of those Italian comedies with what's-his-name," Bernie said. We were following Marvin Winkleman. Nothing to it, really: the pickup's lights were on, freeway traffic was light, and he wasn't driving fast. "You know," Bernie said. "Good-looking guy, divorce, Marcello something?" He was quiet for a while. Winkleman took an exit not far from the North Valley Mall—the lights from its huge parking lot made an orange haze in the sky. "Divorce must be funnier in Italy," Bernie said. "Why is that?" I had no idea, didn't quite know what he was talking about, although some of it, like divorce, when Leda had packed up Charlie's stuff and taken it away, and Italy, which was connected to pizza—sausage and pepperoni, no extra cheese, being our favorite, mine and Bernie's—was pretty solid in my mind.

We followed Winkleman past the mall, then swung up into the Pottsdale hills, one of the nicest parts of the Valley. Downtown Pottsdale has lots of art galleries where Leda had tried to drag Bernie before the divorce, plus fancy restaurants that didn't want me and my kind around, and weren't the sort of restaurants Bernie liked anyway. We like the same kind of restaurants, me and Bernie, our favorite right now being Max's Memphis Ribs. Max's Memphis Ribs—in Rosa Vista, pretty far from Pottsdale—is owned by Cleon Maxwell, a friend of ours. We're friends with lots of restaurant owners. That's working out real well for us.

Winkleman drove past a bar with people sitting at outdoor tables, candlelight flickering on wine glasses and silverware, a pretty sight, and turned a corner. "Pepe's Mandarin is down this street," Bernie said. "Best Chinese food in the Valley—ten to one that's where he's going." Chinese food's a big subject, no time for it now, but there's something called pineapple chicken balls that's hard to beat. Meanwhile, Winkleman kept going. A restaurant with lanterns in the window went by and Bernie said, "Owe you ten," losing me completely. Winkleman drove another block or two, passing some storefronts, the windows dark now, and finally parking in front of a place with a big coffee cup sign hanging over the street. Hey! I knew where we were: Livia's Friendly Coffee and More.

Bernie pulled over quick, parked behind a car. We watched Winkleman getting out of the pickup. He glanced up and down the street. "Is it possible?" Bernie said.

Winkleman moved toward Livia's Friendly Coffee and More. It was dark, closed for the night like the other stores on the block, but I knew from the Chatterley case—no time for that now, a complicated affair I never really understood, although we somehow ended up with an emerald necklace, later pawned to Mr. Singh when the piston rods did something bad, can't remember what, and . . . what was I . . . ?

The Chatterley case. From the Chatterley case, I knew that Livia's Friendly Coffee and More being closed for the night didn't mean much. Winkleman glanced around again, then knocked on the door, a soft knock, but sound was carrying well on the quiet street. After a moment or two the door opened and Winkleman disappeared inside.

"How about a little visit with Livia Moon?" Bernie said. Fine with me. Livia Moon—I think I mentioned her already, some-thing about Popo's smell reminding me of hers that first time I saw him with the white face, red mouth, green eyes, and nasty orange hair, with the added male element, of course—owned the coffee shop, and knowing coffee shop owners was like knowing restaurant owners, a good thing, and her blueberry muffins were very tasty if you like muffins, which I don't, really, no offense, but the point is that when the coffee shop shut down for the night, Livia's wasn't quite dead, on account of her house of ill repute doing business in back.

Bernie knocked on the door, a heavy wooden door, the kind you see on the old ranches in the Valley. I heard footsteps approach-ing, a click-click of high heels. Houses of ill repute come up from time to time in our job—I've liked every one.

The door opened. A young woman in a short black dress looked out. "Sorry," she said, "we're closed." Behind her the cof-fee shop was dark except for the white glow of a cooler and tiny green machinery lights here and there.

"Too late for coffee anyway," Bernie said. "I'd never sleep." Don't ask me what that was about; the young lady didn't appear to get it, either. But then Bernie took out our card and we were back on track. "Mind showing this to Livia?" he said. She nodded and closed the door. We waited. A patrol car went down the street, didn't slow down.

"What does that tell you?" Bernie said.

I didn't know.

More clickety-clicks from inside. The door opened, and the young woman looked out again, this time with a friendly smile. "Mr. Little? Please come in."

Which we did.

"I'm Autumn," the young woman said, closing the door.

"That's a nice name," Bernie said.

"I found it online," Autumn said.

"Oh," said Bernie.

She looked at me. "Is this Chet? Livia asked me if he was with you."

"Yup," Bernie said.

"Can I pat him?"

"He hates that."

"You're joking, right?"

Of course he was. Bernie's quite the joker at times, not always the right ones. But in this case everything worked out fine. Autumn turned out to be an excellent patter. The young ladies in houses of ill repute were always excellent patters, although why I wasn't sure. What the whole business was about, meaning what was actually for sale—for example, Max's Memphis Ribs sold ribs—remained a mystery to me.

We followed Autumn across the coffee shop, through a door, into a storage space with sacks of coffee beans—lots of complicated smells but no time to sort them all out—and then through another door and into a nice sort of living room with a soft rug, some puffy-looking sofas and chairs, and a small bar, a room I kind of remembered, mostly from a heavy perfume smell. Another young lady in a black dress, but barefoot rather than in high heels, lounged on one of the sofas, leafing through a magazine, and a somewhat older woman wearing a dark pantsuit and a string of pearls sat at a desk in front of a laptop. She saw us and jumped up—or maybe not jumped on account of her being a big woman, big and curvy—and hurried to us.

"Bernie!" She threw her arms around him, a big woman and not that much shorter than Bernie.

"Hi, Livia." I could see Bernie'd had enough of hugging after a while, but Livia didn't let go till she was good and ready.

She stepped back, still gripping Bernie's upper arms, in fact, giving them a little squeeze. "You look just great," she said.

"Uh, no, um, thanks," Bernie said, which made Livia laugh, a nice big sound, not a boomer like Uncle Rio's but impressive for a woman. "And you, too," Bernie said.

"Oh, go on," she said. "I've put on so much weight."

"No, no, no," Bernie said. "And it suits you."

Livia laughed again. "Those are mutually exclusive, Bernie. Pick one, preferably the first."

"Um," Bernie said, and then he was laughing, too.

"Tulip?" she said. The young woman on the sofa tossed her magazine aside and rose right away. "A nice big bourbon on the rocks for Bernie here, and a small one for moi," Livia said. Tulip went behind the bar, reached for a bottle.

"Sweetie?" Livia said. "We're pouring from the top shelf tonight."

Tulip took a quick glance at Bernie, picked out a different bottle. Autumn went over to help her. Anyone could see this was a well-run place.

Soon Bernie and Livia were on a couch having drinks—Bernie at one end, Livia in the middle and maybe inching closer to him. Tulip gave me a pat. She was an excellent patter, too, maybe even better than Autumn, couldn't make up my mind about that. Autumn herself had left by another door; laughter came from not far off just before it closed.

"His coat is so nice and glossy," Tulip said.

"Chet's a looker, no doubt about that," said Livia. She reached over, touched Bernie's knee. "Nothing shabby about his partner, either."

"I don't," said Bernie, "uh . . ."

She gave his knee a squeeze. "We go way back, Bernie and I."

"Was he one of your husbands?" Tulip said.

"Oh, never," said Livia. "I'm genuinely fond of Bernie." She turned to him. "Remember how we met?"

"Well, it was a long time ago," Bernie said, "as you say, and . . ."

"This was near Fort Hood, Tulip," Livia said. "I had a very small establishment then, doing what I could for boys in the service—I've always been very patriotic, and by the way, you're not wearing your flag pin."

"It must have fallen off somehow," Tulip said.

Livia seemed to think about that. Then she sipped her drink and continued. "A small establishment, but with a nice enclosed patio in back, where we sometimes had dancing, and one night things got a little out of hand—I wasn't quite so knowledgeable then—and Bernie just happened along and saved my bacon."

He did? Then where was it? No bacon smell in the air, but that didn't mean none was around, in a fridge, for example, although I could usually sniff out bacon in fridges. Still, the possibility of bacon was out there; this was turning out to be a great evening.

"But," Livia was saying, "Bernie's probably not here to reminisce—never been much of a reminiscer, have you, Bernie?"

"I wouldn't say I never—"

"So let's get straight to whatever prompts this very welcome but unexpected visit. Goes without saying that any of our services are on the house, specialties included."

Tulip's eyes widened; why, I didn't know.

"Thanks, but not tonight," Bernie said. "We're actually

working." He nodded toward Tulip, a tiny quick nod, barely noticeable.

"Sweetie pie?" Livia said. "Go relax for a few minutes."

"With who?" said Tulip.

"With yourself."

"With myself?"

"Watch TV. Check your email. Do your nails."

"I just did them." Tulip showed her nails, wine-colored, I thought, but don't trust me when it comes to color.

"Do them again."

Tulip left the room. Livia set down her drink. "What's up?" she said.

"Marvin Winkleman," Bernie said.

"He's in number four," Livia said. "Want me to interrupt the proceedings?"

"Just tell me a little about him."

"Do you know the word *schlub*?"

"No."

"Means like it sounds. That's Marvin, a schlub. On the other hand, he's a very good customer, never makes trouble, pays cash, tips appropriately, wears deodorant."

"A very good customer?" Bernie said.

"Not the weekly kind of regular—that's our bread and butter—"

Bread and butter went well with bacon. Didn't smell any bread and butter either, but I moved closer to Livia just in case some of this food she was talking about made an appearance.

"—more of a semiweekly, I'd say. Or is it bi when you mean every second week?"

"That's a tough one," Bernie said.

"Come on, you know—you're just not telling. No need to be modest with me, big fella."

"Bi," Bernie said. "How long has he been a customer?"

"Years and years," Livia said. "Ten, at least."

Bernie rose. "Thanks," he said.

"That's it? You're not even finishing your drink?"

"Work comes first," Bernie said.

"My philosophy, too, but sometimes it's nice to blow off a little steam."

"That's where I get in trouble," Bernie said.

Livia gave Bernie a careful look. Her eyelashes were amazing! "How's divorce treating you?" she said.

"Not too bad."

"Got a lady friend?"

"Sort of."

"Want some advice?" Livia said. "From—let's face it—a pro?"

"I'd be crazy not to," Bernie said.

"Take her on a long walk. Hold her hand. Keep your mouth shut."

"Got it."

"Kiss me good-bye."

Bernie gave her a kiss. I thought it was meant to be quick, one of those pecks, but Livia had other ideas. When she finally stepped back and opened her eyes she said, "I've got a lot of know-how if you're ever interested."

"My heart couldn't take it," Bernie said.

Livia started laughing, then stopped quite suddenly. There are times when humans can't be understood, and this was one of them.

We followed Winkleman from Livia's for a few blocks, onto Pottsdale's main drag. He pulled over at a takeout place and went inside.

"Worked up an appetite," Bernie said. We parked behind him, got out of the car, stood on the sidewalk. "Long walk," Bernie said. "Hold hand. Shut mouth. Sounds so easy."

Winkleman came out of the takeout place, a brown bag in his hand. With a BLT inside, meaning bacon, but I tried not to think about that. Life has some frustrations, such as now all of a sudden a subject like bacon comes up over and over and yet you're not getting any—but I tried not to think about that. Winkleman saw us and stopped.

"Bernie?" He patted his comb-over. "This is a surprise."

"Couple things," Bernie said. "First—your stalking adventure is over."

"What the hell?" said Winkleman. Spots of color appeared on his face. "I don't know what you're talking about." He looked my way, stepped back a bit. My mouth was wide open for some reason.

"You've been stalking someone who has nothing to do with your case," Bernie said. "Stalkers piss the DA off more than just about anything. That's what got him elected."

"The DA? What the fuck are you—"

Bernie made a quick chopping motion with his hand, not something I'd often seen. "Second—your revenge fantasy is over, too."

"Huh?"

"Think, Marvin. Are you really in a good stone-casting position?"

Winkleman's mouth opened and closed, always a good sign for us.

"Get divorced," Bernie said. "Move on."

"I thought you were working for me."

"In a big-picture sense. You'll be grateful one day."

"I want my twenty-five hundred back."

"Less time worked and expenses."

"Time worked?"

"Tonight," Bernie said. "Tailing you."

Hey! Was Bernie being tough about money? I wanted to see that more often.

# TWENTY

Bernie called Leda from the car. Charlie answered. His voice came through the speakers. "Have you found Peanut yet?"

"No."

"When are you going to?"

"I don't know."

"I told the class you were finding Peanut."

"Did you say when?"

"No."

"Good. Put your mother on."

Leda came on. "Everything's taken care of," Bernie said. "A case of mistaken identity. You won't be bothered again."

"Whose identity was mistaken?"

"Just about everybody's," Bernie said.

"I don't—"

"No time to discuss it now, Leda. We're on a job."

"Okay," Leda said, and her voice softened. "And thanks."

Bernie hung up. "This marriage has got to work," he said. "Work and be a model for every single marriage till the end of time. Otherwise I couldn't live with myself."

No problem—I could live with him. In fact, forever. So everything was cool, although a bit confusing, so it was good that the phone started ringing.

The next voice over the speakers was Popo's. "Can we meet somewhere?" he said. "I've got something to show you."

"Should we come to your trailer?" Bernie said.

"It's not mine anymore," said Popo.

We met Popo in the lobby of this old hotel called Copperman's in the West Valley. I knew Copperman's from a case we'd worked on long ago, all about a Japanese restaurant and some stolen tuna. We found the tuna, but too late—I knew that before we even got out of the car on that last day.

But back to the lobby. It had ceiling fans, a palm tree—I know palm trees from the big leaves—and a few clusters of leather chairs here and there. Very nice, the leather smell. Leather is good for gnawing: that was my first thought.

The lobby was deserted except for Popo. He sat in a leather chair in one of those clusters, his face even thinner than the last time we'd seen him, the bones underneath showing in a way that made me uneasy. We sat beside him, Bernie on another leather chair, me on the floor, a black-and-white tile floor that felt nice and cool.

"Drummond fired me," Popo said.

Uh-oh. Humans got fired from time to time, meaning they had no job. Having no job: that would be bad. Couldn't happen to me and Bernie. There was always divorce work.

"Why?" Bernie said.

"He's going in a different direction."

"A circus without a clown?"

Popo shrugged, just a little shrug. A big shrug means not caring. A little shrug means you're beat. I didn't like seeing that from

Popo. I moved closer to his chair. And what was this? Down near one of the wooden legs, a small corner end of leather had come loose and was just hanging there, like something meant to be.

"What are you going to do?" Bernie said.

Popo shrugged again.

"You must have contacts."

"Contacts?"

"In the clowning world."

"I suppose," Popo said. "But what if your heart's not in it?"

"Maybe you just need some time," Bernie said.

Sometimes humans get this look that makes me think they hadn't heard what had just been said. "Has that ever happened to you?" he said. "Your heart not being in your work?"

"Divorce cases sometimes do that to me," Bernie said. "But my head's always in it."

Popo gave Bernie a quick look. "That's probably why you're the way you are."

Did Popo mean that in a good way or bad way? I didn't know. As for Bernie, he was shrugging the big shrug, the non-caring kind. Bernie's tough—don't forget that. And so am I.

"With me there's not much separation," Popo said, "so my head's not in it either, at least not now." He gave himself a shake, not much of one, more like a shiver, but I loved seeing that. "Not fair to you, talk like this," Popo said. "Obviously not in your line. But I was sorting through Uri's—effects? Is that the properly detached terminology?—and I found something you might be interested in." He opened a laptop. "This was Uri's. There were no bad surprises, if that's what you're thinking, but I found this video. It's from twelve years ago, before we even met." Popo turned the laptop in our direction. "I think it's for some sort of school discussion video hookup."

Popo tapped at the keyboard. A close-up face appeared, a face I didn't recognize at first, but then I noticed the pencil mustache and even though he looked younger than in the video with Peanut, I knew it had to be DeLeath: mustaches interest me, especially the pencil kind, and there wasn't another one in this case, not that I could remember.

First came a woman's voice. "Welcome to Eleanor Roosevelt Middle School, Mr. DeLeath."

"Thank you," DeLeath said. Hey! He had a very nice voice, strong and kind of deep, in fact a lot like Bernie's. Although not quite as nice as that—goes without saying.

"The students really enjoyed their visit to the circus when you were in town last winter," the woman said, "and they have some questions. Can you hear me all right?"

"Perfectly."

"Great. How about we start with Jeremy?"

There was some banging around and then a kid spoke. "Hi."

"Hi," said DeLeath, starting to smile.

"My dad says you have to hurt the elephant to make it do tricks."

The human smile when the smiling feeling stops suddenly inside them: that's an interesting sight, and I saw it now on DeLeath's face. "Jeremy?" he said, and now the smile was gone. "The most important thing I've learned in my life is that you should never be cruel to animals. And to treat an animal badly just to get it to do a trick is not worth it."

Hard to describe the look on DeLeath's face at that moment, but it was one of the best human looks there is. I've seen it on Bernie's face once in a while. I think it's the look of a leader.

The woman spoke. "Does that answer your question, Jeremy?"

"My dad says they poke the elephant with this hook thing," the kid said.

DeLeath's face hardened a bit, not as hard as a real hard guy like Mr. Gulagov, now breaking rocks in the hot sun, but hard enough. "That does happen, and I've been guilty of it, too, but that was in the past. If we—human beings—are so smart, then we're smart enough to persuade animals to do what we want without violence."

This was not so easy to follow. On top of that, I all of sudden found myself thinking about how we'd found DeLeath in the desert, and the horrible snake. I got a bit confused, and the next thing I knew I was right next to Popo's chair, and gnawing on that loose bit of leather—in fact, already at the stage where there's almost nothing left.

Meanwhile, the woman was saying, "Well, Jeremy, that seems to answer your question, don't you think?"

And Jeremy was saying, "My dad says it's a big hooked thing, real sharp. You dig it into—"

Popo closed the laptop. His hands—long and thin—were trembling a bit. "I wanted you to see him in life," he said.

"Why?"

"It might make you more determined."

"To do what?"

"Find the truth," Popo said. "And if that's impossible, at least keep looking for Peanut."

"Determination comes with the service," Bernie said.

"Sorry. No offense."

"None taken."

"Do you need another check from me?" Popo said.

That was the kind of talk I liked to hear. "We'll settle up when it's over," Bernie said. Oh, Bernie.

"I'm staying here for the moment—the owner's a friend," Popo said.

Bernie rose; me, too. "Did Uri go to Mexico much, or have any dealings down there?" Bernie said.

"Nothing I'd call dealings," Popo said. "We went to Cabo once. Why?"

"Where we found him was practically on the border."

"I know," Popo said. "That's just another thing I don't understand."

We went outside. I felt something flapping on my lip, licked at it, tasted leather. Uh-oh: a little scrap of leather, actually not that little, was stuck to my teeth and hanging out for all the world to see, had maybe been like that for some time. I hopped in the car, started trying to put things right.

Bernie glanced over as we drove off. "What are you up to?"

I sat up straight: quiet, alert, professional.

"You have papers for the dog?"

Late at night, crossing the border. I've done it before; we worked Mexico from time to time, me and Bernie. Bright lights, the kind that buzzed, shone down from above, and the uniformed guy in the booth held out his hand. Bernie said, "Sí," gave him a sheet of paper, and then said something else, the sound of his voice changing in a hard-to-describe way. All I know is when that happens I can't understand him at all, except for a few words like *amigo, cerveza,* and *croqueta.*

The uniformed guy eyed the paper, handed it back to Bernie, and said, "Enjoy your visit, señor."

Señor—I knew that one, too, another way of saying dude. I glanced back at the uniformed guy as we rolled away, saw him pick up a phone. Meanwhile, Bernie shifted gears, and—VROOM

VROOM—we were south of the border, down Mexico w
knew that because Bernie had started singing those very wo
There's a little woo-woo thing I can do for joining in, and I
it now.

We drove through a small town, not well lit, and into th
countryside. Things are different down Mexico way, for example
the days are brighter and the nights are darker. Does that make
sense? Not to me. Soon the yellow line disappeared from the middle of the road, then the road got narrower and bumpier, and traffic thinned out to just us. The wind rose and blew scraps of this
and that through our headlight beams. Yellow eyes glowed from
time to time off the side of the road, and once we passed a barefoot man standing under a scrawny tree. I kept my eyes on him as
we went by—I can turn my head practically around backward if
I want, strange how little turning the human head can do, but no
time for that now—mostly to get a long look at those bare feet,
bare human feet being an interest of mine, hard to explain why,
and saw the man take a cell phone from his pocket just before we
rounded a curve.

The moon rose, low, huge, orange. I love the moon, but
what's going on with it is hard to say. Soon, I knew from experience, it would be higher, smaller, and white. What was up with
that? And there were other nights when part of it was missing,
sometimes almost all, and that complete disappearance thing happened, too—nights with no moon. One thing for sure—I knew
because Bernie made the point a lot—we were in the Milky Way. I
felt good about that, although milk isn't my drink. Cats like milk.
Have you ever seen how cats lap it up? In real tiny sips, very neat
and tidy, never spilling a drop. Cats will do just about anything
to irritate.

In the distance rose a dark mountain, or maybe two moun-

tains. Bernie was looking that way, too. "Dos Jorobas," he said, "meaning two humps. And down in the valley between them— that's San Anselmo." I could see a cluster of yellow lights between the humps, very dim. We were headed in that direction, but Dos Jorobas seemed to be moving with us so we couldn't get closer. I'd seen that happen before—it wasn't just a Mexican thing. I shifted over, rested a paw on Bernie's knee.

"Hey, Chet," he said. "You all right?"

Of course I was all right, and if not at the very top of tip-top, then pretty close.

He patted my head; so nice. "Getting a bit tired, big guy? It's been a long day."

Tired? I never got tired. I wagged my tail, not easy to do when you're sitting down in the shotgun seat. It swished back and forth on the smooth, worn leather, making a sound I liked so I kept doing it till I got tired. I yawned a big long yawn.

"Maybe," said Bernie, "we should call it a night."

Fine by me, if that's what he wanted. We climbed a rise, started down the other side, and there, just ahead, lay a crossroads with a few low buildings and a flashing neon sign. I like neon signs. My favorite's this one with martini glasses we'd visited on a case, couldn't remember any details at the moment, my mind getting a bit fuzzy, like dreamland was trying to close in, maybe close in fast.

"Looks like a motel," Bernie said, slowing down. A motel— exactly what we needed! One thing about Bernie: he can make things happen.

# TWENTY-ONE

We parked and went into the office, a very small office but full of interesting smells. I'd forgotten all about Mexican air and what's in it. This is a big subject that I promise to get to later, but for now let's just say Mexico's a great place if you're interested in smells.

A woman with gray hair in a long ponytail sat in a lumpy old chair, watching TV and smoking a thin cigar. Bernie said something in that way he did when we were down in Mexico. The woman said, "Three hundred pesos for a single, or twenty U.S."

Bernie took out his wallet. "Your English is great."

"Should be," said the woman. "It's my first language."

"Yeah?" said Bernie.

"Graduated from New Trier High back in the day. Plus a year at Central Illinois."

"Hey," said Bernie.

"Now I'm back down here."

"Oh?"

"Papers," said the woman.

"Ah," said Bernie.

Human speech could be very easy sometimes—yeah, hey, oh, ah. Bernie was a master. As for what they were talking about, that was anybody's guess. I didn't dwell on it; in fact, the whole thing vanished from my mind right away, because all of a sudden a mouse popped out of nowhere, ran right by me—smelling strongly of butter, by the way—and disappeared into a tiny hole in the wall. I looked up. Bernie and the woman seemed to have missed it all.

"Room number seven," she was saying, and Bernie took a key off a wall peg.

"Get many Americans staying here?" he said.

"Some," said the woman. "Especially around festival time. Plus birdwatchers and hunters passing through."

"Hunting what?" Bernie said.

"Whitetail, mostly," said the woman. "Some turkey." She nodded toward a table in the corner. "There's brochures if you want."

I was hoping Bernie would go pick one up—turkeys are another interest of mine—but he didn't. Instead he said, "Had any Americans recently?"

"One or two."

"Gentleman named Darren Quigley, by any chance?"

"Doesn't ring a bell," the woman said.

"An acquaintance of ours," Bernie said. "We're trying to catch up with him, maybe get in some sightseeing." He took something from his pocket. "Here's a picture of him." We had a picture of Darren? One thing about this job: there were lots of surprises.

The woman glanced at the picture. "Never seen him," she said.

"Too bad," Bernie said. "We should have organized this better. Kind of a reunion thing, actually—three old buddies." Three old buddies? I was lost. "The third buddy should have passed this way as well—big fellow."

The woman shook her head.

"Wears a bandanna," Bernie said. "Name of Jocko Cochrane."

She stopped shaking her head in mid-shake, then shook it once or twice more. Her gaze fell on me. "It's fifty pesos extra for the dog."

"You didn't mention that," Bernie said.

"I forgot."

Bernie paid some more money and said good night. We went outside, headed toward our room. I realized my tail was down, kind of just dragging along after me, and raised it back up. Fifty pesos extra for me? What was that all about?

Bernie switched on the bedside light, a dim brownish light that left the corners of the room in shadow, even though it was a pretty small room. He tried the overhead light; it didn't work. I sniffed around. There'd been a man and a woman in here, but not recently, and they'd had a burger or two. Other than that, nothing of note. Then I spotted a strange picture on the wall, a picture of a bull and a dude dressed up in a glittery costume. The dude held a sword and seemed to be about to stab the bull with it. Could that be? I tried to look away but couldn't, at least not for long. Has that ever happened to you? Meanwhile, Bernie was unpacking, pouring water in my bowl, brushing his teeth. Those little teeth humans had—they brushed them every day for some reason. Mine are big but only get brushed when Janie's Pet Grooming Service—We Pick Up and Deliver comes to visit. So: the smaller the teeth, the more you need to brush them? Was that it?

"Let's catch some zzz's, big guy." Bernie turned down covers, got in the bed, reached for the switch, but the light went out before he touched it; at the same time the AC stopped humming. "Uh-oh," Bernie said. He rose, crashed into a chair sitting in plain sight, and went to the window.

I squeezed in beside him. Bernie parted the curtains. The whole village was dark, dark and silent; although actually it was a silvery kind of darkness because of the moon, and not quite silent, either: I could hear a car, far off, but coming closer.

"Either a power failure or they switched off the generator," Bernie said. He opened the window and a nice little breeze flowed in. Bernie gazed at the village, not a light showing. His voice grew quiet. "That's how nights were in olden times," he said. I waited for more, so maybe I could get the point, but no more came. Bernie climbed in bed. I lay down beside it, stretched my legs way out, then pulled them back in, got comfortable. Dreamland rolled over me right away, like a tall, dark wave.

Things are different in dreamland. For example, I was flying. Not flapping my wings or anything—I don't believe I had wings in the dream—but just soaring high up over the desert. Way down below something was moving. I drew closer. Hey! It was Peanut! I took a nice deep sniff, trying for a whiff of that powerful Peanut smell, and I picked up a powerful smell, all right, but kind of confusing.

I opened my eyes, saw the bed beside me, remembered where we were. I rose and looked at Bernie. He was sleeping, one arm outside the covers, chest rising and falling. I watched that arm for a while, and might have kept that up for some time, but then a gust of wind blew through the open window, carrying a powerful smell, the powerful smell from my dream. The dream itself was gone, but did I care? No. I was already at the window, sticking my nose out into the night. That smell, the very most powerful smell in the nation within the nation: need I mention it's the smell that females of my kind sometimes get when they . . . have wants—let's leave it at that.

The next thing I knew I was outside. I'm a pretty good leaper—in fact, the very best leaper in my K-9 class, which actually led to all that trouble on the very last day, meaning the day I would have gotten my certificate—but with such a low window even a bad leaper, Iggy, for example, could have done it. Well, maybe not Iggy.

Ah. So nice to be outside on a soft and beautiful night, all silvery dark, the moon now in a different part of the sky and lower, nothing stirring, and that special scent a snap to follow. Was this the way things were in olden times? I began to see why Bernie went on and on about them, whatever olden times actually were.

The scent led me away from the motel, across the hard-packed dirt street, still warm from the day, and into an alley with a bar on one side—easy to tell from that barroom smell, which I must have described already, probably more than once—and a crumbling wall on the other. The alley ended at a cross street, also dirt, with deep ruts here and there like black holes. Bernie talked about black holes a lot. They were dangerous, capable of swallowing up everything, so I was careful to avoid them. I made my way down the street, low ramshackle dwellings on both sides, the scent growing stronger. A moment or two later, just beyond a rusted-out car up on blocks in someone's front yard, I glimpsed a bushy tail, pure white in the moonlight and raised up high.

I trotted on over, not fast; no need to scare anybody. And there she was! Nice and big, although not nearly my size, of course; mostly black and white, with some other colors, too; a longish snout and small, watchful eyes: I liked her! She gave me a look with those small, watchful eyes and then turned and trot-

ted away. But not fast—we were in tune on that not-fast thing.
I trotted after her, gave her a sniff. Ah, yes. After that, it got not
so easy to keep events straight in my mind. But did she give me a
sniff back? Pretty sure that happened. Did we circle around a bit?
Probably. And there's no doubt that I bumped up against her and
she kind of pushed back a bit. Then we were in the shadow of the
rusted-out car, a very private space. My eyes were on the moon,
but I wasn't really seeing it.

All of a sudden a woman called out from the nearest ramshackle house: "Lola! Dónde estás? Lola?"

Lola? A cool name, but the interruption was inconvenient. A
flashlight went on, and the beam began sweeping the yard.

"Lola! What the hell?" The beam passed over us, came back,
and stayed, circling us in bright light. "Dios mío! Ven aquí!"
Very inconvenient, because we were occupied. And then just like
that—in the way the very best things can sneak up on you—we
weren't! Lola scooted away and took off toward the house, glancing back once. Those small, watchful eyes: I'd never seen anything
quite like them. The next moment something got thrown at me,
missing by a mile, whatever that was. "Mal perro-vete!" Meaning
what? Not sure, but I caught the tone and ambled off. I felt tip-
top, just about the highest tip-top I can feel. It was great to be
south of the border down Mexico way.

I headed back to the motel, taking my time. Funny, the way
I'd been so tired before I'd lain down beside Bernie's bed, and now,
long before morning, I was full of pep and all set for another day,
and not only that but working up a bit of an appetite. No trouble
finding my way back in a new place, a simple matter of following
my own scent, a scent—if I haven't gone into this before and I
should have on account of the importance of knowing your own
scent in the nation within—made up of a faint, almost undetect-

able, smell of old leather, plus salt and pepper, mink coats, and just a soupçon of tomato; and to be honest, a healthy dash of something male and funky, especially tonight for some reason. And so, not really paying much attention to my surroundings, my mind on other things, such as the likelihood of coming upon a tidbit or two in this dark little village with everyone but me fast asleep, I was just dimly aware that I might not be the only one up and about. The faint sound of soft, quick footsteps; a shadow darting around a corner: hey! What was going on? I snapped out of it, hurried toward that same corner.

Not a shadow, I saw, but a man, and a big one. He ran across the main street toward the motel, carrying something that picked up a few moonlit sparkles. At the same time, the big man's scent drifted to me, a nasty, stale smell I remembered. Those bad guys I get close enough to sink my teeth into tend to have smells that stay with me. I charged across the street just as the big guy threw the shiny thing through a window in the motel: our window.

From inside came a flash, bright as day, and then a huge boom that blew out all the window glass and a chunk of the wall. The big guy turned and I got a real good look at him—bandanna, sideburns, twisted nose: Jocko. He saw me and took off toward a pickup parked down the street. I wanted to go after him, wanted that real bad. Instead I leaped through the hole in the wall.

The room was on fire—the bed, the walls, everything—with sheets of flame bursting up to the ceiling and tearing right through. And so much smoke, hurting my eyes, filling my nose in a horrible way. Where was Bernie? I couldn't see him, couldn't smell him, could only smell smoke. I barked and barked again.

"Chet?"

And there he was, almost lost in the smoke, crawling on the floor, but in the wrong direction, toward one of the burning walls.

I ran over—the air so hot now, crackling all around—and pushed at Bernie, turning him around. He got a hand on me, staggered to his feet. Then came another boom and the whole outside wall vanished and burning stuff started pelting down on us like a fiery rain. We dove through the space where the wall had stood, rolled into the street, got up, and ran, me and Bernie together.

KA-BOOM!

We turned to watch. The motel went up in flames. They rose to the sky and from their very tips hurled red fragments of curtains and bedding and furniture even higher. Maybe it was kind of beautiful in a way.

# TWENTY-TWO

Lucky," said Captain Panza, the chief of police. He sat straight behind his desk, a thin little guy with gold braid on his shirt and creases in his uniform pants, smelling strongly of the same kind of shaving lotion favored by Skins Barkley, now sporting an orange jumpsuit at Central State. Creases always got my attention: Bernie's pants never had them. "You're very, very lucky to be alive," Captain Panza went on. He took a thick gold pen from his chest pocket and wrote something on a sheet of paper.

"I'm aware of that," Bernie said. He sat in a chair on the other side of Captain Panza's desk; I stood beside him. Bernie wore sweats he kept in the car—all the rest of his stuff had burned in the fire. I wore my brown collar; the black one, back home, is for dress-up. "Got any leads yet?" Bernie said. "Clues about who did this?"

"The term *leads* is familiar to me," said Captain Panza. "Leads are being developed even as we speak."

"Such as?" Bernie said.

"Perhaps in El Norte the police discuss ongoing investigations," Captain Panza said. "Procedures are different here."

"I appreciate that," Bernie said, "but—"

"My office is grateful for your cooperation," said Captain Panza. "Enjoy your visit to our beautiful country."

"I'm sorry?"

"You may go."

"That's it?" Bernie said. "You've hardly asked any questions at all."

Captain Panza glanced at the sheet of paper. "You testified that you were asleep when the incident occurred, escaped with the help of your dog, and saw no one. Is there more?"

"Yeah," said Bernie. "Lots. Starting with the fact that someone tried to kill us and I'd like to know who."

Captain Panza's gold pen moved across the page. "We have no indication that you were the target."

"Someone blows up my room and I'm not the target?"

"As you may know, we have a violent element among us in this state. Dangerous, yes, but often careless, prone to mistakes."

"They were going after someone else?"

Captain Panza nodded.

"Who?" said Bernie.

"That information must remain confidential."

"Did any of the other guests get hurt?"

"There were no other guests."

"What about the woman who runs the place?"

"Rosita?" said Captain Panza. "Lucky, like you. She was elsewhere at the time."

"That's interesting," Bernie said.

"Is it?"

Bernie and Captain Panza gazed at each other. They'd been having a polite conversation, but I got this uncomfortable feeling—it happens down the back of my neck—that they actually weren't big fans of each other.

"I've got an odd question for you," Bernie said.

"I'm listening," said Captain Panza.

"Ever heard of puff adders out in the desert?"

"Puff adders?"

"It's a kind of poisonous snake."

"We have poisonous snakes, certainly," Captain Panza said. "That's no secret."

"The thing with puff adders," Bernie said, "is that if they show up here in Sonora they're lost. Puff adders come from Africa."

One of Captain Panza's eyelids made a tiny fluttering motion. "You're a naturalist?" he said. "That is what brought you to Mexico?"

"I'm a private investigator," Bernie said. "I thought you knew."

"Why would you think that?"

"Because you didn't ask."

More eyelid fluttering. I was glad to see it, although I couldn't have explained why. "Private investigators from El Norte have no status here," Captain Panza said. "You must be on vacation."

"Yeah," said Bernie. He rose. "We're just starting to have fun."

Captain Panza smiled. Hey! He was missing a tooth. I couldn't help feeling a little bad for him. "We want all our visitors to have fun," he said. "But before you go, it's my duty make sure that your dog has papers."

"They were checked at the border," Bernie said.

"I will have to see them."

"They're in the car."

Captain Panza gestured toward the door. Bernie moved that way, and so did I. "The dog can remain," Captain Panza said. "I like dogs."

Bernie gazed at Captain Panza, then nodded. "Stay, Chet," he said, and went out the door. I stayed.

Captain Panza stopped smiling. He stared at me. I stared at

him. If he was a fan of me and my kind, his face kept it hidden very well. "I saw what you did last night," he said. "Muy bien. We would make a good team, you and I." He opened a desk drawer, took out a big bone-shaped biscuit, the size I like the best. Captain Panza held out the biscuit. "Ven aquí," he said.

I stayed where I was.

He laughed. "Jocko fears you," he said. "Imagine that!" Captain Panza put the biscuit away, closed the drawer. Jocko? This guy knew Jocko? What did that mean, if anything?

The door opened and Bernie came back in. He crossed the room and laid the papers on Captain Panza's desk. Captain Panza glanced at them real quick, if at all.

"These papers are not in order," he said.

Bernie gave Captain Panza a look that showed nothing, at least to me.

"You must leave Mexico at once," Captain Panza. "Alternatively, you may stay, in which case the dog will be seized."

Bernie kept giving him that look. "Do you have a specific amount in mind?" he said.

"Amount, señor?" said Captain Panza. "For your sake, I will pretend I did not hear that word."

Bernie was silent for a moment. Then he said, "We can pretend all kinds of things."

For some reason, Captain Panza didn't like hearing that; it kind of stung him—I could see from this tiny flinch in his eyes.

Bernie turned to me. "Let's go," he said.

I followed him to the door. Captain Panza said, "Maintaining a safe speed, you will reach the border in"—he checked his watch, thick and gold, like the pen—"seventy-five minutes. Naturally I will receive a telephone report from the aduana the moment you pass through."

"Adiós," Bernie said.

"Hasta la vista," said Captain Panza.

"It stinks," Bernie said, as we got in the car.

It did? I sniffed the air, rich with smells, although I wouldn't call any of them stinking.

We drove for a while, back in the direction we'd come from, away from Dos Jorobas, that two-humped mountain. "Hasta la vista," Bernie said. "Probably not a good idea if that actually happens, at least not down here."

That one zipped right past me. I watched the outside go by, hilly and rocky, with saguaros here and there, the kind of country we like. Normally Bernie would switch on the music and we'd do a little singing, but his hand didn't move toward the knobs, just stayed on the wheel, maybe gripping it harder than usual. We passed a donkey pulling a cart with an old man riding on top— the donkey's big eye seemed to watch me going by, sitting up tall in the shotgun seat, but I couldn't tell, and anyway got distracted by the sight of tiny white worms crawling around on the donkey's face. Only for a moment, though, and then we were zooming on down the road.

"What's a border, Chet?" Bernie said. I waited to hear. "Just a line on a map, drawn by politicians. Is that supposed to impress us?" I didn't know. We came to a crossroads, the pavement continuing straight ahead, a dirt track leading off to the side. Bernie pulled over, shut off the engine.

It was real quiet. Bernie twisted around in his seat, gazed at Dos Jorobas. In between the humps lay a little clump of white. "San Anselmo," Bernie said. "That was our plan. Do we cut and run, let ourselves get pushed around?" Were we getting pushed around? By who? I didn't know, but getting pushed around was out of the question. I barked. Bernie laughed and gave me a pat. Then he opened the glove box and took out the .38 Special and a box of ammo. "Don't know about you," Bernie said, loading the rounds—those rounds, glittering in the sun, a sight I always liked seeing!—into the cylinder. "But I'm in the mood for pushing back."

Me, too. That was exactly my mood, to a T, whatever that means. There were golf tees, of course, and once in a pro shop I'd gotten into a bit of a—but forget all that. How could this be about golf? Had golf come up in this case, even once? Hey! In fact, it had. I remembered Colonel Drummond on the practice tee—whoa, another T—and those yellow pants. So maybe this was about golf, after all. Fine with me. I was ready for anything, including golfers in yellow pants trying to push us around.

Bernie tucked the .38 Special in his belt, started the car, steered off the paved road, and onto the dirt track. Almost at once, his hand relaxed on the wheel, let it go, wandered over to the knobs, and then: music! All our favorites, like "It Hurts Me Too," with Elmore James and his slide guitar, "If You Were Mine," with Billie Holiday and Roy Eldridge on trumpet—that trumpet always does things to me—and "Honky Tonk Blues" with Hank Williams. By then Bernie was singing at the top of his lungs, I was joining in with my woo-woo thing, and we'd made another turn, so now the two-humped mountain stood dead ahead, getting closer and closer.

The road switchbacked up the nearest hump of the Dos Jorobas. I like switchbacks—you get to look down on where you just were, and then again and again. Sometimes that can make me pukey, but not today. Soon the road leveled out, widened, became paved, and a bit of traffic appeared. We drove into San Anselmo, through narrow cobbled streets, all bumpy, and then into a square with a fountain in the middle and white buildings all around, gleaming in the sun. We parked beside a rusty old flatbed with a load of flowers in back. The smells: lovely.

We got out of the car, walked over to an outdoor café near the fountain. It made nice splashing sounds. I leaned in and lapped some up. Delicious. Coins glittered down at the bottom. A skinny barefoot kid passing by on the other side reached in and grabbed one of them. A waiter yelled at him and the kid ran away. The waiter came to our table.

"Señor?" He had a cigarette sticking out the side of his mouth, a plume of smoke curling up into the still air. Bernie couldn't take his eyes off it. His nostrils seemed to expand a bit, like his nose was making a play for some of that smoke. Poor Bernie.

"Café," he said,

The waiter went off. We sat in the sunshine. The skinny kid returned and fished out another coin. The waiter came back, yelled at kid. The kid ran away. The waiter lowered his tray, a tray bearing a cup of coffee and a dish with some cigarettes on it.

Bernie took the coffee, gave the waiter a quick glance. "Yeah," said Bernie, "don't mind if I do." He plucked out a cigarette and handed over a greenback.

"For one cigarette and one coffee is twenty pesos," the waiter said. "You have nothing more small?"

"Keep the change," Bernie said.

The waiter nodded, just once, a careful sort of nod. Bernie stuck the cigarette in his mouth. The waiter produced a lighter and held the flame under the tip of the cigarette. Bernie's cheeks got hollow and the cigarette end glowed. I loved seeing all that; if I could smoke I would, no second thoughts, whatever those are, about it.

Bernie blew out some smoke, reached into his pocket, laid the photo of Darren Quigley on the table. The waiter's eyes shifted to it, then away.

"Know him?" Bernie said.

The waiter shook his head, just once, a careful sort of head shake. Some kind of interview was going on. Bernie was a great interviewer. That was one of our strengths at the Little Detective Agency. I bring other things to the table. Maybe they'll come up later.

"But you've seen him," Bernie said.

The waiter didn't reply. He stuck the lighter in his apron pocket, took a slow glance around.

"Suppose our friend in the picture likes a drink or two but doesn't have a lot of money to spend," Bernie said. "Where would he go in San Anselmo?"

The waiter tilted his chin toward a narrow street leading away from one of the corners of the square. "La Pulquería," he said.

"Gracias," said Bernie.

The waiter picked up his tray and left without another word. The skinny kid reappeared.

I've been in dives before—that comes with the job—but never one as divey at La Pulquería. Dark and smoky with walls stained brown and a floor that stuck to my paws with every step, plus a smell of human urine that was off the charts, if off the charts means the most powerful I've ever come across, except for that one time on the freeway when a truck carrying a load of portable toilets wrecked right in front of us.

There was one customer at the bar, slumped over it and motionless, his hand around a glass, drool coming from the corner of his mouth. We stood as far from him as possible. The bartender approached. She was hefty, wore a low-cut top and gold hoop earrings that touched her shoulders, looked kind of puffy and tired.

"Pulque?" she said.

"Cerveza, por favor," said Bernie.

She opened a bottle, took a glass off a shelf, and set them on the bar, said something in that Mexican way I didn't understand. Bernie laid a greenback on the bar. The bartender seemed to perk up. She said something else. Bernie said something that made her laugh. Did it also make her lean forward, giving Bernie an even lower-cut view? Bernie tried and failed not to look; I'd seen that happen many times. He raised the bottle as though to fill the glass, then paused.

"Salud," he said.

"Salud," said the bartender.

Bernie drank, but right from the bottle. I couldn't help noticing the fly at the bottom of the glass. Bernie was fussy about things like that. That was one difference between us. There may be others, but none came to mind at that moment.

"You like?" the bartender said. "Is good beer?"

"Yeah," said Bernie. "Real good. I like bourbon, too."

"Bourbon?"

Bernie pointed to a bottle on the shelf behind the bar. The bartender brought it down, put it on the bar. "Cuatro Rosas?" she said. "You want?"

Bernie nodded. The bartender poured bourbon in a shot glass. Bernie took out another greenback, laid it on top of the first one.

The bartender's eyes narrowed. "Is too much," she said.

"Got a friend who had some trouble with Cuatro Rosas," he said.

"Amigo?"

"Sí." Bernie laid down another greenback. "We're trying to find him. Darren Quigley's his name." Down at the end of the bar, the lone customer tightened his grip on his glass, but otherwise made no other movement. "He looks like this." Bernie set the photo of Darren on top of the greenbacks.

The bartender glanced at the photo, then sucked in her breath and made a quick motion with her hand over her chest, up and down, side to side. I'd seen that before, although what it meant was a mystery. "No sé nada," she said.

"I don't believe that," Bernie said.

"No Inglés," she said.

Bernie switched to the Mexican style of talking. The bartender shook her head. "No comprendo," she said, and shook her head some more. At the same time she kept sidling away down the bar, toward a bead curtain at the end.

"Qué pasa?" Bernie said.

The bartender raised her finger, like she'd be right back, and disappeared through the bead curtain.

We waited. Some kind of creature scratched inside the wall. Bernie was thinking hard and fast: I could feel it. All at once, he looked down at the greenbacks, still lying on the bar. "Christ," he said, and then he was up and running around the bar, and I was running with him. We charged through the beaded curtain and into a small room with a dented fridge, cases of beer, a rusty sink with a dripping tap. No sign of the bartender. Bernie opened the only door. It led to a narrow street with tall whitewashed walls on both sides, the sunshine glaring bright, and no one around.

"Can I be so stupid?" Bernie said.

Bernie stupid? Never.

We went back inside. The only customer was still there just as before, sprawled on the bar. Bernie picked up the greenbacks and the photo, and was putting them in his pocket when the customer suddenly raised his head and looked right at us. He was a scary-looking dude in lots of ways, but what stuck in my mind was the sweat now on his face, just dripping, the way humans get after running a long way. He opened his mouth—his teeth were black, same color as the fly in Bernie's glass—and spoke in a deep voice, maybe the deepest I've ever heard.

"Jesús Malverde," he said.

"Quién?" said Bernie.

The dude pointed to a ceramic—ceramic means breakable if you knock it over—statue standing by one of those big, old-fashioned cash registers, the kind of statue that's just the head and shoulders, in this case a dark-haired unsmiling man with a thick mustache.

"I don't get it," Bernie said.

"Él sabe," said the guy.

"He knows?" Bernie said. "Knows what?"

The dude gazed at us, sweat rolling off his chin. "La respuesta," he said in that deep deep voice.

"Jesús Malverde knows the answer—is that what you're saying?" Bernie said.

The dude's eyes rolled up and he pitched forward onto the bar, knocking over his glass. It toppled off the edge and smashed on the floor. His hand twitched once or twice, like it was trying to find something.

# TWENTY-THREE

ack in the square: ah! The air smelled so fresh after La Pulquería. I took a nice deep breath, felt tip-top.

"Let's go to church, big guy," Bernie said.

Church? I've been in churches a few times—a perp name of
Whizzer DuPuis tried to hide from us under a pew at St. Domi-
nic's in South Pedroia—and never felt comfortable. Churches
were big and hushed at the same time, a combo I didn't like, but
also—what were they all about? I know what a restaurant's about,
for example, or a grocery store, or Petco. But if Bernie says we're
going to church, then that's that.

The church stood at one corner of the square, a white stone
building, actually pretty small. The wooden door, old and cracked,
squeaked when Bernie opened it. No one inside, but it wasn't
hushed: I heard a guitar, not far away. So far, not too bad for a
church. There were no pews, just card-table-type chairs set up on the
cool stone floor, with an aisle down the middle. We were walking
down it when the music stopped abruptly and a side door opened.

Did I get a fright then or what? A woman—I knew it was
a woman, but only from the scent—appeared in the doorway.

She gave me the same feeling I'd gotten when Bernie and I went through a period of watching horror movies, a short period because they turned out to be too scary for both of us. I got right next to Bernie, even maybe a bit behind him; I'm not ashamed to admit it, or if I am I'll get over it soon. The woman wore a strange kind of long black robe, and also had a black hood thing with weird side flaps sticking out, everything black except the insides of those flaps and the tight white covering that hid her neck and ears, came up practically to her chin.

"Hola, sister," Bernie said.

Sister? Do you know that human expression—my heart skipped a beat? At that moment it happened to me for real: I felt a pause deep in my chest. I was shocked, more shocked than I could ever remember. Bernie had a sister and I was just finding out after all this time? He had a mother—a piece of work, can't go into that now—but besides her and Charlie, no other family. Life was full of surprises, like when out of the blue someone says, "Let's pick up some dog treats on the way," but this wasn't that kind of surprise.

"Buenas tardes, señor," the scary woman said. "You're American?"

Huh? Yeah, Bernie was American—me, too—but wasn't that a pretty basic thing to know about your own brother?

"Yes," Bernie said. "You speak English?"

"I do."

"Good," said Bernie. "My Spanish is a little rusty."

I knew rust—could actually smell it sometimes, which had led to me digging up a knife that cracked a case, all the other details of which are gone—but I wasn't getting even a whiff of it now, had no idea what Bernie was talking about.

The scary woman looked at me. "Your dog seems a bit shy."

"Shy?" said Bernie. Me, shy? My thought, exactly. Then he glanced back, saw that I was now pretty much completely behind him. Bernie smiled. "Probably the first time he's seen a nun, sister—at least in full habit."

The woman smiled, a nice smile, with even white teeth and happy eyes. "He's very handsome," she said. And just like that, whether she was Bernie's sister or not, this nun person wasn't scary anymore. Life is full of surprises, in case I haven't pointed that out in a while. I came out from behind Bernie, not that I'd really been behind him, more at his side, in truth, or even a bit in front.

"I'm Sister Mariana," the nun said, coming forward.

"Bernie Little," said Bernie. "And this is Chet."

So they were meeting for the first time? And still, she was calling herself sister? I made up my mind never to think about this again.

"May I pat him?" Sister Mariana said.

"I've never seen him object," said Bernie.

Sister Mariana gave me a pat, not an expert-type pat, but still nice. "I hope you're not here for the blessing of the animals," she said. "It was last week."

"Chet might have enjoyed that," Bernie said. "Or maybe not. But we're looking for information about Jesús Malverde."

The smile faded from Sister Mariana's face, starting with her eyes, the way a human smile fades. She backed away. "This is a church," she said.

"Isn't Jesús Malverde a saint?"

"Most surely not," said Sister Mariana. "The church is for peace."

"If he isn't a saint what is he?" Bernie said.

Sister Mariana glanced around. Sunlight shone through a stained-glass window—I knew what those were on account of we had one once, but Leda took it with her after the divorce—and made a splash of color on the floor. "Is your purpose good?" Sister Mariana said.

"I'm a private investigator," Bernie said. "We're looking for a guy named—"

She held up her hand, long, thin, pale. "No details," she said. "Is the purpose good? That's all I want to know."

"Yes," said Bernie. "Our purpose is good. The results sometimes end up mixed." My tail started wagging, which it sometimes does on its own, not sure why.

Sister Mariana gazed at Bernie, her face kind of hard. Then she looked at me and softened a bit. "What I said is true: Jesús Malverde is not a real saint, not from the church. But he is the saint of the outlaws. They have shrines by the roadside, with fresh flowers when someone is killed."

"Any of those shrines around here?"

"One," said Sister Mariana.

Bernie left some money in the box by the door as we went out.

Our purpose was good. What did that mean? I tried to figure that out on the drive but didn't get anywhere, even though it turned out to be a long drive—out of San Anselmo, up the side of the second hump, steeper and more rugged than the first, the road much worse, just a narrow, rocky track with sheer drop-offs on one side and cliffs on the other, nobody around, like it was only me and Bernie in the world. Once we had to stop and roll a boulder out of the way. Bernie did the actual rolling. I tried not to get too excited.

"Watch it there, Chet. I don't want the goddamn thing to—"

But it did—no way I had anything to do with that happening—making the one extra roll like when a golf ball pauses at the rim of the cup, which reminded me of a little adventure that maybe had been my fault and . . . where was I? Right. The one extra roll that took the boulder right to the edge and then—boombity boombity boom. Way way down it fell, bouncing and tumbling and finally ending up as only a puff of distant dust, hardly visible. We gazed down at that puff of dust, both of us leaning over the drop-off, watching the wind carry it away.

"The past is so strong here," Bernie said. "Like the whole mountain's full of ghosts."

Ghosts? Uh-oh. That was very bad. What is it about Halloween that brings out the worst in humans? I had a quick look around, saw no ghosts, nobody of any kind; just me and Bernie, up on this cliff edge. He gave me a pat.

We hopped back into the car—me actually hopping, Bernie using the door, but I knew he was capable of hopping into the car because I'd seen him do it, sort of, on a day Suzie happened to be around—and headed up the switchbacks. They took us across the face of the second hump, higher and higher, the desert floor shimmering way down below. Hey! Was this how the birds saw things? Maybe, but if so why did they always have that mean look in their eyes? And the air, so clean and pure: maybe they didn't appreciate that, either. But I sure did. And so did Bernie. I put my paw on his knee. The car made a sudden swerve toward the drop-off.

"Chet—what's with you?" Bernie jerked the wheel, got us back on track.

Nothing. Nothing was with me. I sat up tall, a pro and on the job.

We worked our way around the mountain, came to the other side. In the distance lay a great plain, spreading on and on, with towns here and there and thin black highways connecting them, sunlight flaring on shiny things. We followed the track around a huge outcrop and into a narrow canyon with steep slopes rising on both sides, coming closer and closer and finally coming together.

"Box canyon," Bernie said.

I'd been in box canyons twice before that I could remember. Once was on a camping trip and Bernie had played his ukulele by the fire. The other time there was lots of gunfire.

Or maybe it was the same time.

We followed the track to the end of the box canyon. A village lay there, reddish like the countryside, with a few small trees growing nearby and nothing stirring. As we got closer I saw that the village was mostly rubble, houses with no roofs, crumbling walls. The tallest ruin, a kind of guard tower, maybe, stood near the trees, at a point where the track narrowed to a footpath that climbed the steep slope beyond the village.

Bernie stopped the car by a pile of rocks and we got out. The pile had been flattened on the side facing the road, and in the carved-out part was a painting of the dark-haired unsmiling dude with the thick mustache. "Jesús Malverde," Bernie said. Someone had laid flowers on the ground in front of him, maybe a while back, since they were all brown and stiff; there were also a few empty shotgun cartridges lying in the dirt. Bernie kicked at them with his toe, then turned toward the trees. They stood close by, but down a little slope, in a kind of hollow, and among them were some wooden crosses.

We walked down into the hollow. "Might have been a pond here at one time," Bernie said. No water to be seen now, but I could smell it. We took a look at the crosses. "No names on any of them," Bernie said. "Meaning . . . ?"

I didn't know. We came to the last cross, just two twigs nailed together. This cross had an empty bottle lying on the ground beside it. Bernie picked it up. "Four Roses," he said. "I wonder—" he began, but by then I was barking.

Bernie hurried up to the car, came back with the folding shovel, pulled the cross out of the ground and started digging. I dug, too, somewhat faster than Bernie. I can dig all day if I have to, especially with this kind of dirt, dirt that had been dug already. In this case we didn't have to dig all day, or even very long at all, before a face appeared, eyes open, and dirt in those open eyes. But the face itself was undamaged and I remembered it no problem.

"Christ," Bernie said. "A dumb guy, but he still ended up knowing too much. Why couldn't he get lucky, just once?"

We dug carefully around Darren Quigley. He had a hole in his chest, the big kind that comes from a close-up shotgun, and maggots were quivering inside it. Bernie stuck the shovel in the ground and bent down to pull Darren out of the grave. At that moment, a sound came from back up the slope, the sound of a hard heel snapping a dried-out twig. We turned.

Uniformed men stood at the top of the slope, handguns and rifles pointed at us; more men were appearing from behind the guard tower wall. I knew one of them: Captain Panza. He wasn't smiling—in fact, his face was hard and mean—but I got the feeling he was enjoying himself.

Bernie reached for his cell phone.

CRACK. A gunshot—and the cell phone, all in bits, flew from Bernie's hand.

"Hands to the sky if you want to live," Captain Panza said. A breeze had sprung up, bringing with it the smell of his shaving lotion, the kind Skins Barkley liked, but too late for that as well. Bernie raised his hands. "You are under arrest for murder," said Captain Panza.

# TWENTY-FOUR

We were outnumbered, some big number against two. When it comes to numbers, two is as far as I go, but it's enough, in my opinion.

"Easy, boy," Bernie said, his voice low, between us. "Don't move a muscle." How did he know I was just about to charge up that hill at my very fastest, first taking out Captain Panza and after that—well, I had no real plans for after that, but so what? "Sit," Bernie said.

I sat. Bernie would think of something—he always did. That was one of the things that made the Little Detective Agency such a success, except for the finances part. At that moment I remembered the .38 Special, all chambers loaded and hidden in Bernie's pocket. Bernie's a crack shot—which I hope I've already gotten across, what with so many examples out there that it was hard to think of even one—so that had to be the plan. Gunplay was a great plan, had worked for us many times. Any second now—and seconds flew by pretty quick—out would flash the .38 Special and blam blam blam! Yes, the .38 Special, blam blam blam, and then—

"Very, very slow," Captain Panza said, "and at the same time hands up very, very high, you will now walk this way."

Bernie raised his hands a bit higher. But his hands up there and the .38 Special down in his pocket. Was that going to be a problem? Bernie started up the slope. I moved beside him.

"The dog stays," said Captain Panza.

"No," Bernie said. "He comes with—"

BLAM! But not from the .38 Special. This was one of the uniformed dudes firing from the top of the slope. Dirt kicked up at Bernie's feet, real close, and a sharp stone went airborne and hit my shoulder. Didn't hurt, not one little bit, and I showed no pain at all.

"You don't hear well, Señor Little," said Captain Panza, "a fact I know for sure from you being out here in wild country instead of safely back across the border. So I say again, and for the last time—the dog stays. We have no time for dogs, and especially this one." A uniformed dude behind Captain Panza spoke in the Mexican way. "You catch that, Señor Little? Sergeant Ponson says we forgot to bring the ark today."

Bernie knelt beside me, real slow, and also real slow, lowered his arms and wrapped them around me. He looked me in the eye. Bernie has the best eyes. I saw no fear in them and I didn't smell any, either. He spoke so softly there was hardly a sound at all. "Chet," he told me, "when I say run, you run. Just as fast and as far as you can."

Something about running. We were going to be running together, right? So why would I have to be running my fastest, or anywhere near? No criticism of Bernie, but he didn't run that well, not even for a human, on account of his wound from the war.

Bernie let go and stood up, eyes still on me. "Stay," he said, louder now. Then he turned and started up the hill again, hands raised.

Stay? But if I stayed, how were we going to run together? Maybe Bernie was going to blast them all with the .38 Special first, and then we'd be running. Did that sound like good strategy, strategy being how we were going to come out on top, me and Bernie? I thought so. And so I stayed, although as Bernie got farther and farther away I shifted some in his direction, but still on my backside, which is a form of staying.

As Bernie reached the top of the rise, a couple of Jeeps drove out from behind the watchtower. The uniformed dudes closed around Bernie, pointing their guns. One of them began to pat him down. Oh, no. What if he found the—

And he did. He took the .38 Special from Bernie's pocket and handed it to Captain Panza. Captain Panza held the .38 Special up in the light, squinted at it. "What luck," he said. "This must be the murder weapon."

"I didn't murder anyone," Bernie said, not screaming or even agitated; just the same calm voice he'd use any old time.

Captain Panza pointed the .38 Special down at Darren Quigley, lying in the open, shallow grave. "That looks like a murder victim to me." He turned to the others, "Muchachos?"

"Sí, sí," they said. A few of them were grinning, like something funny was going on.

"He's a murder victim all right," Bernie said, "but it wasn't me."

"No?" said Captain Panza. "If not you, any idea who was the real murderer?"

"I'd like to think it was you," Bernie said.

Silence up on top of the rise. Everyone went still.

"Maybe," said Captain Panza, "my English is very bad. Maybe so bad I didn't understand what you said. Please—por favor—tell me again."

Bernie took a deep breath—I could see his chest swelling up.

Then, in a loud booming voice, a tremendous voice I'd never heard from him before and didn't know he had, Bernie shouted, "Chet—run!" And he batted the .38 Special out of Captain Panza's hand.

I ran. The loud boom of Bernie's voice was like a wave, carrying me, pushing me along even faster than my very fastest. CRACK! A shot rang out. PING! Dust exploded off a rock, right beside me. Then from behind came a thud, and another thud, sounds I knew well, sounds of fighting. I slowed down, looked back, and there was Bernie, still on his feet, locked in a struggle with the uniformed guys. One or two lay motionless on the ground and Bernie was a great fighter, but there were so many of them! I stopped running. Hadn't Bernie told me to run and not stop? Yes, but now he needed me. I couldn't make those two things fit together. Meanwhile, I found I was sort of inching my way back down the footpath, toward Bernie. And what was this? Still down in the graveyard but definitely moving my way—a uniformed guy with a rifle.

I knew what rifles could do, of course, one of the most important things I'd learned on this job, but I kept inching down anyway. Bernie—still fighting on that little rise above the trees and the graveyard—needed me. What had he told me to do, again? Couldn't quite remember and also had no big desire to. I inched down some more, maybe not inching now, more like walking. The uniformed guy stopped. I was still pretty far away, but suppose I sprinted at him, my very fastest, and then sprang right at his throat and—

He raised the rifle. At the same instant came Bernie's voice, that booming shout, like thunder from the sky. "Chet—run!"

I didn't want to run, couldn't leave Bernie like this but at the same time I had to do what he said, or at least give it the old college try, whatever that happened to—

Muzzle flash, bright orange. CRACK! Thump. All those

things came together practically at once, and at the same time the top of a cactus got blown off right by my head. White droplets from inside the cactus went spraying in the air. I felt some on my face. Once this real bad perp took a bullet as he stood beside me, and some of his blood dripped down on my fur.

"CHET!"

I remembered that sticky feeling of blood on my fur, and the smell, too, one of the richest smells there is. I rolled around in the dirt plenty after that time with the bleeding perp.

"RUN!"

I turned and ran back up the hill, not my fastest at first, but another CRACK sped me up. Blood had gotten me going, hard to explain the connection. I tore along the footpath. It got steeper and steeper and vanished forever in a jumble of rocks. From behind I heard ACK-ACK-ACK. I knew that was automatic fire from back in my days at K-9 school—it would have been nice if I'd gotten the certificate on the last day, the day things went wrong—so it shouldn't have been a big surprise when the dirt in front of me erupted in dust-spewing pockmarks, like during the monsoon rains, but it surprised me just the same. I started taking switchbacks of my own over hard ground, whipping past spiny cacti that whipped back at me—uh-oh, the stinging kind—and all the time behind me: ACK-ACK-ACK, ACK-ACK-ACK. *Run! Run! Run!* I heard Bernie's voice now, but not from Bernie actually speaking. Instead I was hearing Bernie in my mind, which happens a lot. ACK-ACK-ACK. I swerved, swerved back, swerved the other way, my whole body low to the ground—steep steep ground that kept trying to tip me over and roll me all the way down—the wind in my ears, high and scary, me not really running now, more like climbing, digging in with my front paws, pushing from the back. ACK-ACK-ACK—and what was that?

I felt a buzz right through the fur on my back, a buzz like a big hard insect might make, and then PING—close by a fiery spark shot off the face of a rock. The next moment I was suddenly over the top, going so fast I flew straight up in the air—ACK-ACK-ACK—and then I fell, landing hard on my stomach, but on the far side of the hill, almost a cliff, really; on the far side and safe from human weapons.

I lay there, trying to get my breath back. So weird, that feeling of getting the breath knocked out of you. But no big deal. The point was I heard no more gunfire, heard nothing at all, except for a cascade of pebbles and stones I'd knocked loose on the other side, and soon that went silent, too.

My breath came back. I breathed. Should I be getting up? I really didn't feel like it at the moment. I felt like just lying on the ground and breathing. Was that a good idea? I didn't know. Then Bernie spoke in my mind: *On your feet, big guy.*

I got on my feet. Maybe that hadn't been Bernie speaking in my mind, but Bernie in real life. Oh, I hoped so. I crept back up to the crest and stuck my head over, just the smallest bit. Wow. I was up so high, had come such a long way. I gazed down the slope—yes, a cliff in places—all the way to the bottom of the box canyon with the graveyard and the trees, trees that looked like tiny garden plants from where I was, and on to the ruined village with the crumbling watchtower. Not a soul in sight, which is human talk for no people. There was at least one soul around, if I understand the term properly, and that was me. But I could be wrong; words were tricky. Not important anyway; what was important was the absence of people. Bernie, Captain Panza, the uniformed men, the rifle dude and ACK-ACK-ACK dude, the Jeeps: all gone. Did I spot a dust cloud on the far side of one of the humps of the two-humped mountain? Maybe. But it might have been an ordinary cloud, the kind that sometimes brings rain. I checked the sky: not another cloud in it, bright blue and the sun kind of glaring. I realized I was a bit thirsty.

Maybe Bernie was down there in the box canyon and I just wasn't seeing him. I checked again. No Bernie. I barked. Bark bark. And from the box canyon came a bark bark. I barked again. Bark bark bark. And bark bark bark came back. None of my guys were down there, not that I could see. I trotted back and forth on the crest, this trot that happens sometimes when I'm getting beside myself. That's an expression of Bernie's. You didn't want to get beside yourself—that was important in this business. I remembered another important thing—you were never supposed to show yourself at the top of a crest: *No better target than that, big guy.* I moved down the back side a short way, out of sight.

But soon I found myself trotting back and forth on top of the crest again. Where was Bernie? I barked. The bark came back. And that kept up for a while and then I was beside myself again. I had a faint memory of Bernie explaining the barking thing that was going on, maybe explaining it a thousand times, which had to be a lot. The actual explanation wouldn't come, but just knowing that Bernie had cleared it all up made me feel better, put me back inside myself.

I stood on top of the crest and breathed. This was Mexico. Things were different in Mexico: that was another saying of Bernie's. Mexico was different. So therefore? Bernie said that, too, sometimes with his head in his hands. *So therefore?* Then, after *so therefore?* things would get real quiet, so quiet I could feel his thoughts, like gentle breezes in the air. Meanwhile, the air around me, this warm and clear Mexican air, was perfectly still.

# TWENTY-FIVE

This one here flunked out," the handler said.

"Yeah," said Bernie, although I didn't know he was Bernie then, just knew I liked his smell—apples, bourbon, salt, and pepper, plus a little extra something that actually reminded me of me. "I saw."

"Too bad," said the handler. "He's the fastest and the strongest of the bunch."

"And the smartest," Bernie said.

"Think so?" said the handler. "Then how come he's out of the parade?"

"I don't know," Bernie said. "There's something about him. What's his name?"

"We've been calling him Chet. Must've had some other name before. Some tenth precinct guys found him in a crack house when he was just a pup."

"What's going to happen to him?"

"Shelter, I guess," said the handler.

"Tell you what," Bernie said.

Which was how we got together. Funny that I'd be thinking

about that now, up on this crest in Mexico where things were different, because there were probably lots of other things I should have been thinking about.

Such as?

Such as—that was another saying of Bernie's. He used it on people, to make them . . . I'm not sure what, but to make them do something. I used it on myself: such as, big guy? Such as?

Nothing happened.

I gazed down into the box canyon, and especially at the graveyard. Too far away to really tell, but I thought the body of Darren Quigley was gone. You see dead bodies in this job, and for a while at least they look like they could be sleeping, but they don't smell like they could be sleeping, far from it, and that's from the get-go. The life smell goes, and that's that.

A shadow passed over the box canyon, moving fast. I glanced up, saw a big dark bird. I'm not a fan of birds. This one reached a place in the sky high above me and started circling. That gave me a bad feeling, hard to say exactly why. I moved off the crest, down the back side a few steps. When I looked up again, the big dark bird seemed to have moved with me, circling slowly in the blue, not bothering to flap its wings, just gliding.

Meanwhile, my mouth was real dry. On the patio at our place on Mesquite Road, we have this fountain Leda had installed a long time ago—oh, those poor workers!—a fountain in the shape of a swan. When Bernie turns it on, a sparkling stream of water flows from the swan's mouth. I love to stick my tongue in that stream. Is that the best water I've ever tasted or what? Actually, it's not. Once Bernie and I went for a hike, somewhere very high up, and on this rock face hung an icicle. Wow. First and only time I've seen one. We couldn't quite get to the icicle, but it was dripping water off the pointy end, and that water ran down the face of the rocks and I licked some off. That was the best water I've ever tasted. I could taste it now, pure, cold, rocky. I got thirstier.

I gazed down from the back side of the crest. The ground fell sharply away, down and down, just as steep as the other side, or steeper. At the bottom lay a plain, and beyond that endless hilly country, on and on, with rock formations here and there, plus desert plants that looked like green dots. But on the plain itself—funny how first it wasn't there and then it was—I saw a shimmering blue pond. My mouth started watering right away, and then quickly dried up. But at least now I had a plan. Such as? To head for water.

Yes, the back side was very steep, almost a cliff at first, and a few times I found myself leaning way over an edge, my front claws trying to dig into the rock face and keep me from falling off. At those moments the bird shadow would suddenly grow bigger and pass right over me; *but no looking up, big guy.* My balance is pretty good, better than yours, no offense, but with only two legs—and no tail!—it's a miracle you can even stand up; still, my balance isn't so good I can do a lot of looking up while I'm on a cliff face.

I worked my way down a bit, came to an outcrop that ended in a sheer drop. Down below was a kind of narrow dirt shelf topping another cliff, but off to one side of the shelf the angle evened out a bit, and then things seemed to get easier over that way. The problem was the distance to that shelf. From where I stood, it looked like a long distance. Too long? How did you figure out the answer to that? I crouched on the edge of the outcrop for a while, gazing at the shelf, hoping the answer would come.

The bird shadow passed over me, back and forth. I raised my eyes, gazed at that shimmering blue pond on the plain. What would Bernie say now? I listened real hard but didn't hear him. All I knew was that I didn't want to think about this anymore.

Then I was in midair. I'd been in midair before—it's that kind of job—but never this long. There was lots of time to look around—which I didn't do—or to think about things. I thought about Bernie.

And was still thinking about him, when—OOOMPH! I landed on the shelf. Right now I'm maybe going to surprise you and point out something good about cats. Have you ever seen them land? A thing of beauty.

My landing on the shelf wasn't a thing of beauty. I came down on all fours like cats do, but that was just about the only similarity. You don't hear a loud thud when cats land, and if you're the cat doing the landing, you probably don't feel a jolt of pain that goes up your legs, into your shoulders and chest and through your whole body, and you probably don't find yourself rolling, rolling and rolling right to the edge of the shelf and then shooting off into thin air and starting that long, long—

But not quite off the edge. At the very last second—which I'm sure isn't much time—or even less, with the front part of me already hanging over empty air, the back part got a grip, those two paws digging in, hitting the brakes harder than I've ever hit them; and I pulled myself away from the long, long fall.

I sat safely on the shelf, panting and panting. No good to have your tongue hanging out like that when it's all dry and stiff, but I just couldn't help myself. *Get a grip, big guy.* I got a grip, stood up, moved toward the side of the shelf. Just as I'd thought: things weren't so sheer over this way, more like a regular mountain. I stepped off the shelf and started down.

A breeze rose up the slope from the plain, carrying lots of smells—including a creature smell that might have been goat, although I saw no goats down there, nothing moving at all except for the shimmering on the pond, although for some reason the water smell wasn't in the air. The ground was hard and dry, with lots of prickly pear cactus from which I kept my distance, and—almost at the bottom now—one of those gnarly manzanita trees. I stopped and lifted my leg against it. Surprise: nothing came out! Kind of strange, since when was the last time I'd lifted my leg? Plus I always had a little something in reserve for marking purposes.

I reached the plain and headed toward the pond, still shimmering in the distance. Was there any reason not to ramp up into my trot? I've got a few trots, but there's one I can do forever, my go-to trot, Bernie calls it. I went into my go-to trot and started closing the distance between me and that cool blue water fast. Only here was another strange thing, mixed up in my mind with the strangeness of having nothing to mark with: the distance wasn't closing at all! The shimmering pond kept shimmering, but it seemed to be moving with me. I sped up a little and the pond sped up, too, no doubt about it. I slowed down and it slowed down. Meanwhile, this plain wasn't very big, and the hills on the other side were coming closer—no doubt about that, either—with every step I took. *So therefore?*

I didn't know, so I just kept going. I realized my head was hanging down a bit and raised it up. The pond kept moving away from me; the hills came closer. What was that about? All of a sudden I recalled Bernie talking about this very thing. But what had he said? I was still trying to remember, trying my very hardest, when the pond stopped shimmering, stopped looking blue, and vanished completely. There was nothing but the desert plain, with its stones and dust, prickly pears and other spiky things. I crossed the little of it that remained and entered the hills. The bird shadow made interesting patterns in front of me.

*   *   *

For a while I was thirsty, and then not; you've got to be tough in this business. I went up hills, down hills, around hills. Also on the move were the sun, sliding lower in the sky, and the shadows of the hills, growing longer and longer. As for the bird shadow: gone. I felt pretty good, maybe not tip-top, but pretty close. The breeze blew in my face, carrying a smell of smoke, and that made me feel even bet—

Smack. Something hit me from behind, knocked me for a loop. I did a somersault, twisting in the middle of it, landed facing the way I'd come. And there stood a goat, making chewing motions the way they do. All at once I was in a bad mood. I snarled at the goat. It did that bleating thing—the sound actually reminding me of the ACK-ACK-ACK of automatic fire, except toned way down—and lowered his head. I've never had anything against goats, but now that was all changed. I didn't like that ACK-ACK-ACK bleat, didn't like that wispy beard—don't like wispy beards on anybody—and there were probably other unlikable goat things, but before I could get to them he was charging at me again. This time I was ready.

Makes a difference, doesn't it, Señor Goat? That was my thought as I stood over him a moment later. He lay on the ground, looking kind of stupid, in my opinion. I barked in his face, a bark that felt real dry in my throat. He bleated again. Not an ACK-ACK-ACK: this bleat told me he was done. I backed off. The goat struggled to his feet and ran away, kind of stiffly.

I watched him go, and I wasn't the only one: up on a ridge a kid in a sombrero stepped forward and yelled something at the goat. The goat headed toward her. The kid climbed down from the ridge, shook a stick at the goat. I liked the look of this kid and trotted toward her. She saw me, backed away, pointed the stick in my direction. I kept coming, but not so fast, and when I got close I sat down.

She gazed at me, said something in the Mexican way. She was a real skinny kid with a runny nose and a high little voice. My tail swept back and forth in the dust. The kid lowered the stick and asked me some kind of question, no idea what, but for some reason I started panting. She asked me another question, a short one. I wagged my tail and panted. Then from a leather satchel over her shoulder she took out a plastic bottle of water and a tin cup. Oh, water! Now it hit me big-time just how thirsty I was. I needed water and right away, couldn't wait one more single moment. On the other hand, as humans like to say, and then I had a thought: maybe if they had more hands, they would . . . but the rest of the thought wouldn't come, so maybe it wasn't a thought in the first place, and forget about all that anyhow. The point was that sometimes when you want something real bad, the best way to get it is to keep your mouth shut. That was a saying of Bernie's, but it also means just sit still. So I sat still.

The kid approached, slow and cautious, and without taking her big brown eyes off me, she knelt, set the cup on the ground and poured it full of water. Ah, the sight of that little stream, reddish in the light of the lowering sun: so beautiful.

"Hola," she said, backing away and pointing to the cup. "Agua."

Agua—I knew that one from way back, could probably do well in Mexico, given time. I rose, went to the bowl, and drank agua. Bliss. At first I drank slowly, but as I drank—kind of crazy, I know—I got thirstier and thirstier so I drank faster and faster and soon the cup was empty and I was licking the moisture off the bottom.

"Más?" said the kid.

I backed off a step or two. She refilled the cup. This time she didn't move away. I drank another cupful, felt lovely agua spreading through me.

"Más?"

I liked this word, más. I drank some more, all I needed, than sat down by the cup. The kid reached out, still slow and cautious, and patted my head. I shifted closer to give her a better angle. She spoke to me in the Mexican way, said lots of nice things—did it matter exactly what? After a while, she noticed my tags, leaned forward to read them.

"Jet?" she said, or something that sounded a lot like that. "Tu nombre es Jet?" I'm Chet the Jet for sure, but was that what it said on my tags? I'd always thought it would have been just Chet, why, I don't know. Was this another thing that didn't matter? All of a sudden we had things that didn't matter out the yingyang. I tried to hold that thought, but it got away from me.

The kid rose. "Ven, Jet."

Ven? There was Vin McTeague, but he was now up at Northern State—breaking rocks in the hot sun if there was any justice at all—so that couldn't be it.

"Jet," the kid said. "Come. Is late."

She put the cup and the plastic bottle back into her satchel, slung it over her shoulder, and started walking. I walked beside her. The goat went on ahead, glancing back at me from time to time and doing his bleating thing. Our shadows got huge in front of us.

## TWENTY-SIX

We hadn't gone far—at least it didn't seem that way, but all watered up again I was feeling pretty peppy, and distances tend to go by fast when I'm feeling peppy, which is just about always—when we came over a rise and into a little valley. I liked this little valley right away. It had trees, a few white adobe buildings that were actually pink from the setting sun, and a narrow stream with real, smellable water in it.

"Mi casa," said the kid. "Ven, Jet."

We walked side by side, me and the kid. I was getting the hang of things down Mexico way.

We came to the biggest of the adobe buildings—none of them very big, and all of them kind of run-down—which had a shaded porch and looked like a farmhouse. The goat wandered off and nibbled at stunted plants in the yard. The kid and I walked past a hitching post—marked by a coyote, but not recently—and up to the front door.

"Papá! Abuelita!" the kid called, adding some more I didn't catch.

The door opened. I glimpsed a tiny old woman at a stove. Then a man came out. He was a little guy in a torn shirt, had deep lines in his face, and hands that were too big for someone his size. He looked at me, frowned, and spoke to the kid in a way that sounded annoyed. The kid moved closer to me and spoke back to him in a way that also sounded annoyed. I liked this kid.

The man—her father, I had that down—stepped off the porch and came toward me. I backed away; didn't like his smell or those big hands. Bernie has big hands, too, but he's a big man and they look right. The kid's father didn't look right. Also Bernie's hands are beautifully shaped and this guy's hands were ugly, fingers twisted, knuckles swollen. He paused, said something to the girl.

"Jet," she said. "Es Americano."

"Sí?"

"Sí."

The man turned to me and smiled. Whoa! He had silver teeth. Never seen that before and I didn't like it, not one bit. I backed away some more. "Hey, Jet," he said, holding up his hands the way some perps do to show you there's nothing in them; but that wasn't the point—the hands themselves were the problem. "You nice dog," he said. "I like you."

Uh-huh.

"You want food?" he said.

Sure. But I didn't go any closer.

He went back into the house. The kid gave me a pat, so gentle I could hardly feel it. Have I mentioned her big brown eyes, just about the nicest human eyes I'd ever seen?

"Eres guapo," she said. "Muy, muy guapo."

No idea what that was about. The kid's dad came out of the house holding a bone, a real nice one with a bit of meat still on it. And what a powerful smell, wiping out all other smells! He approached, offered the bone. I didn't take it, didn't back away, didn't do anything except try to make up my mind. But what a bone! He smiled his silvery smile, said something to the kid, and gave her the bone.

"Take, Jet," he said, "take."

The girl held the bone right in front of my face. Who could have resisted? Not me. I took the bone, careful not to hurt her hand, so tiny and pretty compared to the hands of her dad. And at that moment, when we were finishing up with the exchange of the bone, me concentrating to get it just right, the man came fast from the side and tried to loop a lasso over my head.

I writhed away from that lasso and took off, running and running and—

And then—oh, no! Something squeezed tight around my neck, stopping me dead. My feet flew out from under from me and I got stretched out to my fullest in midair—upside down and tail first—for what seemed like a long time. And then—thud!—I came crashing down on the ground. I scrambled up right away, or almost right away, and tried to run. But at the same moment the man yanked hard on the other end of the lasso and took all my breath away. Even worse, he seemed to be smiling: his silver teeth glinted in the fading light.

"Papá!" the kid cried, and reached for the rope. He raised the side of his hand to her. The kid flinched even though he didn't hit her, then turned and ran into the house. I sank to the ground, no air at all, and things turning black. Meanwhile, the man was tying his end of the lasso to a ring in the hitching post. The squeezing around my neck slackened a bit. I breathed in some air and the blackness cleared. This was my chance! I had to bring him down before he got me tied to the post. I charged. He looked up, saw me coming, his big hands working frantically at the knots. Then he jumped up and darted toward the house. I leaped onto the porch, dove at his back. But too late: the door closed in my face.

Anger took over. I tore at the door with my front paws, barking and barking. At some point I heard the man laugh, safely inside the house. I went quiet, backed off. The kid said something. Then came a smacking sound. The old lady said, "No, no, no." The man yelled at her. But there was no more smacking, just silence.

I left the porch, walked across the yard, kept going until the rope drew me up short. I pulled the other way, pulled harder and harder, but all that did was bring the blackness, so I stopped. I went back to the hitching post and gnawed at those knots, but got nowhere even though I'm a pretty good gnawer; the rope was thick and the knots were big and hard.

Night fell and stars came out. I was still gnawing, but not at the knots around that hitching post ring. Instead, I was off in the shadows and on my back, working on the part of the rope closest to the loop around my neck. The smell of food cooking over a fire came drifting from the house and, yes, I was hungry, but gnawing always takes the edge off hunger. And was I getting anywhere? I thought so: when you gnaw on a rope for a while you realize that it's actually not one solid thing, like a bone; a rope turns out to be made of many many thin strands, thin strands that parted if you gnawed hard enough. Was I gnawing hard enough? Better believe it. I could feel those thin strands giving way against my teeth, one after another. It wouldn't be long before—

Headlights appeared on a hillside above the house. They swept down in one long curve and then a truck, kind of like a UPS truck, drove into the yard, and stopped. A man—oh, no, could it really be him?—got out, stepped onto the porch, and knocked on the door.

I gnawed that rope as hard and fast as I could. But gnawing isn't one of those things that can be speeded up much. I tried to speed up anyway. One strand split, and another, and one more, and—

The front door opened and light spilled out. In the light stood the kid's father—this farmer or whatever he was—and another man, a much bigger man with sideburns, bandanna, a big crooked nose: Jocko, for sure. The kid appeared between them. Her father pushed her back inside.

I rolled over, jumped up, bolted right out to the full length of the rope, strained against it with all my might. It began to give, the tiny strands breaking and breaking, the rope weakening. Any moment now I'd be free! Free and gone. I dug my claws deep into the dirt for better traction and was giving it all I had, the strands snapping apart so hard and fast I could hear them, when out of nowhere this strange thing came down over my face. I jerked my head to get away from it, but couldn't. Something clicked, like a buckle snapping into place, and someone very strong jerked on the rope around my neck, lifting the front part of me right off the ground. I twisted around, tried to bite whoever had me.

But biting wasn't possible. Some kind of cagelike thing was clamped around my nose and jaw. I could barely open my mouth. Jocko held me up, just my back paws on the ground.

"Will you look at that," Jocko said. "Practically gnawed his way through the goddamn rope." He tugged at it with his free hand and the last strands gave way, the long rope end falling to the ground. I'd come so close.

"Es muy malo," said the farmer.

"Talk English, for Christ sake."

"He very bad."

Muzzle: the name came to me. No one had ever muzzled me before, but I'd seen muzzles on others of my kind, always felt bad. Biting was now impossible, but why should that mean I couldn't fight? I barked—not much of a bark with that muzzle on, mostly trapped in my throat—and went at Jocko with my front paws.

I got him a good one right on the side of the face, a good one that brought blood. Jocko staggered back but didn't let go of the remaining short end of the rope, still around my neck. I pawed him hard again, this time on the throat, and the rope began to slip from his hand. I was twisting away from him, wrenching the rope free, when the farmer sneaked in from the side, raising a big stick, or something like a big stick; I saw him coming, but too late.

San Diego: what a place! It takes a while before I stop trying to herd Bernie back to the beach. "Chet, for God's sake—I can swim." After that we paddle out with the surfboard. "Think you can stand up on this, big guy?" Turns out I can! A wave rises up and I ride and ride, higher and higher, having the time of my life, till I fall off, a long long fall followed by a hard hard landing on the desert floor.

The desert floor? My head hurt. I opened my eyes, saw only blackness. Maybe I was a bit confused, but I knew one thing for sure: I wasn't in San Diego. No surf sounds. Couldn't miss surf sounds; they were surprisingly loud—I'd learned that on our trip to San Diego.

*Bernie!*

Things—none of them good—came back to me in a jumble. As for the here and now—another saying of Bernie's, the here and now—I couldn't see or hear anything, but smells were in the air, one in particular—rich and powerful. I tried to place that smell and got very close to actually remembering.

I rose. My mouth sometimes needs a good wide stretch when I wake up, so I opened it wide and—only I couldn't. The muzzle! That part hadn't come back with the rest of the jumble. I shook my head from side to side, tried to shake off that horrible muzzle, but it wouldn't even budge. I went at it with one of my front paws, then the other, felt metal bars, straps, some kind of buckle behind my head, and attacked them all, with no result. I sat down, tried again with my back paws, found the angle much better but the ending was just the same. The next thing I knew I was charging around frantically, banging into walls of some kind, falling, getting up, charging around harder, at the same time doing my best to bark and bark, although I could hardly make a peep. I was out of my mind.

THROOMPH: a strange sound and all at once came light, so bright it blinded me. I went still. Soon my eyes adjusted and the first thing I saw was a man watching me, a small man like the farmer, except he wore a gun on his hip; a big tarp lay rumpled at his feet. The next thing I noticed was the steel cage all around me. I barked at the man, made that puny muzzled sound. The man laughed. I dove at him. Why did I bother when I'd already seen the cage, knew it was useless? I don't know.

I smashed my body against the steel bars.

"Loco," said the man. He folded the tarp, carried it toward a big, low building that looked like a warehouse, and disappeared around a corner. The sun beat down.

I sniffed my way around the cage, sniffed no way out. This had happened before: certain humans—and they'd all paid eventually—had a thing about trapping me in cages. But what hadn't ever happened was the second cage, the small one over my face.

These particular humans had me in two cages at the same time. That enraged me. I threw myself around some more.

*Easy, Chet. Everything's going to be all right.*

Bernie! I heard him! I hurried to the bars, looked out. No Bernie. I waited for the sound of his voice to come again. It did not. But I felt calmer just the same. Also my head didn't hurt so bad. I hated being in a cage, and I hated the muzzle so much I had to force myself not to think about it or else I'd go crazy, but I felt calmer.

What did Bernie always say when we were in a new place? *Get the lay of the land, big guy, that's step one.* Bernie was always right about things like that, one of the reasons the Little Detective Agency was so successful. I looked around. The back of the cage stood against an adobe wall. From the front I saw a flat plain with a road crossing it, and beyond that some steep hills. Right away I had a plan: get out of the cage and into those hills. That was what happened when you did things Bernie's way. Ideas came out of the blue.

Getting out of the cage had to come first. I sniffed around again for a way out. Didn't find one, but I picked up that rich smell again, so strange and powerful. And this time—now that I was calmer—I placed it. It was Peanut's smell, for absolute sure.

I thought to myself: Chet the Jet! You go!

# TWENTY-SEVEN

*G*et the lay of the land, big guy, that's step one.

*G* I already had the lay of the land down pat: the back of the cage against the adobe wall, the big warehouse, the road cutting across the plain, the steep hills in the distance. Nothing moved except the sun, and you couldn't really see it moving, but it had to be, because the next time you looked it was somewhere else.

*Down pat:* that expression stayed in my mind. A pat from Bernie would have been real nice long about now; even a pat from just about anybody. Meanwhile, heat was building up in the cage, pressing down on me from the tin roof. No water to be seen, and how would I have drunk it anyway, wearing that horrible muzzle? I tried to stay calm, and during the staying-calm period, I spotted something up on a ridge in the steep hills, a strange kind of something, like a skinny fire hydrant with an umbrella on top. Once some stray bullets hit a fire hydrant in Los Olas, and water came shooting out. I was thinking about how much fun that had been, and feeling more and more thirsty, when a long tractor-trailer—the kind they call an eighteen-wheeler but don't ask me to count them—appeared on the road, raising a long cloud of dust. It came closer and closer, went right by me, and parked by the warehouse. The red roses on the side panel were hard to miss.

I heard the cab door slam shut but couldn't see who got out. Silence fell. I explored the cage, searching for some little gap I could work on, or some weak spot, but there were no gaps, no weak spots. I found myself just standing there, poking my muzzled face through the bars. Up on that distant ridge the skinny fire hydrant with the umbrella top seemed to be on the move.

Another dust cloud appeared on the road, smaller than the first, with a white dot out in front. The white dot grew, changed shape, became a car, a long, white convertible I thought I knew, and when it turned off the road and parked in front of the warehouse I was sure.

Colonel Drummond, a cigar in his mouth and a straw hat on his head, got out of the car and entered the warehouse. After that nothing happened except that the umbrella-topped hydrant thing was still on the move, coming down the distant slope. Also I was getting hotter and thirstier.

Some guys came out of the warehouse, carrying paint cans and rollers. I knew rollers from back in the Leda days, when she decided to change the color of the kitchen to what it had been a few changes before, and Bernie got the idea of painting it himself to save money. The less said about that the better, but I learned one thing for sure: I hated having my coat shaved.

The guys went to the side of the eighteen-wheeler, opened up the paint cans, and went to work. Pretty soon the red roses were gone, the whole side of the truck all white with no pictures. It was interesting to watch, so interesting I forgot about the cage around me and the muzzle on my face. Then I all of a sudden remembered. It made me so mad I rubbed and rubbed my head against the bars real hard, tried to rub that muzzle right off. But it wouldn't budge. I stood with my muzzled face between the bars.

The paint guys went away. The sun beat down, and we were back to the nothing moving thing, except for the umbrella-topped hydrant slowly descending toward the flatland. After a while the umbrella turned into a big sombrero, and the hydrant became a person, most likely a small one.

The small person in the sombrero came a little further down the distant slope. Then the warehouse door opened and out walked not the paint guys, who I was kind of expecting, but two other men. One was Colonel Drummond; the other—a big, round-faced guy with a handlebar mustache—looked familiar but I couldn't place him. Then I noticed his snakeskin boots and remembered: Tex Rosa, owner of Cuatro Rosas trucking, some kind of buddy of Jocko's. I backed away from the bars, deeper into the cage.

They walked toward me, side by side but not close, like maybe they weren't buddy-buddy. Tex Rosa said something about trouble, and Colonel Drummond said, "You're blaming me?"

"Who else?" said Tex Rosa. "You started it."

They stopped in front of the cage. Human fear has a smell, a sweaty smell with some nasty sourness thrown in—and it was coming off Colonel Drummond in waves. Was he afraid of me, locked in a cage and muzzled? That didn't make sense.

They gazed at me. "Fine-looking animal," said the colonel.

Tex Rosa nodded. "I'm giving him to Jocko as a bonus," he said. "That's if there're no more goddamn screw-ups."

"I'm sure everything's going to end up just—"

"Shut up," Tex Rosa said. "And lose the cigar. It stinks."

The colonel dropped the cigar. Rosa ground it under the heel of his snakeskin boot.

"Gonna need some scratch from you," he said.

"What for?"

"Bernie Little."

"I don't get it," said Colonel Drummond.

Neither did I. But they were talking about Bernie, so I listened my hardest.

"Think Panza's just gonna up and hand him over?" Rosa said. "That not how it works down here."

"You have to buy him?"

"We," Tex said. "Meaning you and me. You put up the money, I'll do the deal."

"How much?"

"He's asking sixty grand."

"Christ."

"I'll talk him down."

"How far down?"

Rosa turned to the colonel. "There are no guarantees. How come you don't know that by now?"

Colonel Drummond looked down at the ground. I'd seen lots of duos like them in the nation within the nation. Tex Rosa was the winner and the colonel was the loser.

"It's just that I can't lay my hands on that kind of money right now, not even close," the colonel said.

"Don't want to hear it."

"And when you do . . . buy him, then what?"

Rosa shrugged. "Have to take care of business."

The colonel blinked. "The way you took care of DeLeath?"

"Nope," Rosa said. "That was pretty much of an accident, Jocko getting carried away. Not that DeLeath didn't deserve it—interfere with a character like Jocko, what happens happens. But the point is that taking care of Little will be more a matter of policy, all planned out, see my meaning. Unless you got some other idea."

Colonel Drummond shook his head. "Little knows way too much."

"Now you're thinking."

"But our problem is receipts are in the toilet since . . . since the Peanut thing."

"*Our* problem?"

Some humans—never Bernie, of course—fell into whining when things weren't going their way. You couldn't tell whiners from how they looked. The colonel, for example: would I have picked him out as a whiner, with his long white car and yellow golf pants? No. But he started whining now. "Be reasonable, Tex. Peanut was the star attraction."

"Shoulda thought of that before."

"I did think that—always thought it. I just never imagined you'd go to such extremes."

"Extremes?" said Rosa. "Tell you a quick story about extremes. Back in the Depression my great-granddad was trucking booze across the border and he had this junior partner—kind of like you and me. Comes a day when junior partner gets the bright idea of cutting my great-granddad—they called him Tex, too, by the way—out of one little truckload. And guess what."

The colonel shrugged.

"Mister Junior Partner was never seen again," Rosa said. "And here you are, alive and well." He clapped the colonel on the back the way humans do to each other sometimes when they're being palsy, except harder. "Turns out I'm a big softy—lot of people miss that."

The colonel gave Rosa a quick sideways look. He was scared, no doubt about that, but he managed to lower his voice and stop whining. "I learned my lesson. And we're not talking about a truckload of booze—it was just a goddamn parrot."

"One of three left in the whole world." Rosa bent down, picked up a small stone. "Went to a lot of trouble to get that parrot—think I was going to let something like that slip by?"

"Did I know that at the time?" the colonel said. "Plus I offered to pay you every penny I got for the stupid bird. Can't we move on?"

"Move on where?" said Rosa, tossing the stone up and down in his hand. "It's not about money."

"It's not?"

Rosa shook his head. "It's a moral issue," he said. "A matter of principle."

"Tex," said the colonel. "Money's part of it. Don't we need money to pay Panza so you can . . . do what you have to do?"

"No denying that."

"Good. At least we're agreed on that. Cash flow's the real issue right now, but supposing we could bill the miraculous reappearance of Peanut, then in one fell—"

"Not happening," Rosa said. "Can't do that to the memory of my great-granddad. But tell you what—I'll lend you the money."

"You will?"

"Whatever Panza's number turns out to be."

"Why, thanks, Tex, I'll pay you back as soon as—"

"Don't even think about it."

"Don't think about paying you back?"

"Nope," Rosa said. "In return I'll just—what's the word? Assume?"

"I don't know. Depends what you're—"

"Yeah, that's it," said Rosa. "Assume. I'll assume majority ownership of the circus."

The colonel licked his lips, thin lips, dry and chapped. "My circus?"

"Uh-huh."

"But it's been in my family for generations."

"You can still be minority, no problem," Rosa said. "And I'll keep the name—Drummond Family Traveling Circus. Has a nice all-American sound." Their eyes met. "Shake on it?" Rosa said.

Handshaking is one of those human things I'm always on the watch for in my line of work. And just because my situation might not have been perfect at that moment didn't mean I wasn't on the job. We'd been in lots of scrapes, me and Bernie.

The colonel looked away from Rosa, sticking out his hand at the same time. Rosa gave the colonel's hand a hard squeeze and held on until the colonel's eyes were on him again.

"Deal?" Rosa said.

The colonel nodded. Rosa let go of his hand. Drummond walked away, back toward the warehouse, shoulders slumped.

Rosa smiled at me through the bars. "See how it's done?" he said. "And the kicker is Panza's only asking ten."

I didn't get what he was talking about, just knew I didn't like him, not one little bit. All I wanted to do was grab him by the pant leg—the actual truth being I wanted to sink my teeth into his ankle, right through one of those snakeskin boots—and bring him down for good. I growled at him, just in case he was missing where he stood with me. That made him smile even more. Then without warning he winged that stone at me real hard, hit me right on the nose between the bars of the muzzle cage. That's a sensitive spot, meaning it stung pretty good, but I didn't make a sound.

Rosa went off. The sun slid across the sky, away from me and sinking lower. The distant slopes got all shadowy, the small person in the sombrero nowhere in sight. I went back to trying to rub off the muzzle, and when that didn't work, I had another search for any weak spots in the cage, finding none just like the last time. A little later I had another try, and I was getting ready for a repeat after that when activity started up at the warehouse.

First, the eighteen-wheeler backed up to a loading dock. Then a forklift appeared, and what was this? A cage rested on the forks, and in that cage stood a lion, the kind with the huge head of hair; not standing, really—he was actually pacing back and forth, kind of like me. The forklift drove into the eighteen-wheeler, emerged a few moments later without the cage. Then it disappeared inside the warehouse. When it came out again, another cage stood on the forks, this time with a black leopard inside, not pacing, but just lying down in a slumped kind of way.

Back and forth rolled the forklift, loading caged-up creatures into the eighteen-wheeler: another big cat I recognized from Animal Planet, although the name escaped me; some monkeys; brightly colored birds; a huge lizard; a chimp with his hands on the bars and his mouth open wide the way humans do when they're about to scream. Plus there were other crates I couldn't see inside. After a while the forklift returned to the warehouse and didn't come out again. The door to the eighteen-wheeler rolled down and the truck drove away. Not long after that, Colonel Drummond left in his white convertible, followed by a big SUV with Tex Rosa at the wheel.

Then it got quiet. The sun went down beyond that distant slope, and the sky turned all sorts of colors, a beautiful sight, but I couldn't concentrate on it on account of my thirst, and my tongue being so hard and dry and crusty. I decided to try rubbing off the muzzle again, and when that didn't work I had another search for weak spots in the cage. But if there were weak spots, I couldn't find them and maybe I got a bit frustrated because the next thing I knew I was up on my hind legs, hammering at the bars with my front paws. That was when the skinny kid stepped out of the evening shadows.

She took off her sombrero and put her face between the bars. "Jet," she said in a low voice. "Pobre Jet."

I liked kids in general, and had liked the look of this particular kid from the get-go.

# TWENTY-EIGHT

Pobre Jet," said the kid. She had beautiful eyes, big and dark. I moved toward the bars of the cage. She patted my head. "Pobre Jet," she said. Jet was me, Chet the Jet. Was Pobre her name? Was she saying we were some sort of pals, me and her? Made sense to me.

She touched the muzzle over my mouth, ran her fingers over all the straps and clamps and other stuff I could feel but not see. Her face got still and thoughtful, reminding me of Bernie's face when he was deep in one of his thinking spells. Her thoughts drifted in the air. I didn't know what those thoughts were, but they felt a lot like Bernie's. Hey! This Pobre kid reminded me of Bernie! How weird was that? She was just a little kid and didn't smell at all like Bernie. That combination of apples, bourbon, salt and pepper was his and his alone, while Pobre smelled more like honey and those little pink manzanita flowers that turn out to be kind of tasty. I realized I was hungry as well as thirsty. But that wasn't important. The important thing was this strange likeness between Bernie and Pobre, even though they weren't alike.

Pobre glanced around. A quiet evening, the sky turning purple except for a fiery band shining above the distant slope, and nothing stirring, no one around but us. Pobre knelt and laid her sombrero on the ground and then rose—one of those humans who moved so nicely it was hard to take your eyes off them—and said, "Silencio, Jet, silencio." Whatever Pobre meant had hardly finished zipping right by me when she reached behind my head, fiddled around for a moment or two, and then—and then that horrible muzzle was off me! She tossed it away, into the shadows and out of my life.

I gave my head a quick shake—ah, felt so good—and then pressed my face against her, through the bars. She stroked between my ears with her soft little hand. Meanwhile, my tail was going a mile a minute, which means pretty fast. Pobre laughed, a low, gurgling laugh, very nice to hear, and then her face got serious again. "Por qué no?" she said. She stood on her tiptoes—always an interesting sight, considering how close to losing their balance humans were even when standing flat-footed—and reached as high as she could. Then came a squeak and a soft chunk and the cage door swung open. I stayed where I was, not sure why.

"Ven, Jet," she said.

I walked out of the cage. Nothing happened, nothing bad, shots ringing out, for example. I was free and clear.

Pobre gave me a pat. "Libre," she said. "Libre."

I licked her face. It tasted salty. She turned away, laughing that lovely laugh again, and was still laughing when headlights appeared on the road.

"Oh, no," she said. Her eyes and mouth opened wide and I caught the smell of fear. "Papá." And just like that she took off toward the distant hills. I took off after her of course, but she stopped, took my head in her hands, and said, "No, Jet, no."

Meaning what? I wasn't supposed to go with her? The headlight beams came closer. Pobre ran off again into the shadows. I hesitated, waiting for some idea, trying to make up my mind. Then the headlights found me, blinding me with their brightness. I took off, too, but the other way, back into the shadows beyond the cage.

The headlights came closer and closer, like two big yellow eyes; angry eyes, I thought, but what sense did that make? A rattly old car pulled up in front of the warehouse and a man got out. He left the car running, headlights on, and in the spillover of the headlight beams I got a good look at him: the little silver-teethed man with the huge hands. Didn't like him, not one bit: I stayed where I was, motionless in the darkness.

He moved toward a small door by the loading dock, started to open it, and paused. Then he began walking my way. I shrank back, around the far corner of the warehouse, just poking my head out to see.

This guy—farmer, Pobre's papa, and also a perp of some kind, no doubt about that—approached the cage. He stopped abruptly, yelled something I didn't understand, swung the door back and forth, pounded his fist into his open hand and yelled again. Then he noticed the sombrero, lying in the dirt. I just knew that was bad. He picked up the sombrero and yelled more angry things, and was still yelling when his gaze fell on me.

Or seemed to; in fact, I went unseen. No surprise: human eyes pretty much stop working at night; I'd learned that time and time again. He banged the cage door shut, walked back to the small warehouse door and went inside, carrying the sombrero.

I came out from my hiding place. I wanted that sombrero. My problem was how to get it. No idea. I listened real hard, hoping to hear Bernie speaking inside me, telling me the plan. Silence. But in those moments when I was standing there, kind of confused, I again caught that knockout smell in the air, Peanut's scent. I followed it, the easiest tracking I'd done in my whole career.

The smell—growing stronger with every step I took—led me along the front of the warehouse to the door the silver-teethed dude had entered. He'd left it open. I stopped in the doorway and peered inside. This was called recoy or recon or something like that, a very important part of our job according to Bernie, and if he said so, then that was that.

What did I see? A real big dirt-floored space lit only by a few bare bulbs hanging here and there, a mostly empty space except for some crates, a small cage with a monkey inside—actually a mean-looking sort of monkey I knew from the Discovery Channel—baboon? was that the name?—and much more important, another cage, really the whole far end of the warehouse, walled off by floor-to-ceiling chain-link. There was a big gate in the chain-link, and the farmer dude had rolled a wheelbarrow full of bananas next to it and was busy with the lock. Beyond the chain-link, against the back wall: Peanut.

Peanut! I was doing good, no doubt about it. This was the Peanut case and here was Peanut. Were there problems? Maybe, like for example the way Peanut wasn't standing up, instead lying on her side, her trunk flopped in the dirt, her eye dull and unseeing. The sight made me feel bad, hard to say why. Meanwhile, the baboon's eyes were real lively. They gave me a look that was too close to a human look for comfort. Then the baboon showed me his teeth. I've got a nice set of big sharp teeth myself, but this baboon's teeth were something else.

I turned back to Peanut. Even lying down she was huge, as tall sideways as the silver-teethed dude standing up. He opened the lock, laid Pobre's sombrero on the floor, and swung the gate open. Peanut, I thought, up and at 'em! But Peanut just lay there, which wouldn't have been my move in this situation, better believe it. The next thing I knew I was no longer in the doorway, but actually inside the warehouse, moving softly. For one thing, I wanted that sombrero. Pobre's sombrero had to be important and whatever made it important would be clear to Bernie right away. My job was to get it to him, plain and simple. Just like that, I understood the whole case.

The silver-teethed dude grabbed a pitchfork and began heaving bananas through the open gate, in Peanut's direction. I crept across the dirt floor, closer and closer to that sombrero. It lay at the silver-teethed dude's feet, but his back was turned, what with how busy he was heaving all those bananas. I got right up to him, no problem, and was just lowering my head over the sombrero when the baboon cried out. Crying out hardly describes the sound, maybe the most horrible sound I've ever heard, kind of a shrieking and howling combo that raised the hair from the back of my neck all the way down to the tip of my tail.

After that, things happened fast. First—and maybe this wasn't even first, real hard to say: that's how fast things were happening— the silver-teethed guy—which is what I've been calling him, on account of how uneasy I am about calling him Pobre's papa— whipped around toward where that awful sound had come from, and of course when he whipped around he saw me, just about to snatch up the sombrero.

His eyes opened wide, although not very wide, because of how narrow they were to begin with. He recognized me, no doubt about that, and the sight of me ticked him off big-time. That had happened before with perps too numerous to mention, Zutty Yepremian, for example, or Sing Jong Soo, and didn't bother me at all. But when he jabbed the pitchfork right at my head—that bothered me. I darted away from those sharp, pointy ends, then came at him from the side, real quick, but he turned out to be real quick himself, getting the pitchfork between us and jabbing again. I dodged, tried to go underneath, take him out by the ankles, one of my best moves, but down came the pitchfork, blocking my path. And what was this? Holding the pitchfork in one hand, the silver-teethed dude reached into his pocket with the other and drew a gun.

"Perro loco," he said. He raised the gun. I saw down the barrel, a small round space, black and empty. Bernie's voice spoke inside me at last: *Run, big guy.* But I couldn't. Somehow that tiny black emptiness had me frozen in place. That thick, oversized trigger finger started to squeeze.

And at that moment came a surprise. Somehow, without making any noise, or at least not any that I heard, Peanut was on her feet, and not only on her feet but—you couldn't call it running, maybe, more like lumbering—yes, lumbering with surprising speed, up and at 'em but even more so than I could have dreamed, and heading right in the perp's direction; dudes who point guns at me are perps, case closed.

This little perp with the big hands, one on the pitchfork, one on the gun, heard Peanut coming at the last instant—hard to miss now, and come to think of it, the floor was shaking—and spun around. Now his eyes really did get big, big as any human eyes I'd seen. He dropped the pitchfork, tried to bang the gate closed. Ha! That gate bounced right off Peanut and came swinging back, so hard it knocked the perp to the ground and flew off its hinges. He rolled over, and—oh, no, he still had the gun. I dove for his arm, too late. Blam. He got off a round, and a little red hole appeared in Peanut's shoulder. The perp was adjusting his aim for another shot, swinging the barrel so it pointed at Peanut's head, when she came rumbling through the space where the gate had been, trampled right over him, and kept charging across the warehouse floor. Did she take out a crate or two on the way? I thought so, because suddenly overturned crates were all over the place, splinters flying, and what was this? Snakes! Masses of snakes of different sizes and colors, tangled up with one another, writhing and hissing in clusters all over the floor. Also the baboon's cage was a twisted mess and the baboon was on the loose, hooting in that scary voice. And the perp? The perp was writhing around kind of like the snakes, and also hissing, but not the snake-type hissing, more the sort of hissing humans sometimes do when they're in a lot of pain. He rolled into the space where Peanut had been, dragging the remains of the gate after him, trying to cage himself in but having a lot of trouble since one of his arms was hanging in a funny kind of way.

Meanwhile, Peanut was on the move, that bullet she'd taken not slowing her down at all. She—you couldn't call it running, exactly, or trotting, although it was pretty close to trotting, but in a gigantic way—made her way to the door that led to the loading dock, one of those metal roll-down doors. The door was closed, of course, so Peanut was about to come to a halt, pull up, stop this trotting or whatever it was, right? Only she didn't. Peanut just kept going, right into that door. It crumpled and got ripped away, with a metallic tearing sound that thrilled me, I'll admit it. What else was there to do but follow her? Stay in the warehouse with the snakes, some of whom seemed to be slithering my way? Not my cup of tea, as humans say, and speaking personally tea isn't my cup of tea, water being my drink, and just then I saw a trough filled with water, standing near the loading dock. Why hadn't I smelled it? I tried to smell it now and couldn't: Peanut's smell smothered all others.

I hurried over to the trough, lapped up my fill—oh, water!—

my eyes on all those snakes the whole time. Some of them were enormous! And the fangs! At that very moment a big green one sank its fangs into an even bigger black one and all the writhing sped up and all the hissing grew louder. This was a nightmare.

I ran onto the loading dock. Still some light left and I could see Peanut clearly. She was on the ground, walking toward the perp's old—what was the word?—jalopy. That was it. She walked over to the jalopy, lifted one of her huge round feet and stomped down, crushing the whole front end. Why? I had no idea, but I liked it, liked it a whole lot. Then Peanut raised her trunk high and blew a beautiful trumpeting sound up toward the darkening sky. I loved that trumpeting sound—as good as Roy Eldridge or better—and was hoping for more, when the baboon blew right by me with a whoosh of air, flew out into the night and disappeared from view, although not before I saw that he had the sombrero.

I jumped down onto the ground and went over to Peanut. This was the Peanut case, meaning she was my responsibility. First, I had to get her attention. That probably meant waiting until she'd finished crushing the jalopy's back end. It didn't take long.

# TWENTY-NINE

I tried barking, not too loud: I had the feeling that making lots of noise long about now wouldn't be the best idea. But— what's that expression Bernie uses, something about being on the same page? I had a faint memory, my very earliest, even before my puppy days in the crack house, a memory of a litter box and paper training. How did that explain the being-on-the-same-page expression? I got a bit confused. Then I remembered the main point. We weren't on the same page, me and Peanut. How did I know? Because there she was lofting her trunk high —sending this enormous scent wave over me, by the way—and doing her trumpeting thing, again, just blasting to the skies.

After that it was quiet, the strange sort of muffled quiet you hear after a plane has flown over you real low. By then there was just the tiniest bit of light left over the distant slope; everywhere else night had fallen. Peanut was this enormous shadowy figure beside me, like something jutting out of the earth. That was the feeling I got: like standing next to a mountain, a real smelly one. Not a nice feeling, so I barked. How feeble that sounded, reminding me of one of Iggy's yips when he's just about ready to give up jumping up and down in his window.

I tried barking again, louder. Yes, that was better, much more like me. And one more, even louder. Back in action, no doubt about it, and now I had Peanut's attention. She looked down, those big eyes gleaming like two fiery lights in the sky—at that moment I realized the warehouse was on fire—and turned her head in my direction. More of a swing than a turn, really, and all of a sudden her trunk came whipping at me with surprising speed. That trunk hit me hard—and it felt hard, too, more like a block of wood than some giant nose, which is what it was, right?—and the next thing I knew I was tumbling backward in the dirt.

I came to a stop, got my breath back, and rose to my feet. By that time Peanut was on the move, headed away from the warehouse—which wasn't really on fire in a total way, more like just showing some flames here and there—and toward the road. Was that a good idea? I didn't think so. The road was for humans and except for Pobre the humans around here weren't friendly. I hurried after Peanut.

She was walking, and not in a hurried way, but somehow covered a lot of ground anyway, so I had to trot to catch up, not my fastest, but not my slowest, either. I trotted out in front, turned to face her, and barked. I have lots of different barks. This one was short and snappy, and meant hit the brakes, sending that message loud and clear.

But not to Peanut. She just kept walking, at the same time doing that head-turning thing, and here came that trunk again, lashing in my direction. Not this time, baby. I darted out of the way, then darted back, getting out in front of her again, and barking short and snappy. This was herding, something I just knew how to do, hard to explain. My job now was to get Peanut turned around, away from the road and headed the other way. This was a point Peanut didn't seem to be getting, because she showed no sign of turning around, just kept coming in that lumbering walk that made the ground tremble under my paws and that was starting to irritate me, I admit it. Was it possible she didn't know how to be herded? That was going to make my job harder, no doubt about it.

But I'd done hard jobs before, including hard herding jobs. My mind returned to the Teitelbaum divorce, not the excellent kosher chicken at the celebration dinner, but before that, when I'd actually had to herd Mr. Teitelbaum and a bunch of his angry supporters back into the steam bath. If I could do that, then was there any reason to doubt that—

Whoosh! That trunk came swinging at me once more, and I suppose I hadn't been paying close enough attention because I was airborne again, spinning through the air and thumping down. What the hell was going on? I'm a hundred-plus-pounder, if I haven't mentioned that already, and if there's any knocking down to be done, I do it. I jumped back up, then rose in front of Peanut and pawed at the air. From that angle I caught my first real good look at her tusks, glinting in the night. Were they a kind of teeth? I remembered Charlie saying something about that. Yes, teeth, but blown up to the nth degree, whatever that meant. I stopped barking, stopped pawing the air, just stood there up on my hind legs, a brand-new thing for me. While I waited for a new idea, a snake came slithering out of the shadows, right between me and Peanut. I'd forgotten the snakes—we had snakes out the yingyang, and soon, with the warehouse on fire, they'd be all over the place. I dropped down and growled at it. The snake coiled up and flicked its tongue at me. At that moment Peanut seemed to become aware of the snake—was it possible she was like Bernie, couldn't see diddley at night? Bo Diddley's a favorite of ours, by the way, but no time to go into that now—because she stopped in her tracks and screamed, a sound like her trumpeting but harsher. It hurt my ears. Plus I didn't like the look of that snake. Nothing was going right. All at once I lost my temper. I circled the snake, went right up to Peanut, well within range of that trunk and those tusks, and started barking, real loud. And—surprise: Peanut took a step back. I took a step forward, in fact more than that, one of my steps not covering enough ground, and kept barking. Peanut backed up another step and I closed in, staying in her face and barking hot and angry barks. Way up there her ears—she had to hear amazingly with ears like that—started flapping. I felt the breeze, and was still feeling it when Peanut turned and began walking, and not just walking, but in the direction I wanted, away from the road. I trotted after her. This was herding, kind of like with Mr. Teitelbaum and his steam room buddies, but harder, for sure.

Peanut and I took a route away from the road, away from the warehouse, now throwing up more flames, and onto a flat plain with no lights showing, not as far as I could see. The firelight flickered across Peanut's huge hind end, and what was this? She had a tail all right—not easy to imagine life without one—but how small considering the size of the rest of her, a ropey thing with a tuft of hair at the end. And that was all the hair she had on her whole body. What was up with that?

I watched her tail bounce around for a while, sometimes swinging back and forth as though she was in a good mood, although in truth her mood was a complete mystery to me. That thought bothered me, so I ran in front of her and did some zig-zagging, just to let her know who was in charge. Did she get the message? I wasn't sure but she kept going, and in the direction I wanted, meaning I was getting my way, and therefore wasn't

I in charge? Me, Chet the Jet! I raced around Peanut in a tight circle, ears flattened by the wind I was making, and maybe my attention wandered a bit because I almost didn't see one of Peanut's back feet—a foot bigger around than the Hungry Dude with Everything from Dude's Pizza, our go-to pizza joint in the Valley—kicked out sideways at me without warning. I veered away, my very quickest veer, and that foot barely grazed me, but somehow that was enough to send me flying, the whole somersaulting thing again, ending with another hard thump on the ground.

I bounced right up. Get knocked down and you bounce right up: that was one of our core beliefs, mine and Bernie's, a big reason for the success of the Little Detective Agency. No time to go into the other reasons now, but I couldn't help thinking: *Bernie.* Have I already mentioned that he had the best smell of any human I ever met? If so, why not mention it again? It's important.

Where was I? Bouncing back up. Peanut was turning out to be hard work. Was I afraid of hard work? No. Hard work cracks cases: that's something Bernie says and I believe it. What Peanut had forgotten, or maybe not understood in the first place, was—what again? I stood on the desert floor, somewhere down in Mexico, watching Peanut as she kept walking. Does that ever happen to you, needing to remember something that wouldn't quite- -

And then, out of the blue, I had it. Peanut was forgetting that I was the one doing the herding and she was the one being herded. I ran around in front of her, turned again, and was about to try barking one more time, and time after that if I had to, when all at once the night, which had been very dark, turned brighter.

Peanut halted. That ear-flapping thing started up. She raised her head toward the sky. I looked up, too. The moon had risen over some faraway hills. I'd never seen it so big and fat and yellow. We gazed at the moon, me and Peanut. So beautiful; I mean the moon, not Peanut. Her having no hair except for that tuft at the end of her tail—how could that be beautiful? But the moon, big and fat and yellow: that was another story. After a while, I became aware of a very pleasant woo-woo, woo-woo, kind of sound. Hey! That was me! I was sitting back on my haunches, singing to the moon, or at least making nice noises.

Peanut looked down at me. Her trunk was on the move. Not again. But this was different. Peanut's trunk curled up and then unrolled in a slow and gentle sort of way, and then the tip of it touched me, actually right between the ears where I like to be scratched. I just sat there, feeling no threat at all, despite the dust-up we'd already had. Peanut didn't actually scratch between my ears— the trunk being just a way over-the-top kind of nose, and how can you scratch with a nose?—but she did rub my head. Here's something funny about the tip of Peanut's trunk: it felt a lot like a human fingers.

She withdrew her trunk. I rose, wagging my tail. She squatted back a bit and peed, a downpour, enormous and shocking. I lifted my leg and peed, too, trying to lay my mark on top of hers. All I can tell you is that I did my best. When the peeing was over—hers went on long after mine, on and on like the monsoons—she gave me a little swat with her trunk, not hard. I barked at her, not loud, just a low rumble to let her know it was time to hit the road, me herding, she getting herded. We hit the road, side by side, headed in the direction of the moon.

A cool night with a soft breeze in our faces: funny how the moon, just as big as the sun right now and almost as yellow, brought no heat. The sun was just another . . . what? Something or other; Bernie'd gone into this maybe a million times, whatever that was. While I was trying to remember—but mostly thinking about Bernie's interest in the sky, and then just plain about Bernie—I began to notice a few things. Like for example how the moon was on the rise now, shrinking and losing its yellowness, and how the distant hills it rose above appeared a bit familiar.

We walked on—Peanut walking, me at a slow trot that's just as easy for me as walking—the ground trembling slightly with every step she took. I was getting used to that—even starting to think I liked it—when I noticed something about those hills. There seemed to be a giant human form on top. Not possible, of course. Meaning . . . hey! It had to be a saguaro, and then I remembered about the biggest saguaro I'd ever seen, and knew one thing for sure: home was on the other side. I changed course slightly, aiming right for that tall black form. Peanut changed course with me.

We walked all night, nice and easy, no problems of any kind. The stars began to fade—the moon being long gone—and over to one side the sky turned milky and then colors spilled all over the place. The hills seemed closer now, but still far away. Around us spread the plain, flat, rocky, and treeless, except for a single big and shady palo verde standing in a dry wash that cut across our path. We had one a lot like it off our patio on Mesquite Road. Leda wanted to chop it down because of the pods it dropped, but the divorce happened first. But forget all that. The important thing was a smell I was just starting to maybe pick up, perhaps a—

Peanut took off. How did something that big get up to speed so fast? I shot after her. By the time I reached the dry wash she was already in it. Not quite a dry wash: a small pool of water gleamed under the rising sun. Peanut came to the edge of the pool, stopped, dipped her trunk into the water, curled it to her mouth, and drank. She kept that up for quite a while, then plodded into the pool and sat down, very little of her disappearing beneath the surface. Her eyes closed. Then she just sat there.

I felt a bit thirsty myself, not the horrible, crusty-tongued thirst I'd had in the cage, just the normal kind you get after a long walk. I went to the water's edge and lapped some up. Dusty-tasting water, but not bad, not bad at all. I lapped up some more.

Peanut's eyes opened. She watched me drink. I watched her watching. She dipped her trunk in the pool, so of course I thought she was taking another drink. Surprise: her trunk bent in my direction and out came a jet of water, soaking me through and through. Bernie sometimes did that with the garden hose: it was one of my favorite games. I started running around that water hole, darting this way and that at my very fastest, Peanut sitting on her butt and spraying me whenever I got near. Were we having fun or what?

By the time the fun ended, the sun was high in the sky. I turned to the hills. We still had lots of ground to cover. I gave Peanut one of those low rumbly barks that meant up and at 'em. Peanut didn't get up. Instead she began giving herself a shower. I barked louder. No effect, not even after the shower was over. I stood by the pool barking my head off. Got nowhere. Peanut didn't swing her trunk at me or seem to get angry in any way. She just ignored me.

After a while I climbed up on the bank, sat in the shade of the palo verde. The next thing I knew I was more curled up than sitting. I heard showering sounds. My eyelids got heavy. I dreamed I was riding on Peanut. It made me pukey.

# THIRTY

I awoke feeling tip-top. Tip-top and hungry. I sniffed the air, smelled no food; pretty much no other smells were in the air except for Peanut's, crowding out all the others. No surprise there: when I looked around I saw she was lying right beside me, back to back, rising like a wall, crowding my space, too.

I rolled over, rose, and had a nice stretch, butt up high, front paws sticking way out; can't tell you how good that feels. Then I took a good recoy or recon or whatever it was, very important in this line of work. I knew right away—from the reddish tinge in the sky and the long shadows—that the day was getting late. The hills topped by that giant saguaro, with home on the other side, still seemed far away. All around lay the flat plain, treeless except for the palo verde we were under, me and Peanut. Then, off to one side, I noticed a low dust cloud on the move, all red and gold. It was coming closer, but not exactly in our direction—a good thing, because Jeeps were raising all that dust, the sort of green Jeeps that Captain Panza and his guys rode in. I glanced over at Peanut, still sleeping in the shade of the palo verde. She made a few sounds, somewhere between moaning and snoring, but showed no signs of getting up—also a good thing, because spotting upright elephants was probably pretty easy, even from a distance. But then another thought came, hitting me hard: what if Bernie was in one of those Jeeps?

The next thing I knew I was charging across that flat plain with everything I had, not directly at the Jeeps but trying to cut them off somewhere up ahead. I ran and ran thinking, *Bernie, Bernie,* ran faster than I could ever remember, and soon made out the rough track the Jeeps were on. I scanned the track, spotted some low bushes they'd have to pass, and made them my target. What did Bernie call this? Heading them off at the pass, that was it: one of our best techniques at the Little Detective Agency. I dug in and found one more gear; loved when that happened. The wind whistled in my ears. It was saying Chet the Jet!

But even with me in that extra gear, and the wind urging me on, the Jeeps reached those low bushes first, close enough to me so I could see the shapes of the people inside, far enough so I couldn't tell whether Bernie was one of them. I kept going, running on the track now, maybe eating dust, maybe feeling like I was bursting inside, but not caring. I just cared about Bernie.

After a while, I realized I was no longer eating dust; also not seeing the Jeeps and not even hearing them. I forgot all that and kept running. Then I remembered again and stopped. I stood on the track and panted. They were gone. I wanted to—I don't know, maybe sink my teeth into the tires of those Jeeps. Humans and their machines: a big subject for later. Right now the big question was whether Bernie's scent lingered in the air, very faint? I wasn't sure. Maybe if I sniffed around a bit, I'd—

At that moment, I heard a trumpeting sound, somewhat distant but very clear. I looked back in the direction I'd come from. There was Peanut, a huge form standing beside the palo verde tree, and almost as big. Hard to be sure at that distance, but I thought she had her trunk raised up high, almost the way Bernie sometimes waved his arm when he wanted me to come. A crazy thought, but there it was. I turned and went back. Peanut was my responsibility.

By the time I reached her, Peanut was in the pool again, taking another shower. She took no notice of me, just kept scooping up water and dowsing herself, flapping sheets of water off her ears. It suddenly struck me, maybe kind of late, that Peanut was a performer. Oh, brother. I'd worked with other performers before— Weedy Willis, the country singer, for example, or Princess, the best-in-show champ—and they were trouble each and every time. Besides, I was hot and dusty, no longer in my best mood. I went to the edge of the pool and drank, felt a bit better—in fact, pretty close to tip-top.

Peanut sat down. Was she planning on a nice long pool session? I gazed at the hills, darkening in the late afternoon light. Did we have time for a nice long pool session? No. Why wasn't Peanut getting that? I barked. She ignored me in that still and heavy way of hers, showing no reaction at all. How annoying was that? I waded into the pool, barged up to her, and gave her a nudge on the side, not the least bit gentle. And what was this? She got right up, so fast that a wave sprang up, sweeping me out of the pool. I rose, gave myself a good shake, and started off toward the hills. Peanut followed along, no problem. I didn't have to look back, just felt the earth trembling under my paws.

Night fell. The moon, yellow but maybe not quite as big as before, like a piece was missing, rose over the hills. That missing piece bothered me—where did it go? That was the kind of thing Bernie knew. I thought about Bernie for a while. Then I thought about food, the ribs at Max's Memphis Ribs, for example, the way the juicy meat comes right off the bone—and then you've still got the bone!—or a big biscuit the judge gave me one time when I went to court, Exhibit A in this case where Exhibit B was a .44 Magnum I'd dug up in a flower bed, the perp now breaking rocks in the hot sun, and then back to Bernie. Soon the ribs again, the whole time this light boom-boom happening in the earth, like drums. Have I mentioned Big Sid Catlett yet? Maybe some other time. But with all this thinking going on, presto: before I knew it the hills were right there, rising in front us, that single huge saguaro on top. *Presto* was a word Bernie sometimes used, like just before turning the key that time he was jump-starting the DA's car. The DA had a fire extinguisher in the trunk, so there turned out to be no problem.

I paused at the base of the hills. Peanut stood beside me. The moon was high overhead now, pouring down this silvery light. It glinted on her tusks, and also on a hard-packed path that led up the mountain. Home lay on the other side. I started up. And after me: boom-boom in the earth.

The path cut back and forth in long, easy switchbacks, easy for me, anyway, and I heard no complaints from Peanut. Up and up we went, the air nice and fresh and every step a step closer to home. I was rounding a bend, thinking about my bowls beside the fridge at our place on Mesquite Road when the boom-booming stopped. I looked back. Peanut had gone still, all except for her trunk, raised up high and sort of feeling at the air, reminding me of those things submarines poke out of the water, the name escaping me at the moment; we love submarine movies, me and Bernie, but no time for that now because without any warning Peanut was off and running, and if you couldn't call it running, there was no denying how fast she covered the ground. She bowled me over and rounded the bend.

I rolled down a steep slope and came to rest in a gully. I hopped right up, a bit annoyed. Had I had it up to here, wherever that is, with Peanut knocking me around? Pretty much. Plus this turned out to be a very deep gully with scratchy things growing all over the place. By the time I scrambled to the top, Peanut was out of sight. Nothing easier than following her smell, of course, which I did, around the bend, up and around another bend, and then onto a flat part: the very top, with the saguaro towering overhead. I knew this place: it was where we found—

And there was Peanut, lit almost white by the moon, standing at the edge of the shallow dip where we'd found DeLeath's body. At first she was perfectly still; then her ears moved a bit and she stepped down into the dip, steps that seemed to me very careful, like not to disturb anything. At the bottom she paused again, then lowered her trunk and swept it gently back and forth over the ground. I sat down and watched, didn't move, didn't make a sound. The sweeping of the dirt—more like patting or stroking, really—went on for some time. Then Peanut picked up a rock, maybe the size of a basketball or a little smaller, and kind of . . . what was the word?—cradled it in the curve of her trunk. She cradled that rock and swung her head from side to side: it reminded me—kind of odd how the mind works, hard to explain—of this one night back when Charlie was smaller and he couldn't sleep and Bernie had rocked him back and forth.

After a while, Peanut put down the rock, slow and careful, and then began raising lots of dust with her trunk, throwing it in the air, and stomping around, maybe even smacking herself with dust from time to time, dust that made silvery boiling clouds in the moonlight. Actually a bit frightening—not that I got frightened myself—and I was glad when all that came to an end and Peanut raised her trunk again and did some more trumpeting; by now I was used to the trumpeting, even starting to like it. Her eyes glistened, and so did a wet track under each one. Something was going on, but I hadn't figured it out before lights shone, down on the plain we'd crossed.

I walked over to a ridge, took a gander. That's an expression of Bernie's, hard to understand, maybe something to do with wild goose chases, but I've never been on one even though it's come up time after time, so I really couldn't tell you. What did I see down on the desert floor? That's the important point, and what I saw were two Jeeps moving our way. They came closer, then swung around a bit, headed toward a nearby rise, and when they swung around, sideways to me, I could make out uniformed guys in the first Jeep, Captain Panza—I could tell from all his shining gold braid—sitting beside the driver. There were uniformed guys in the second Jeep, too, two in the front, two in the back, and in between those two guys in the back, their rifle barrels glinting in the moonlight, sat one guy not in uniform.

My heart started beating fast immediately and I had one paw raised, all set for takeoff, when I remembered Peanut. She was my responsibility. I looked back. There she was, still down in the dip, back to stroking the ground again with her trunk. Was she going anywhere? Not to my way of thinking. I took off.

Tore off, was more like it, forgetting all about steepness and sharp or scratchy things underfoot, my eyes on those two Jeeps, especially on the non-uniformed guy in the backseat of the second one. I couldn't see his face, but I knew the expression that would be on it: hard and calm at the same time. We didn't scare easy, me and Bernie; that's the calm-faced part. Also we didn't take to getting pushed around; that's the hard-faced part.

As I ran, the Jeeps reached the rise—kind of a low round hill, really, rising on the plain—and disappeared from my view. I flew down the last slope, raced across the plain, leaped right over a dry wash, darted around to the back side of the low round hill, pebbles scattering beneath my paws, and saw: nothing. The Jeeps were gone, and so were all the uniformed men, and Captain Panza, and Bernie.

# THIRTY-ONE

G one: but where? This low round hill—how many had I seen like it in my career? Some big number, bigger than two, which is as far as I go with numbers, but why isn't that enough? Back to the low round hill. It had some tall saguaros down at the bottom with bushes growing in between, then got bare farther up. Nowhere for those Jeeps to have gone: that was the point.

Could they have somehow shut off their lights and zoomed away, so far and so fast that I'd missed them in such a short time, or at least what seemed like a short time? Tracking exhaust fumes—it doesn't get easier than that, so I sniffed out the exhaust fumes, starting with where the Jeeps had come from, following them to the base of the hill, and then—But there was no then. The fumes led nowhere. I sniffed at the saguaros and the bushes, noticed a pickax blade, old and rusty, the kind miners used. Lots of empty mines in the desert, but they always had openings and I saw none. Kind of weird, in fact it got me going a little bit, and I ran around in circles, finding the scents of men, one of which I thought I remembered—Captain Panza's—and another I knew for sure: Bernie's.

I ran around in circles—really just one big circle—with all those scents of Jeeps and uniformed guys and Captain Panza and Bernie inside. Strong fresh scents, meaning they came from close by: but I was alone! So therefore . . .

I didn't know. Bernie handled the so-therefores. Where was he? *Bernie,* I thought, and ran faster and faster in my circle. *Whoa, big guy.* That was Bernie, inside my head, a nice sound. I stopped running, sat down, sniffed the air. Smells can be separated out and followed on their own, kind of like . . . I couldn't think anything that was like at the moment, but separating and following Bernie's smell was a snap—and led me back to the hillside.

I was standing there, maybe panting a bit even though I wasn't winded, when I heard the sound of a motor, close by—not a car motor, more like our garage door opener on Mesquite Road, in the days when it used to work. The crazy thing was the closeness, like it was coming from right inside the hill, impossible, on account of how could motor noises come from inside the earth?

And then the hillside began to move. I remembered a mudslide during the monsoons and jumped back. But this wasn't monsoon season, no mud at all, not a drop of rain for ages, so—

Whoa. The hillside—at least a small part—turned out to be a sort of door, like this was some kind of mine after all. As it rose up—yes, like our garage door, except with lots of spiky vines laced over the outside—a shaft of light came spilling out and I saw way too much to take in at once. First: the two Jeeps about to drive out with Captain Panza and his men, Captain Panza tucking something into his shirt pocket. In the background: what looked like a mine, all right, with rock walls. And there was the eighteen-wheeler I'd last seen getting white paint spread over the red roses. Now two dudes were sticking on this enormous circus decal—clowns, ringmaster, lions, a big top. I knew decals—we had one from Max's Memphis Ribs on our back bumper—but that wasn't the point. The point was that a guy stood leaning against the rocky wall and watching the two decal dudes work, and the sight of that watching guy made the hair on the back of my neck stand straight up. It was Jocko. No mistaking that crooked nose or nasty eyes. And then—oh, no. Lying on the ground beside Jocko, partly hidden from my view, was Bernie.

Why that *oh, no*? Because of how bad Bernie looked, his face bloody, one of his eyes swollen shut, clothes all torn. Also he was cuffed, hands in front of him. Growling started up, deep in my chest.

The two Jeeps came rolling out of this cave or underground garage or whatever it was. I slipped out of the shadows, away from the headlight beams. That was something we'd worked on a lot, me and Bernie, staying out of sight. As soon as the Jeeps passed by, I was on my way, headed toward that opening in the hill. Did I have a clear plan? No. All I knew—

The door was closing and closing fast. I took off for that narrowing gap, but what was this? Boom-boom, boom-boom. From out of nowhere came Peanut, cutting me off, getting to the door first. The gap was already way too small for Peanut to pass through, if that was her plan. At that moment, Jocko looked out. Did he see Peanut? I was pretty sure he did, from how his mean little eyes got bigger. Did Peanut see him? I didn't know about that, but her whole body began to shake and I felt a huge kind of anger—more than anger; what was the word?—fury, yes, I felt this fury coming in waves off Peanut. She charged toward that gap—now maybe even too small for me—and I charged after her. Peanut was my responsibility.

She hit the tiny gap, mostly hitting the whole hillside, just about back in place. KA-BOOM! And suddenly there was nothing but gap. We ran inside, me and Peanut. From behind came enormous crashing sounds, like the roof was caving in. No time for that. I had one thing in mind—Jocko—and I knew Peanut was thinking the same thing. From inside the trailer of the eighteen-wheeler came the lion's roar.

"Jesus Christ," Jocko shouted. He reached for something hanging on the wall, something I recognized: an ankus. Jocko held it up so Peanut could see, and . . . and Peanut slowed down? Just from the sight of that horrible thing? I didn't understand, only knew I felt bad. But for no time at all, because when Jocko brandished that horrible hook, a look came into Bernie's eyes— or eye, really, the other one being shut—that I'd never seen before. Suddenly he was up—yes, staggering a bit, but on his feet. He rounded on Jocko. Jocko saw him and jabbed with the ankus, but not quick enough. Bernie was already swinging his cuffed hands, hands squared off in hard fists, right at Jocko's face, swinging with all the strength in his body, meaning a whole lot and never forget it.

What a wonderful sound that blow made! Jocko's bandanna flew off his head and he keeled over at once, eyes rolling up, showing nothing but white. The next thing I knew I was with Bernie, reared up and licking his poor face. He couldn't hug me on account of those handcuffs but he wanted to, no doubt in my mind on that subject.

"Good boy," he said. "You're a good, good boy."

Did I feel great or what?

"I'd sure like to know how you did this."

Did what, exactly? I wasn't sure. But what was better than right now, being with Bernie and on the job?

Bernie looked past me. Those two dudes who'd been working with the decal were moving on us, one holding a machete, the other a crowbar. Bernie sprang to the cab of the eighteen-wheeler, reached in, and whirled around, a gun now in his hands.

"Not another step," he said. They dropped their weapons without being told, a good sign. These weren't real tough guys. The real tough guys were us, me and Bernie.

"Facedown on the ground."

They got facedown on the ground. I went over and stood beside them in case they got any fancy ideas, such as maybe they were tough guys after all. Meanwhile, Bernie rolled Jocko over with his toe, knelt beside him, laid down the gun, and fiddled with some keys dangling from Jocko's belt. A moment later the cuffs were off Bernie's wrists and on Jocko's, behind-the-back style, the way we did things at the Little Detective Agency. Bernie rose, gestured with the gun at the two dudes.

"Don't fire," one said. "We don't know shit."

"A weak argument," Bernie said. "On your feet." They stood up, hands raised. "Get lost," Bernie told them.

"Yeah, sure, right away," they said, and turned to where the door had been. No door, but also no way out: the rubble from the roof caving in blocked the opening.

Bernie sighed. "Facedown," he said.

They went back to the facedown position, me standing over them. I noticed that Peanut was on the move again, not running, in fact going quite slow, but in the direction of where Jocko lay.

"Peanut?" Bernie said, lowering the gun. "Got something in mind?"

No doubt about that. I knew Peanut. She kept coming.

"I understand your position," Bernie said. "Not saying he doesn't deserve it, because he does. But we're building a case here, and—" Peanut's ears flapped a bit but that didn't mean she was listening; from the look in her eye, I was pretty sure she wasn't, and Bernie must have gotten that, too, because he tucked the gun in his belt, grabbed Jocko by the scruff of the neck, dragged him over to the cab of the eighteen-wheeler, and stuffed him inside. "There," said Bernie, "all taken care of."

He smiled at Peanut. Peanut kept coming, was now just a few steps from Bernie. I hurried over and stood in front of him.

"No, Chet," Bernie said. "Come here."

Go there? Not what I wanted, but if Bernie said so, then that was that. I backed up a little, stood beside him.

Peanut came closer, then paused, towering over us, gazing down. My heart beat hard and fast, and I could hear Bernie's heart beating, too. Peanut was awesome.

Nobody moved—not me, not Bernie, not Peanut. Then, very slowly, Peanut extended her trunk. Just as slowly, Bernie reached out and touched it with his fingertips. He spoke gently, "Been through the mill, haven't you?"

Meaning what? I had no idea, but whatever it was didn't get Peanut riled up, so it must have been right.

"Bet you're hungry," Bernie said.

Hey—me, too.

"Think I saw bananas around here somewhere."

Peanut's trunk twitched.

"Hey," Bernie said, turning to the facedown dudes. "Any bananas around here?"

They both pointed to a shed.

"You," said Bernie, "with the chin."

"Me?" said one of the dudes.

"You," said Bernie. "Get the bananas." The dude with the chin—that very long kind you see sometimes on humans—rose and moved toward the shed. "And you," said Bernie to the other dude.

"Me?" said the other dude.

"Roll that ramp up to the back of the trailer."

The second dude—one of those real chinless human types—rose and walked over to a ramp that stood by the wall. Meanwhile, the chin dude was tossing bunches of bananas into a wheelbarrow.

"Easy, there," Bernie said. "That's someone's dinner."

"Huh?" said the chin dude. But he stopped tossing the bananas, placing them carefully instead. Bernie smiled. Uh-oh. His mouth was all bloody inside. What had they done to him? I glanced over at the cab of the eighteen-wheeler, wondered how I could get in; I already knew what I'd do when I got there.

The chin dude pushed the wheelbarrow, now piled high with bananas, over to us. Bernie plucked a banana, held it out for Peanut. Peanut swung her trunk toward the banana, swooped over it and down into the wheelbarrow. She scooped out a whole big bunch of bananas and scarfed them up. The chin dude cowered against the wall.

"It's like that, huh, Peanut?" said Bernie. He glanced at the chin dude. "Wheel that thing into the trailer."

"What if I get trampled?"

"Then your buddy will have to do it."

Eyes on Peanut the whole way, the chin dude pushed the wheelbarrow over to the back of the truck. The no-chin dude got the ramp in place. The chin dude went up the ramp. The lion roared again. The chin dude returned, wheelbarrow empty.

"Facedown," Bernie said. The dudes went back to lying facedown. Bernie moved toward the ramp. I went with him. "Come on, Peanut," he said.

Yeah, right, I thought.

But Peanut came. She followed us to the ramp. We stood aside. She walked right up and into the trailer. You never knew with Peanut. Bernie went up and closed the doors, and was just sliding the bolt in place when noises came from the other side of the cave-in. Maybe not that much of a cave-in: lights shone through from the other side.

Bernie jumped down. "Let's go." We ran to the cab—Bernie limping a bit from his war wound—and jumped in. Jocko lay sprawled on the front seat, eyes still closed. Bernie shoved Jocko onto the floor, and there we were, Bernie behind the wheel, me riding shotgun, situation normal. I checked the side mirror, saw a big opening in the cave-in rubble, and Captain Panza and his men making their way through, some with shovels. Maybe not completely normal, but pretty close, except what was this? The guy with the big automatic rifle, the one that went ACK-ACK?

The key was in the ignition. Bernie turned it and the engine fired. His hand moved to the gear shift, gave it a little wiggle. "Wonder where first is," he said. "Here, maybe?" He shifted. The truck lurched forward and stalled. I remembered a difficult afternoon from back in the Leda days where Bernie tried to teach her how to drive the stick. No way this could turn out that bad. Bernie cranked the engine again, tried another gear, and we went through the lurch-stall thing again. Was that the lion roaring? And other creatures joining in? I wasn't sure because at that moment the ACK-ACK guy fired a burst, and then another. I checked the side mirror again, saw one of the Jeeps bump slowly over the rubble, Captain Panza standing up in the front seat, shouting something at the driver. Then the mirror shattered and that whole scene vanished in a spray of tiny glass bits all over my window. Hey! Mirrors were glass? And windows, too? I came close to having a thought about that.

"How come I never learned to drive a big rig?" Bernie said, banging the stick into different positions. No idea; I just knew it wasn't his fault. We lurched forward again, but didn't stall this time.

ACK-ACK. ACK-ACK.

Bernie stepped on the gas. He tried to get into another gear and couldn't. The engine screamed. We barreled through this mine or whatever it was. The walls closed in around us and then we were in a long tunnel, lit only by our headlights. I knew this kind of tunnel from a drug-smuggling case we'd worked once in a border town, the name escaping me and no time to remember it now.

ACK-ACK. ACK-ACK. Sparks flew off the rocky walls of the tunnel and ricochets pinged off the body of the cab. Down on the floor, Jocko moaned.

"Zip it," Bernie said. I looked over, saw him stomp on the gas, down to the metal. The scream of the engine rose and rose, unbearable.

ACK-ACK. ACK-ACK-ACK. Bernie's window blew out, scattering glass all over the place. Up ahead, our headlights shone on a big garage-type roll-up door like the one we'd entered.

"No time to stop," Bernie said. So therefore? I had no clue, but that didn't matter. I had Bernie back and he handled the so-therefores. He reached up to a gizmo on the visor, kind of like our remote thing for the garage door at home, which no longer worked, if I haven't mentioned that. "This should do the trick," Bernie said, pressing a button.

The metal door—closer and closer now—didn't budge.

ACK-ACK. Bullets tore through the metal door, leaving twisted holes in zigzag patterns.

"Or maybe this one," Bernie said, trying another button, "although wouldn't it make sense that red would—"

But whatever that was about never got finished, because the door began to rise—oh, so slow—with us hurtling right toward it and that ACK-ACK closing in behind. And then—zoom, a sort of zoom with a metallic scraping from above that shrieked in my

ears all the way to the tip of my tail and back—we were out! Out
of the tunnel and into the great outdoors!

Bernie slowed down. Was now a good time for that? Bernie!

He looked over at me and smiled. "Don't worry," he said.
"They won't follow us—we're home." Home? In the middle of
nowhere, empty desert all around? Bernie reached over and rubbed
my head. "In the good old U.S.A., big guy, safe and sound." He
circled around, shining our lights on where we'd come from, a low
rise I'd seen before: the spot where Jocko had given us the slip on
the way down to Mexico.

Safe and sound in the good old U.S.A. Fine by me. We followed a track, silvery and smooth in the desert. Bernie found a
gear that didn't hurt my ears so much. Down on the floor, Jocko
stirred and opened his eyes.

Bernie glanced at him. "Was it Churchill who said there's
nothing more exhilarating than being shot at without result?"

Jocko had no answer. Neither did I. Churchill? Probably a
perp of some sort. He'd be breaking rocks in the hot sun, sooner
or later. We had ways of getting things done, me and Bernie. Back
in the trailer, Peanut blasted out some of her trumpeting sounds.

# THIRTY-TWO

We drove through the darkness, Bernie at the wheel with the gun in his belt, me in the shotgun seat, Jocko on the floor, maybe a tiny bit uncomfortable. "Any food on board, Jocko?" Bernie said.

Good question. Could I think of a better one? No.

"I got nothin' to say," Jocko said.

"Is that the kind of loser you want to be?"

"Huh?"

"We take down a lot of losers in this business," Bernie said. "Ends up there are only two kinds—losers who want to keep losing and losers who want to cut their losses. Guess which ones get the most jail time."

I thought about that and was pretty close to making up my mind when the whole problem kind of went away, and I felt better. And that better was on top of how good I was already feeling, back with Bernie.

After that came a long period of silence, and then—surprise—Jocko spoke. "Try the console," he said.

A little light shone in Bernie's good eye—the one I could

see—a little light that usually goes with a smile, but not this time. He opened the console, fished around, and said, "Well, well. What do we have here?"

Of course, I already knew: the smell of a Slim Jim is distinctive, not something you're likely to forget. And the next moment, I was going to town on a wonderful Slim Jim, the best I'd ever had. A funny thing about Slim Jims—every one is always the best I've ever had. Great folks, the Slim Jim people. I tried to make my Slim Jim last, but that's never been my best thing, have to be honest.

"Chet?"

Was that my paw, scratching at the console? Oops.

"Sorry, big guy—there's no more."

I put a stop to that scratching right away, and if not right away, then real soon, Bernie only saying Chet? hardly any more times at all.

He glanced down at Jocko. "You're in a pretty good position, stop to think about it."

"What are you talkin' about? My back's killin' me."

Bernie has a face for when he really cares and a face for when he wants someone to think he really cares. I know the really-cares face very well because that was always how he looked at me; right now the other face was on the job.

"We're talking about your future, Jocko. Ever hear that expression—get there first with the most?"

"Nope."

"Nathan Bedford Forrest—ring a bell?"

"Nope."

"Maybe not the best role model, come to think of it," Bernie said. "But here's the point, Jocko—this is your lucky day."

"Huh?"

Jocko was no favorite of mine—in fact, that urge-to-bite feeling I get in my jaw sometimes, hardly ever, really, was suddenly quite strong, but I was with him on this. How was it lucky to be crammed and cuffed down on the floor of the cab, with a big knot swelling on the side of your head; a bald head, it turned out, now that he'd lost the bandanna, a baldness that didn't go well with the bushy sideburns, just my opinion?

"Because," said Bernie, "you're already first. Now all you have to do is get most out of the way and you're free and clear."

"Free and clear?" said Jocko. "You'll let me go?"

"Next best thing," Bernie said. "I can set you up with the DA—he's a personal friend. And since we're a capital punishment state and there are two murders in this case, you won't want anyone in there first, plea-bargaining ahead of you."

"Don't know about any murders," Jocko said.

"Uri DeLeath," Bernie said. "Darren Quigley."

"News to me," Jocko said.

"You can try that line on a jury," Bernie said. "The problem is—no fault of your own, accident of birth—when juries think of a killer they picture someone like you. Lethal injection is the usual method, but the state still offers the gas chamber option. None of my business, but that's what I'd choose."

"Gas?"

"No question."

Jocko's eyes shifted. He went silent.

What was going on? I wasn't sure, just knew that this was a sort of interview, and Bernie was a great interviewer. A pink glow appeared in the distant sky. "The Valley," Bernie said.

Jocko's eyes narrowed. Whatever he was thinking, I didn't like it. "Can't talk too good like this, can I?" he said.

"Like what?"

"Cuffed. It hurts, man. Interferes with my concentration."

"Just have to tough it out."

Jocko got a real mean expression on his face, but Bernie wasn't looking. "Know what I think?" Jocko said. "You're yellow."

Yellow? I'm no expert on color, as I should have pointed out by now, but Bernie doesn't look at all yellow to me. He has beautiful skin, kind of darkish, with red tones mixed in.

"Yeah?" said Bernie.

"Yeah," Jocko said. "Chicken."

Humans could lose you just like that, and this was one of those times. I knew chicken, of course—that kosher chicken at the Teitelbaum divorce celebration dinner was often in my thoughts—but what was Jocko talking about? Was it possible he had a line on kosher chicken, could hook us up with some? I waited to hear.

"What's on your mind, Jocko?" Bernie said. "Spit it out."

Oh, no, not that; and in the cab? Some humans—men, just about every time—had this very bad habit, plain nasty. And chewing-tobacco spit? Don't get me started.

"You're afraid of talking to me man to man," Jocko said. "Makes me wonder what kind of man you actually are, see what I mean."

Bernie stopped the truck. "Bring your bat?"

"Bat?"

"I forgot," Bernie said. "Metro PD has your bat. Prints matched ones they lifted off the hook you lost that night."

Jocko's voice got lower and meaner. "Won't need no bat," he said.

Whoa. What was going on? In no time, Bernie had stuck the gun in the console, unlocked Jocko's cuffs, and they were climbing out of the cab.

"You stay right there, Chet," Bernie said.

Stay right here? They'd moved out in front of the truck, seemed like they were about to throw down. How could I—

"I mean it, Chet," Bernie said, and was still looking my way when Jocko wound up and threw a tremendous punch at Bernie's head, on the bad eye side. Somehow Bernie saw it anyway and ducked, and not only that, but while ducking grabbed Jocko's wrist, spun around and pulled down like he was snapping a towel—oh, we've had fun with towel-snapping, but no time to go into that now—and then came this CRACK, reminding me of when Bernie and Suzie did that wishbone thing on Thanksgiving, only much louder. Next was Jocko lying on the ground, yelling and moaning and twisting around.

"Broke my fuckin' shoulder. Oh, Christ!"

"Just dislocated would be my guess," said Bernie. "But I'm no doctor."

He got Jocko to his feet, walked him to the cab, and shoved him back on the floor, cuffing Jocko's good wrist to something under the seat. And then we were off again, hardly any time lost at all.

Bernie turned to me. "I guess that was childish."

Yes! And that was just one of the great things about it.

We came to a paved road and the ride smoothed out.

"Nice and easy from here on in," Bernie said.

Jocko spoke. "Quigley—that was Tex all the way. Tex don't take kindly to blabbermouths, plus Quigley was starting to ask questions—like he was thinking there might be something in it for him."

"And DeLeath?" Bernie said.

"An accident," Jocko said.

"He accidentally got bitten by a snake thousands of miles from its habitat?"

"We were just foolin' around," Jocko said.

"Who's we?"

Jocko groaned. "I'm in pain here," he said. "Big time."

Bernie shook his head. "That's not big-time pain."

Pause. "We meaning some of the boys from Mexico," Jocko said. "Miggy, Flip, Cisco—don't know their last names, don't know them dudes at all."

"Panza's men?"

"More like associates."

"Too bad."

"Huh?"

"Just because of how things work down there. Won't be easy, charging them, finding them, bringing them back. Much easier to hang DeLeath's murder on you."

"I didn't mean no harm. He asked for it, want to know the truth."

"How did he ask for it?"

"His attitude, man. I mean, why'd he have to wake up in the first place?"

"This was the night you kidnapped Peanut?"

"Kidnapped? It's a stupid animal."

The muscle that sometimes jumped in Bernie's jaw jumped at that moment. "You think Peanut's stupid?" he said.

"It's an animal."

"She," said Bernie. "And you're repeating yourself."

"Huh? What's your problem? I'm just saying it's property, like a car or something." He shook his head. "Repo work is always full of screwups—I shoulda known."

"You were repoing Peanut?"

"Not me personally. Just followin' orders."

"Rosa's orders?"

"Yeah. Had to teach that dickhead a lesson."

"Colonel Drummond?"

"Colonel, my ass."

"You said it," said Bernie. "What kind of lesson?"

"Drummond was gettin' ideas."

"What kind of ideas?"

"Wanted more of the action," Jocko said. "What other ideas are there?"

Bernie smiled. He has the best smile in the world; if I haven't mentioned that already, I should have. Why he was smiling? A complete mystery.

"And the action is smuggling exotic animals into the U.S.?" Bernie said.

It was?

"Yup."

Hey! But that was Bernie, every time—smartest human in the room.

"Drummond's circus provided the cover?" Bernie said.

"For some of the trade," Jocko said.

"There's more?"

"It's a big business, man, like in the billions," Jocko said, sounding offended. "Second to drugs, but way safer."

"Not safe enough," Bernie said.

Jocko thought about that for a while. The light of the downtown towers appeared, shone faintly in Jocko's eyes. "I'll take that deal," he said.

"Let's hear about the kidnapping," Bernie said.

"Already told you. Drummond pulled this stunt, all about this parrot from some island, the last one in the world or some shit. Tex is the wrong dude to pull stunts on. We took his meal ticket, makin' a point."

"The meal ticket being Peanut?"

"Uh-huh."

"You spiked Quigley's JB?"

"Nothin' to it. Everything was goin' smooth, we got the elephant in the trailer, and then the goddamn thing started acting up—"

"Which was when you used the ankus?"

"That's how you control 'em. But it was too late. DeLeath woke up and came pokin' his nose in, so we had to grab him, too."

"Who decided to kill him?"

"He did."

"DeLeath committed suicide?"

"Kinda. Like he didn't want to write the good-bye note."

"So you threatened him with the puff adder?"

"Just a show, was all. But the goddamn snake got away on us, did its own thing. One scary mother."

"A nice story," Bernie said. "The fact that DeLeath did end up writing the note is the only hole I can see."

There was a silence. I gazed down at Jocko. The biting urge started up.

"What do you want from me?" Jocko said. "I spilled my guts." Uh-oh. I glanced down, saw no evidence of that. I was getting to know Jocko, one of those humans who couldn't be trusted, not one bit.

"DA won't buy it," Bernie said. "You'll have to sweeten the pot."

"Like how?" said Jocko.

"Where does Tex live?" Bernie said.

It was still dark when we pulled up outside Tex Rosa's place in Golden Eldorado Estates, maybe the fanciest development in the Valley, and the one Bernie hated the most. We couldn't see the house itself on account of the high walls around it. Bernie parked in front of the gate. He took the gun from the console, opened the door, and we got out.

"What about me?" Jocko said.

"Stay put."

"What's that supposed to mean? I'm cuffed to the goddamn—"

"And not another peep," Bernie said.

We went up to the gate. Still nighttime, but dark-pink Valley nighttime, and the buzzer was easy to see. Bernie pressed it. Then we slipped back into the shadows. We'd done this very thing once before, couldn't remember the details, except for Bernie forgetting to bring a gun that time, resulting in complications. I glanced over to make sure it was in his belt, caught that friendly gleam.

We waited. Waiting's part of the job, no problem, especially when I'm waiting with Bernie. After a while, I heard footsteps moving behind the wall. Then came some metallic sounds and the gate swung open. Tex Rosa walked out, wearing a silk robe—the smell of silk hard to miss, a big favorite of mine, which had led to some trouble in the past—and with his hair every which way.

He saw the truck. "What the hell?" He moved toward it, his hand sliding down, maybe into a pocket, hard to tell on account of his back was to us. "Jocko? You in there?"

From inside the cab came Jocko's yell: "Shoot 'im, boss."

"Drop it," said Bernie, stepping forward, me right beside him. At the same moment, Rosa whirled, firing straight from the pocket of his robe. PING—that ping pinged off the gate, meaning we were good. Bernie pulled the trigger. Rosa cried out and fell, holding his arm. His gun clattered on the pavement, actually hadn't finished clattering before I was standing over it, the way we'd worked on, me and Bernie.

Bernie came over, put his foot on Rosa's back, nice and hard.

"Boss?" Jocko called from the cab. "You nail him?"

"That whole deal thing, Jocko?" Bernie called back. "It's off the table."

Tex Rosa twisted his head around, groaned in pain. "Going to let me bleed to death?" he said. "That the kind of man you are?"

Bernie gazed down at him. "Shooting from the pocket looks easy in the movies," he said, "but it's really not."

I smelled blood, but hardly any.

Rick Torres and a bunch of Metro PD guys came and took over with the prisoners. Bernie and I got back in the cab. "Meet you at the fairgrounds," Bernie said.

"Nothing rash," said Rick said.

What did that mean? I wasn't sure. There were rashers of bacon, of course—did Rick mean I wasn't supposed to have any? Maybe he didn't realize that except for that one Slim Jim I hadn't had a morsel in I didn't know how long.

The sky was getting light when we drove into the fairgrounds, beautiful colors spreading all over the place. Sometimes, like after you've been up the whole night, for example, things are even more beautiful than ever. What a life!

No one around. We parked in front of the big top and were just getting out of the cab when the box office door opened and Colonel Drummond came out, walking fast and stuffing papers into a briefcase.

"Going somewhere?" said Bernie.

Drummond's head jerked up, mouth falling open, not a good look on him.

"We've got Peanut here," Bernie said. "Don't you want to see her?"

Drummond glanced at the truck. "Too late," he said.

"Because you're on your way downtown?" Bernie said.

"Downtown?"

"To turn yourself in for smuggling exotic animals and obstruction of justice," Bernie said. "That's your best move right now. And getting out front on the whereabouts of that parrot couldn't hurt."

Without another word, Drummond took off, papers flying all over the place, his running style strange and wobbly. Did it take more than a moment for me to chase him down and grab him by the pant leg? No. Case closed.

Drummond lay on the ground, absolutely still; he'd figured that out right away. Bernie came over.

"The goddamn bird died," Drummond said. "I had to refund every cent."

"Dad!" said Charlie. "You did it!" He jumped up in Bernie's arms, gave him a big hug.

"It was mostly Chet," Bernie said.

Soon Charlie was giving me a big hug, too. I gave him a big lick back.

"I told Ms. Creelman you'd come in and tell the class all about it," Charlie said.

"Well, I—"

"And you know what? She said you can stand up on the stage in the auditorium and speak to the whole school!"

"That might not, uh, we'll have to, um . . ."

Suzie found out about this refuge for elephants in Tennessee and made the arrangements. We saw Peanut off at the private strip in Pottsdale, me, Bernie, Suzie, Popo. Peanut was in a cage for the trip, didn't look happy about it. Popo tried to pat her trunk through the bars, but she was having none of it. I gave her that rumbly low bark meaning, let's go. Our eyes met. I felt something from her, no doubt about it. They loaded her on the plane. We watched till it was out of sight. I could still hear it perfectly well, but for the rest of them the plane was gone.

Popo turned to Bernie, his eyes damp. "I can't thank you enough," he said.

"Um," said Bernie, "not, uh, you don't have to . . ."

"Do you have the final accounting?"

"We'll send you a bill."

Now, Bernie. Get the money now. Did anything beat cold hard cash? Never.

"Chet? Something the matter, boy?"

We took Malcolm for a drink at the Dry Gulch Steak House and Saloon. One of my favorite places—great patio in back, with a nice welcome for me and my kind, and what can I say about the food?—but why Malcolm?

"Nice of you to do this, Bernie," Malcolm said. We were by ourselves at a corner table. "Probably good to get to know each other a bit better, what with this marriage coming up and all."

"Exactly," Bernie said. "Marriage is the subject." He fell silent.

Malcolm pushed his coaster around for a bit. Then he said, "You had something to say about marriage?"

"Yeah," said Bernie. He took a deep breath. "Kind of wacky, given my record, but I've got some advice on marriage."

Malcolm sat back, no longer looking friendly, or even the fake friendly he'd actually been doing. He disliked Bernie; you didn't need much in the nose department to sniff that out. "Oh?" he said.

Bernie leaned forward. "Take her on a long walk. Hold her hand. Keep your mouth shut."

Malcolm's eyebrows rose. "That's it?"

"Pretty much," Bernie said. "Just one more thing."

"What's that?"

"Avoid desert motels."

Sometimes the color vanishes from the human face in no time flat. Love seeing that, and I did now.

"Or any motels, really, unless Leda's with you. In this business, we make a lot of contacts with motel personnel, goes without saying." Bernie smiled, a special smile of his that's very bright, like a shiny knife. "Happy homes make happy kids, Malcolm, and Charlie's a happy kid. I wouldn't want to see any change there, not even the tiniest. I'm always armed—heavily. Probably also goes without saying, but I'm saying it anyway, if you get my meaning."

Huh? We weren't carrying now, never carried when we weren't on the job.

"You do get my meaning, Malcolm?"

Malcolm nodded.

Bernie picked up his glass, clinked it against Malcolm's. "Cheers," he said.

We went for a long walk in the canyon, me, Bernie, Suzie. Bernie's eye was looking better now, practically back to normal. After a while he took her hand. He kept his mouth shut.

"You're awfully quiet today," Suzie said.

Bernie's mouth opened. "I," he said. And then after what seemed like quite a long time: "love you."

Some sort of strong emotion began appearing on Suzie's face. A breeze sprang up behind me. I looked back. My tail was wagging like crazy. I must have been happy about something.

# ACKNOWLEDGMENTS

Many thanks to Lily and Josh; to David Brown; and to all the regulars at www.chetthedog.com.